MURDER
AT THE OASIS

Praise for David S. Pederson

Murder at Union Station

"The story is full of engaging, lively characters…I also enjoyed the diversity in the novel, which one doesn't always find in historical fiction. It was a lot of fun to unravel the mystery of what happened…well-written, suspenseful, and smoothly plotted, and it kept me guessing until the big denouement at the end. It's a fast, enjoyable cozy mystery that I enjoyed."
—*Roger Hyttinen (Roger's Reads)*

"Where this story really works is in the 1946 setting…I thoroughly enjoyed this mystery and look forward to the next one."—*Sinfully Good Gay Books Reviews*

"A Clever Murder Mystery. David always delivers an exciting story, always cleverly put together so I can never figure out 'who done it' until it is all pieced together by the detective…There is always an elegance and charm to the stories David writes, which makes them stand out."—*LESBIreviewed*

Murder on Monte Vista

"A great new mystery!…[T]he way everything is described really puts me in the moment. You feel a part of the story, and the way it is written, even though you know Mason is talking to another character, it's as if he is talking to you personally too, so it is so easy to become immersed in the story and really be a part of it. Most enjoyable, super exciting, and a series I cannot wait for more of! What a fantastic mystery!"—*LESBIreviewed*

Death's Prelude

"I highly recommend this story, introducing Heath and giving more insight to his past, as well as setting up the series nicely. The most fabulous thing though was seeing Heath blossom into the detective I met in *Death Overdue*, and I can't wait to read the next mystery he has to solve."—*LESBIreviewed*

Death Overdue

"Deftly drawn characters, brisk pacing, and an easy charm distinguish Pederson's winning follow-up to 2019's *Death Takes a Bow*. Pederson successfully evokes and shrewdly capitalizes upon the time in which his mystery takes place, using the era's prejudices and politics to heighten the story's stakes and more thoroughly invest readers in its outcome. Plausible suspects, persuasive red herrings, and cleverly placed clues keep the pages frantically flipping until the book's gratifying close."—*Mystery Scene*

"David S. Pederson never disappoints when it comes to twisted and suspenseful mysteries...I highly recommend the Detective Heath Barrington mystery series, and *Death Overdue* in particular is suspenseful and an absolute page-turner."—*QueeRomance Ink*

Lambda Literary Award Finalist *Death Takes a Bow*

"[T]here's also a lovely scene near the end of the book that puts into words the feelings that Alan and Heath share for one another, but can't openly share because of the time they live in and their jobs in law enforcement. All in all, an interesting murder/mystery and an apt depiction of the times."—*Gay Book Reviews*

"This is a mystery in its purest form...If you like murder mysteries and are particularly interested in the old-school type, you'll love this book!"—*Kinzie Things*

Lambda Literary Award Finalist *Death Checks In*

"David Pederson does a great job with this classic murder mystery set in 1947 and the attention to its details..."—*The Novel Approach*

"This noir whodunit is a worthwhile getaway with that old-black-and-white-movie feel that you know you love, and it's sweetly chaste, in a late-1940s way..."—*Outsmart Magazine*

"This is a classic murder mystery; an old-fashioned style mystery à la Agatha Christie..."—*Reviews by Amos Lassen*

Death Goes Overboard

"[A]uthor David S. Pederson has packed a lot in this novel. You don't normally find a soft-sided, poetry-writing mobster in a noir mystery, for instance, but he's here...this novel is both predictable and not, making it a nice diversion for a weekend or vacation."—*Washington Blade*

"Pederson takes a lot of the tropes of mysteries and utilizes them to the fullest, giving the story a knowable form. However, the unique characters and accurate portrayal of the struggles of gay relationships in 1940s America make this an enjoyable, thought-provoking read."—*Gay, Lesbian, Bisexual, and Transgender Round Table of the American Library Association*

"You've got mobsters, a fedora-wearing detective in a pinstriped suit, seemingly prim matrons, and man-hungry blondes eager for marriage. It's like an old black-and-white movie in book form..."—*Windy City Times*

Death Comes Darkly

"Agatha Christie...if Miss Marple were a gay police detective in post–WWII Milwaukee."—*PrideSource: Between the Lines*

"The mystery is one that isn't easily solved. It's a cozy mystery unraveled in the drawing room type of story, but well worked out."—*Bookwinked*

"If you LOVE Agatha Christie, you shouldn't miss this one. The writing is very pleasant, the mystery is old-fashioned, but in a good meaning, intriguing plot, well developed characters. I'd like to read more of Heath Barrington and Alan Keyes in the future. This couple has a big potential."—*Gay Book Reviews*

"[A] thoroughly entertaining read from beginning to end. A detective story in the best Agatha Christie tradition with all the trimmings."—*Sinfully Gay Romance Book Review*

By the Author

Private Detective Mason Adler Mysteries:

Murder on Monte Vista

Murder at Union Station

Murder at the Oasis

Heath Barrington Mysteries:

Death Comes Darkly

Death Goes Overboard

Death Checks In

Death Takes A Bow

Death Overdue

Death's Prelude

Death Foretold

Visit us at www.boldstrokesbooks.com

MURDER
AT THE OASIS

by

David S. Pederson

2023

ISBN 13: 978-1-63679-416-7

This Trade Paperback Original Is Published By
Bold Strokes Books, Inc.
P.O. Box 249
Valley Falls, NY 12185

First Edition: August 2023

Credits
Editors: Jerry L. Wheeler and Stacia Seaman
Production Design: Stacia Seaman
Cover Design by Inkspiral Design

Acknowledgments

Special thanks to all my family, especially my wonderful mom, Vondell, and in memory of my dad, Manford.

And to all my terrific friends who are my chosen family.

And as always, thanks and all my love to my husband, Alan, for his support and encouragement.

Finally, thanks also to all my readers, and to Jerry Wheeler, my editor with the most-est, as well as everyone at Bold Strokes Books who have helped me so much, especially Radclyffe, Carsen, Sandy, Cindy, Ruth, and Stacia.

CHAPTER ONE

Friday afternoon, May 31, 1946
The Oasis Inn, Palm Springs, California

Mason and Walter stood at the side of the resort pool, watching the corpse covered by a plain bedsheet being carried away on a stretcher by two attractive young men in starched white uniforms. Walter lit up a Camel, inhaled, and blew out a cloud of smoke as they passed.

"My, my, you boys are strong. I get winded just lifting my martini. And it's so beastly hot. May I get you two a cool drink? I have vodka in my room, and there's ice in the machine."

The man at the rear shook his head at Walter. "Uh, no thank you, sir," he said, as if unsure how to respond to such a comment, especially considering the circumstances.

"Walter," Mason said under his breath.

Walter looked up at Mason as he took another puff on the cigarette and the men moved on with their cargo. "What? I was just making conversation and trying to be considerate. It's so easy to become overheated and dehydrated in the desert, you know, especially when they're wearing all those clothes. I could see they were sweating."

"I don't think offering them a cocktail while they're carrying a corpse is being considerate or appropriate, sweating or not."

"I was just trying to make light of the situation."

"More likely you were flirting with two attractive young men as they carried a dead body away. You never stop."

"I don't plan to until I'm the one being carried out, hopefully by those two," Walter said. He inhaled once more and exhaled another cloud of smoke. "Speaking of flirting, you seemed awfully friendly with that detective fellow."

"I was just answering his questions."

"*And* you gave him your telephone exchange in Phoenix."

Mason blushed slightly. "Just in case he needs to reach me after we've gone back home."

"Naturally," Walter said.

"He asked me for it."

"He didn't want mine."

"He knows he can reach you through me, if necessary."

"Uh-huh. I'm apparently not his type, and he's certainly not mine, but I noticed he's yours."

"What type would that be?"

"Old. He's at least in his mid-fifties. Thinning gray hair, toothbrush mustache, and blue eyes."

"His eyes are green."

"Mm-hmm. Detective Branchwood, isn't it?"

"Branch*ford*. Brian Branchford."

"Nice alliteration. You two *were* quite chatty."

"We were discussing a death, Walter. He's investigating and was asking me questions, that's all."

"I seem to recall you telling me you're not in the market for a man, and even if you were, you wouldn't go looking for one in Palm Springs because it's a five-hour drive from Phoenix."

"I'm *not* in the market for a man," Mason said, "or anything else, but it never hurts to browse."

Walter took another long drag on his cigarette. "Sometimes when you browse, you buy, you know. When you find something just too good to pass up."

"I can't afford to buy."

"Just rent him, then, darling. Ugh, it's all so dreadful. Not you and the detective, though that rather turns my stomach, too."

"Gee, thanks."

"It's true, the way you two were fawning over each other. But by dreadful, I mean this whole thing. Two dead bodies here at the Oasis Inn in two days. It's simply dreadful."

"I agree. Not exactly my idea of a vacation."

"Oh bother, it's not mine, either, you know. You act like I planned all this to happen. Like this was all *my* idea."

"This *was* all your idea, Walter."

"It was?"

Mason scowled. "'Let's go to Palm Springs,' you said. 'Get some sun, some color, and relax by the pool while handsome waiters bring us drinks,' you said. And that's an exact quote, I believe," Mason said, looking down at him sternly.

Walter waved his hand about, the cigarette glowing brightly. "Hmm, I suppose that's all true, if you want to nitpick."

"I do."

"All right, fine. But I certainly didn't plan on two dead bodies. And don't give me that scowl, it's bad for your skin. You don't need any more lines and creases in your face."

"Then stop giving me a reason *to* scowl," Mason said.

"You know, if it wasn't for these dead people, you'd be thanking me for all the fun you had on this trip."

"That's debatable."

"Pish posh, we were having a swell time before the first corpse turned up."

"And now there's been a second. It's all so puzzling. And we're supposed to head home to Phoenix today."

"Good riddance to all of it, I say. I can't wait to leave this behind."

"I know, but still…"

"But still what?" Walter took one more drag on the cigarette and then ground it out on the pavement beneath his sandaled foot.

"You should use an ashtray."

"Oh, Marvin will clean that up, I'm sure. There's no ashtray in sight, so what would you have me do, darling, eat it?"

"I'd like to see that."

"I'm sure you would. You're just beastly to me sometimes, you know."

"Only when you deserve it."

"Maybe I need a spanking."

"Oh no, you'd enjoy that too much," Mason said as he glanced about the pool area of the resort.

"What are you looking at? Or looking for?"

"I don't know exactly. I can't put my finger on it, but the solution to the death of both of these people is here somewhere, I know it is."

"The solution is that one died of a heart attack and the other was a suicide. Or one murdered the other, or something like that. It's all a bit confusing."

"I can't help but think that's not the whole truth."

"Ugh, ever the private eye. *If* there's more to it, let the police figure it out, Mason. It's their job, and no one's paying you to stick your nose into it, darling. Come on, we've got packing to do."

Mason glanced down at his little friend. "Let's stay one more night, Walter. If I haven't come to any solid conclusions by tomorrow, we can leave then, okay?"

Walter shook his head adamantly. "It is most certainly *not* okay. I'm running out of clothes, you know, and frankly, after the second dead body, I'm beginning to wonder if there will be a third. I don't want it to be me, especially in an outfit everyone's already seen. When I die, I want to be dressed in something fresh, fabulous, and stylish."

"Of course you do, and I'm sure you'll be a fashionable corpse. But you're not going to die anytime soon, believe me. I'll protect you. Besides, if things *aren't* what they seem, your friend Marvin's a suspect."

"Don't be ridiculous. Marvin didn't kill anyone. It was a heart attack and a suicide, or one killed the other, like I said. Marvin had nothing to do with it."

"Detective Branchford hasn't closed either case yet, and Marvin had a motive to kill both of them. So, let's stay one more night, please?"

"Ugh, I suppose. If you really think there's more to this, and you can possibly help Marvin."

"Thank you."

"But what will I wear?"

"It seems to me you brought enough clothes for two weeks."

"Goes to show you what you know. I had my ensembles all planned out for each day with no repeats."

"So, what you're wearing now is your Friday afternoon attire?"

Walter glanced down at his blue, white, and red horizontal striped crewneck short-sleeved pullover, khaki trousers, and white leather sandals. "Yes, until it was time to head home. Then I planned to change into my traveling clothes." Walter lit up another Camel, blew a cloud of smoke out his hairy nostrils, looked up at the cloudless sky, and sighed. "Oh, I suppose I can put something together to wear tomorrow, perhaps by combining an outfit or two."

"You are the creative one, after all."

Walter nodded. "That's true, I am. All right, I'll go arrange things with Marvin at the front desk, and then I'm going to go back to our room and sort out my wardrobe, but if you hear me scream, do come running."

"I will, don't worry."

Walter sashayed away, his sandals slapping up and down and a cloud of smoke trailing behind him. Had it really only been a little over three days since their arrival in Palm Springs?

And had it really been just over two weeks since he'd met Walter to discuss the details of this fateful trip? There was no way either of them could have known that their upcoming holiday would lead to mystery and murder, but it had. Twice. So much had happened in a short period of time.

Mason made himself comfortable on one of the loungers, out of sight of the policeman guarding the dead person's room, and closed his eyes, his mind racing as he remembered back on the events. It had all started at the Cactus Cantina…

CHAPTER TWO

Two weeks earlier: Wednesday afternoon, May 15, 1946
The Cactus Cantina, Phoenix, Arizona

Mason parked his blue 1939 Studebaker Champion at the curb and stepped out onto the sidewalk. He put his fedora on his fifty-year-old head, pulled it low, and entered the colorful little café through the solitary glass door. He spotted Walter easily, resplendent in a red checked coat and yellow tie, seated at a small table for two near the restrooms. Mason zigzagged his way through the maze of tables and nodded at him. "Hello, Walter."

"Hello," Walter said as he took a swig of his martini and motioned toward the corner. "There's a place over there for your hat."

"Thanks," Mason said. He hung his next to Walter's, then returned to the table and took a seat.

"What took you so long, darling? I've been waiting."

"What do you mean? We said we'd meet at two, and it's just now four minutes after."

"But you *know* I'm always early. I got here at a quarter to."

"If you wanted me here at a quarter to, you should have said so," Mason said.

"Why? So you'd show up at ten minutes to? Honestly, how long have you known me?"

Mason sighed. "Too long, I think."

"Very funny. You've known me over thirty years, so you should know by now I'm always on time, if not early, and I suppose I should know by now that *you're* always late."

Mason frowned. "That's not true or fair. If you tell me two o'clock,

I'll be there at two o'clock or close to it, anyway. Four minutes past is not late in my book."

"Don't frown, it causes wrinkles. And I've never read your book. Too dull and too many big words."

"And *your* book is just pictures that need to be colored in," Mason said, gesturing toward Walter's glass. "I see you've already ordered a drink."

"I have, my usual martini—though they put in too much vermouth. It should be as dry as those awful biscuits they serve here."

"I like their biscuits. In fact, I was thinking of ordering a plate."

"Only if you want to eat them all by yourself."

"I might, and I'll have a scotch, neat, to wash them down with."

"You'll need it. Have you given up martinis?"

"No, of course not, but I have grown fond of scotch."

"In your old age, as they say. Suit yourself."

"I will, thanks."

Walter snapped his fingers above his head. "Young man, over here."

Mason sighed and closed his eyes briefly. "Walter, you know I hate it when you do that."

"Do what?"

"Snap your fingers like that in restaurants and stores. It's embarrassing."

"It's not. How else is a waiter or clerk supposed to know he's needed? You see? Here he comes now."

"Yes, sir?" the waiter said, glancing down at the two of them with a weary expression.

"Scotch, neat, please, and a small plate of biscuits," Mason said.

"Of course. Would you like menus?"

"No, we're not eating, just drinks," Walter said, nodding toward Mason. "Well, he's eating, but only those dry, stale things you call biscuits. I'm just drinking, and speaking of, I'd like another martini, a little less vermouth this time. In fact, just rinse the glass with the vermouth, toss it out, then fill the glass with gin and three olives."

"All right, sir," the waiter said, shaking his head slightly. He picked up Walter's now-empty glass, turned on his heel, and took it to the bar in the adjoining room on the other side of the café.

"You drank that first one pretty quickly," Mason said.

"I got here early, remember? Besides, I'm thirsty."

"Maybe you should drink some water in between cocktails."

"Ugh, water. That stuff will rust your insides. I try not to touch it in liquid form, unless it's in my bath."

"You *do* know you live in a desert, right?" Mason said, raising a brow and running his tongue over his dry lips.

"Of course, darling, that's why I drink. And speaking of, you really should put some Vaseline on those lips. Who's going to kiss you like that?"

"I'm not looking to get kissed, but I could use something. This dry climate always gets to them."

"Here," Walter said, reaching into his trousers pocket. "I have a tube of Vaseline Camphor Ice. There's not much left, but you can have it, I suppose. You need it more than I do."

Mason reached across the table and took it from him. "Thanks." He took the cap off, applied some to his lips, then put the tube in his own pocket.

"There, you're kissable, or whatever you do with that mouth, and I don't want to know."

"Good, because I'm not telling."

"Fine. Now then, are you all excited about our upcoming little getaway to Palm Springs?" Walter pulled a packet of Camels out of his breast pocket and lit one up.

"I suppose it will be nice to have a change of scenery."

"It will, though you're bringing the best scenery along with you."

"What do you mean?" Mason said.

"Me, naturally, darling. You'll have the pleasure of gazing at me in all my splendor for three full days and nights, Tuesday through Friday."

Mason stared at Walter, all nearly five foot six of him, with a well-trimmed, short brown mustache that complemented his wavy brown hair, parted on the left and combed over the top to cover a small bald spot on his crown. "You certainly are something to look at, Walter, I'll give you that. The getup you're wearing today is as colorful as this cantina."

Walter glanced about the dining room, punctuating the air with his cigarette, which he held between the middle and index fingers of his right hand, his wrist bent back. "The colors in here, the oranges, greens, blues, and reds, are one of the best things about this place. Otherwise the drinks are weak, the food is poor, and the service is just passable."

"I've always been satisfied with the food and drinks here, and I think the waiters do a fine job."

"That's because *you* are too easy to please. Next time, we should go to Roy's Buffet on Roosevelt. The cocktails there are excellent, and they have a new busboy who's just delightful. By the way, have you expanded upon your wardrobe at all for the trip?"

"Just the outfit you picked out for me. The black coat, orange tie, and pea green trousers."

"I simply can't wait to see you in that, darling. Heads will turn," Walter said, taking a drag on his cigarette and blowing the smoke upward.

"So you've said."

"They will, trust me, but why haven't you done any more shopping? We leave in less than two weeks."

"I know, but I'm really quite happy with the clothes I already have. They're in good condition, and they look fine."

"They look dull and old, Mason, and they're out of style." Walter sighed, took another puff, and flicked the ashes into the small metal ashtray. "Oh well, not to worry, I know of a divine little clothing shop on Palm Canyon Drive that I'll take you to as soon as we arrive. You'll absolutely love it."

"I really just want to relax while we're there."

"Of course, and we definitely will. But you do need a few more outfits for the evenings. You can't wear the one I picked out for you more than once while you're there. It just isn't done, it's too small a town."

"I was planning on packing a couple of suits and various ties, and of course my swimming suit and whatnot. What else would I need?"

"Honestly, Mason, are you sure you're one of us? There are seven important S's to remember when packing for a warm weather trip: shirts, suits, short pants, swimwear, sleepwear, socks, and shoes, all in sufficient number for a three-day trip."

"Aren't you a little old to be wearing short pants?"

"In Phoenix, perhaps, but not Palm Springs. I'm bringing at least three pairs, along with four shirts, two suits, a swimming suit in the latest style, and my good red silk pajamas, among other things."

"I don't usually wear pajamas."

"How bohemian," Walter said, taking another long drag on his cigarette and blowing the smoke out through his hairy nostrils.

"I just don't find them comfortable. Typically I sleep in my underwear or nothing at all."

"Well, don't forget we're sharing a room, darling. I don't mind seeing you in your undergarments, but anything else is best left to my imagination. Your long, skinny white legs are enough to give me nightmares."

"I'll try to save you from seeing me naked, then."

"I appreciate that. I'm sensitive, you know."

"Sensitive, right," Mason said, licking his lips once more and noticing they felt much better.

"I can't help it, I just am. Oh, and naturally a tuxedo and a white dinner jacket are a must, along with dress shirts, belts, ties, cufflinks, studs, pocket squares, handkerchiefs, rings, and a fully equipped shaving kit. In addition to all that, I intend to bring my black silk sleep mask, too. I have an extra if you'd like to borrow it."

"Thanks, but I think I'll manage."

"Suit yourself. Oh, and maybe I'll bring my handcuffs," Walter said, a twinkle in his brown eyes and a slight smirk on his face, his mustache twitching.

Mason raised a bushy eyebrow. "Handcuffs?"

He looked around and leaned in to whisper, "I'll explain later. You're not bringing that nasty gun of yours along, are you?"

"I plan to, actually. I know it's a vacation, but I like to be prepared. Don't worry, I'll keep it locked in my suitcase unless I do end up needing it."

"You won't need it. Leave it at home, please. I hate those things. It would be just my luck you'd drop your suitcase and it would go off and shoot me in the behind," Walter said.

"Wouldn't be the first time you've been shot in the rear, but fine. I'll leave it here if it will put your mind at ease."

"Very funny, and thank you," Walter said as he glanced over Mason's shoulder. "Ah, here come our drinks and those dry biscuits you ordered."

The waiter set the glass of scotch in front of Mason and the martini in front of Walter, and placed the biscuits in the center along with a small plate. "Anything else at the moment, gentlemen?"

"No, thank you," Mason said.

"Very good, sir. I'll check on you both in a bit," the waiter said as he turned and walked away.

"That's another thing about this place," Walter said, gazing after him. "The waiters have no pizzazz and flat rear ends."

"Walter, honestly."

"I know you agree, because I know you like a man with a round, firm rear end. But not to worry, I'm sure there will be plenty of those in Palm Springs."

"Keep your voice down," Mason said.

"Oh, you're such a worrywart. There's no one seated near us, and everyone else is too engaged in their own conversations to pay us any attention."

"Be that as it may, I'm not going to Palm Springs to look for men—round, firm rear ends or otherwise," Mason said in a voice just above a whisper.

Walter raised his glass. "When you don't look, you find, they say. Cheers."

"Cheers," Mason said, raising his glass as well and taking a healthy drink as Walter did the same.

"Not as weak this time?" Mason said.

"Not bad, but they're better at the Triada, and so is the scenery if you know what I mean. We'll go there for drinks, too, of course. You can wear that outfit I picked out for you."

"Aren't we staying at the Triada?" Mason said, picking up a biscuit. "Why would we have to go there for drinks when we'll already be there?"

Walter looked embarrassed as he ground his cigarette out in the ashtray. "Oh, yes...well, I meant to tell you about that."

"Tell me about what? We *are* staying there, aren't we? Didn't you call your friend? The one who works there and can supposedly get us a great room rate?"

"I *did* call him, of course."

"And?"

Walter glanced at his fingernails. "Oh dear, I really do need a manicure before we leave."

"Walter, what happened when you called your friend?"

"Oh yes, that. Unfortunately, Marvin left the Triada almost a year ago. I really do need to keep in touch with him more often."

Mason leaned back in his chair and blew out a puff of air. "Oh, Walter, for heaven's sake. One of the main reasons I agreed to go on this trip was because you said he could get us a discounted room at the Triada, and we could rub elbows with all the celebrities staying there."

"I know, darling, but how was I to know he doesn't work there anymore? Not to worry. I found out he's bought the Oasis Inn, and he can get us an even more fabulous rate there!"

"He bought it?"

"Yes, isn't it amazing? After he left the Triada, he found out the Oasis was for sale. Practically brand new, but the owners ran out of money."

"How could he afford to buy a hotel?"

"He has a silent partner, I understand, an investor. So, we're all set. Isn't that marvelous?"

"I've never heard of the Oasis Inn," Mason said.

"That's because it's new. It's a smaller place. Cozy, you see? Only twelve rooms centered around a courtyard pool."

"Sounds *much* smaller than the Triada."

"Well, yes, of course, but it's also more intimate, with a higher guest to staff ratio, so I imagine it has much better service."

"I don't know, Walter. If we can't stay at the Triada, what about the Palm Springs Hotel downtown? That's supposed to be chic."

"Chic? That place? It's over ten years old. The Oasis, I'm told, is less than a year old, practically new! It's all modern and up to date. They started construction the minute the war ended, in anticipation of the travel restrictions being lifted, but then, as I say, the original owners went broke and had to put it up for sale."

"Hmm. So, if it's new and up to date, does it have refrigerated air in all the rooms?"

"Darling, it's only the middle of May. Who needs refrigerated air?"

"But we're not going until the twenty-eighth of May."

"It will still be cool and pleasant there, Mason. If anything, you may need a sweater for the evenings. I certainly intend to bring a wrap."

"So, they don't have refrigerated air in the rooms."

"Well, no. Those big, nasty units are obnoxious anyway. They're loud and block the view out the window. But Marvin did tell me they have electric ceiling fans."

"How progressive."

"Don't be a snob. You don't have refrigerated air in your place, and neither do I. Hardly anyone does. It's too expensive. You're just being difficult."

"Do the rooms at least have private baths?"

"Oh, don't be silly. Of *course* they do. I told you it's brand new!"

"Yes, you did. New and modern, I believe you said. Are there telephones in the rooms?"

"Honestly, what on earth would you want a telephone in our room for? Who are you going to call?"

"Not room service, apparently."

"So what? Marvin got us a rate of only three dollars a night. You'd pay twice that at the Palm Springs Hotel, and probably triple that at the Triada."

Mason furrowed his brow as he considered this. "I suppose that's true. But I doubt they get any celebrities staying at this Oasis place."

"Movie stars are overrated, Mason. Besides, we're bound to bump into a few in the evenings when we go out to the clubs."

"I guess three dollars a night is a decent rate."

"It's a very good rate for Palm Springs, and you know it. I *told* you Marvin would take care of us. He and I are old friends. We know each other intimately."

"So you've said."

Walter took a sip of his drink with one hand while he fiddled with his mustache with the other. "Oh, Marvin's all right, I suppose, but a tad old for me. He's in his late thirties, and you know I like them younger."

"He's in his late thirties? Ghastly! And *you're* fifty."

"Don't be rude, Mason. I'm only forty-nine. *You're* fifty."

"You're only forty-nine for a few more months, Walter."

"There's no point in keeping track past thirty."

"You certainly delight in keeping track of my age," Mason said.

"That's because you're older than I am."

"Only by a few months. So why *did* he leave the Triada?"

"Oh, you know how it is. The Triada caters to the famous and fabulous, which brings with it a certain amount of stress. And I'm told there was also an incident with Marvin and one of the male guests, apparently. It seems the guest's wife walked in on the two of them."

"Ah, now it all comes to light," Mason said, taking another biscuit.

"It certainly did when she turned on the lamp. Honestly, I don't see why the hotel made such a big deal out of it."

"Not surprising. So, they fired him."

"Yes," Walter said. "Personally, I think they overreacted."

"Your friend's lucky he wasn't arrested along with being fired. Homosexual sex is illegal in all forty-eight states."

"Yes, well, rumor has it the wife *was* going to press charges against

Marvin *and* her husband, and *did* plan to have them both arrested. She also called her lawyer right away to start divorce proceedings."

"What happened?"

"She was found drowned in the swimming pool early the next morning."

"How awful!"

"Yes, though it was just an accident. Of course, a few people pointed fingers at the husband and a few at Marvin, but they were both exonerated."

"You must admit it sounds suspicious," Mason said, taking another sip of his drink.

"I suppose, but all's well that ends well, I always say."

"How is a woman drowning, accidental or otherwise, a happy ending?"

"Well, Marvin and the husband weren't arrested, and Marvin got the chance to buy the Oasis Inn. The place sounds simply charming."

"I certainly hope that woman's death *was* accidental. I don't like the idea of staying at a hotel owned by a murderer."

"Oh, don't be a goose, Mason. Of course Marvin's innocent. It was a tragic accident, that's all."

"Hmm. I wonder."

"Of course. It's what you do. Besides, if it *wasn't* an accident, my money would be on the husband. Anyway, Marvin tells me he's been just swamped at the hotel. And on top of that, he does photography in his off time."

"Photography?"

"Yes, didn't I mention that? He's quite the shutterbug, mostly male art portraits. He's sold a few to the muscle and fitness magazines. He has a little shop on Palm Canyon, upstairs from a hardware store."

"He sounds like quite a fellow. How did you two ever meet?"

"Oh, we met a few years ago on one of my many solo sojourns to Palm Springs. He had just relocated from Quebec, and we were both at the same house party. He looked younger in the dark."

"I see."

"I didn't, it was almost pitch black in there. But I felt my way through, and we became friends despite his being older than I'd thought when the lights finally came on."

"Fascinating. I can't wait to meet him."

"You will, soon enough," Walter said. "By the way, he's single. I'm not sure if I mentioned that."

"You didn't, but I really don't care."

"Why not? You like them old."

"He's not old, in fact he's too young for me. I like my men to be at least in their forties, and you said Marvin is in his thirties. Even if I was in the market for a man, I wouldn't go looking for one in Palm Springs."

"What's wrong with the men in Palm Springs?"

Mason let out a loud, exasperated sigh. "Nothing's *wrong* with them, but I'm not going to start dating someone who lives five hours away."

"Oh, for heaven's sake, I seem to recall you had quite a fling with that fellow in Bisbee a few years ago, and he was almost four hours away."

Mason looked thoughtful. "Don Janos, you mean? He was worth the trip every weekend for nearly four months."

"Wasn't something wrong with his legs?"

"He was in a mining accident. Used a cane and wore special shoes. He was amazing in bed, and boy could he kiss. Not to mention he was damned attractive and a hell of a nice guy. Broke my heart when he called it off. And I'm not about to start a long-distance dating thing again."

"His loss. But who said anything about dating, darling? Marvin can be quite entertaining in the dark, no dates required, no commitment, and no questions asked."

"Honestly, Walter, if I'm going to sleep with someone, it won't be someone you've already had and hopefully not someone you even know, not to mention someone who may be a murderer."

"Marvin's a friend of mine, and he's *not* a murderer. And you do like to be secretive about your sex life."

"What there is of it, yes. And I intend to keep it that way." Mason finished his scotch and glared at Walter. "I'll pick you up at your house the morning of the twenty-eighth at eight o'clock. It's about a five-hour drive, so that will get us there around one thirty or two, including stops for gas and lunch."

"Eight in the morning?" Walter looked aghast. "Darling, the sun's not even up yet at that ungodly hour."

"For your information, Walter, the sun usually rises a little after five this time of year."

"Good grief, that's horrible! Why don't we leave at nine if you insist on an early start? I think I could manage that, but just barely. Don't expect me to look too pretty, though."

"Fine, I'll pick you up at nine. And by nine I mean nine, not a quarter of."

"Don't you worry. For that I will definitely *not* be early, and you can feel free to be late!"

CHAPTER THREE

Thursday afternoon, May 16, 1946
Mason's apartment, Phoenix

Mason opened the door of his apartment and gazed out at the woman standing before him on the balcony hall overlooking the courtyard below.

"I brought us doughnuts," Lydia said, smiling up at him as she held up a wax paper bag.

"Thank you, but you're not helping my figure any, Miss Dettling. I have to be swimming-suit ready in two weeks for the Palm Springs trip Walter and I are taking."

Lydia looked him up and down. "You're worried about your figure? You're over six feet tall and, what, a hundred and sixty pounds?"

"A hundred and sixty-four as of this morning."

"Heavens. I *don't* think you have to worry about being swimming-suit ready, Mason. You're in marvelous shape."

"For a man my age, I suppose."

"For a man *any* age. Those gray streaks in your dark hair, your Roman nose, those bright blue eyes. And your tall, lithe figure. No, you definitely need not worry about gaining weight, my love. If anything, you may have to worry about your suit falling down because you're too thin."

"That would be embarrassing."

Lydia laughed lightly, brushing a strand of her red hair back behind her ear. "I, on the other hand, could probably stand to lose a few pounds, but I'm not going to Palm Springs to lounge about a pool. Ugh, I haven't been in a swimming suit since I was thirty-nine."

"Which was only last year, my dear. And you don't need to worry about your weight. You're a lovely woman with a beautiful figure and amazing green eyes."

"That's kind of you, thanks. So, are you going to invite me in or leave me standing out here in the heat?"

"Oh, right, sorry, come on in." Mason stepped back, closing the door behind her. "I've just made a pot of coffee. Let's go in the dining room."

Lydia and Mason walked across the living room and into the small dining alcove where Lydia took a seat, setting the bag on the table. "I got you one with chocolate sprinkles, and I got mine plain."

"You do know what I like. I'll get the coffee and a plate."

"Need help?"

"No, thank you. Sit and relax."

"I have and I am. Don't forget the cream and sugar."

"I won't." Mason stepped into the adjoining kitchen and retrieved two cups of coffee, an empty plate, and the creamer and sugar bowl, which he set on the table. "I'll get some spoons and napkins, too."

"Thank you, love. So, Palm Springs, California. Gee, I haven't been there in a long time. I wish I was going, too."

"It would be fun."

"Thanks. I think so, too, but I wasn't invited. Walter said it was a no-girls trip, as I recall."

"You know how Walter is, but you were invited by me," Mason said, returning to the table with the spoons and napkins and taking a seat.

"True, and I thank you for that, but I have to work at the store anyway, and I really should spend some time with Thad, maybe see a movie or two. There's a double feature at the Orpheum I want to see." Lydia opened the bag and put the two doughnuts on the plate.

"How is Mr. O'Connell? Things still going okay with you two?" Mason said, taking the one with the chocolate sprinkles.

"I guess so. He's a nice fellow, but he's been so busy at the bank, and I've been working a lot at Penney's, so we haven't seen a lot of each other lately."

"I see. So, it probably will be good for you to stay here in Phoenix, then."

"I'd go with you to Palm Springs if I wanted to, Thad and Walter be darned, but the idea of riding in your car with Walter for almost six hours each way is a little much."

Mason laughed. "I must say I agree. I plan on making lots of stops just to escape from his endless chatter for a bit."

"He does like to talk," Lydia said, picking up her plain doughnut and giving it a dunk in her coffee.

"About himself, mostly, or about what he perceives is wrong with me."

"Or wrong with me," Lydia said. "I sometimes wonder why you two are friends."

"Oh, he's really just an insecure fellow who hasn't had the greatest life. He doesn't have a lot of true friends, and I'm happy to be one of them. He drives me nuts, but he also makes me laugh, and he keeps me on my toes."

"But some of the things that come out of his mouth…"

"I know. He can be a bit much."

"Plus when I found out you weren't staying at the Triada after all…"

"Yes, apparently the fellow Walter knows no longer works there. He now owns and works at a place called the Oasis Inn, so he got us a good rate there."

"I've never heard of it."

"Nor I, but I guess it's a new place, small and intimate."

"Well, be sure and send me a penny postcard," she said.

"I will, I promise."

"Good. I collect them, you know."

"I do know, along with lots of other stuff."

"A girl's gotta have a hobby."

Mason wiped his mouth with the napkin. "I prefer hobbies that don't clutter up the place."

"Like your collection of men that come and go," Lydia said, as she finished her doughnut. "They never leave more than an old toothbrush, if that."

"A guy's gotta have a hobby," Mason said with a grin.

CHAPTER FOUR

Tuesday morning, May 28, 1946
Walter's house, Phoenix

Mason pulled up to Walter's house on Monte Vista at nine sharp. He parked his Studebaker at the curb and got out as he placed his hat back on. Walter was waiting on the front porch, surrounded by a pile of matching luggage of various shapes and sizes and dressed in a light blue plaid jacket, yellow tie, and black trousers. His dark sunglasses were perched atop his head as he leaned casually against the wall of the house.

"Good morning, Walter," Mason said cheerfully as he strode up the walk. "I'm right on time."

"I'm not sure it's good, but I suppose it is morning, anyway. So, this is what nine a.m. looks like." Walter briefly glanced up at the clear blue sky. "It's simply beastly."

"Come now, it's a beautiful day. The birds are singing, the sun is shining, the sky is blue, and there's not a cloud in sight."

"And it still feels like the middle of the night. I've been up since seven, believe it or not. I've had my breakfast, bathed, dressed, and made myself up as best I could, considering. And it took me three trips up the stairs to get my things down here, but here I am, so let's get on with it," Walter said.

"You do know we're only going for three nights, don't you?" Mason said, gesturing at Walter's pile of luggage.

"Yes, of course I know that. I hope I've brought enough."

"Four suitcases, a train case, a garment bag, *and* a hatbox? I'd say you're bringing more than enough."

"Hardly, darling. One has to have different outfits for day and evening, so at least two wardrobe changes per day, nicely packed so as not to crowd or wrinkle. And one entire case is just for my shoes. Of course, I also packed all the necessary accoutrements *and* a bottle of vodka, which I'll share if you're nice to me."

"What's that for?"

"Just for sipping poolside. Apparently the Oasis doesn't serve drinks like the Triada does."

"Not surprising. Well, I managed with just one suitcase and a garment bag."

"So I noticed, and I'm sure you crammed it all in. And you're wearing one of your oh-so-stylish gray suits, I see."

Mason glanced down at it briefly. "It's my traveling suit. A bit loose fitting and comfortable, that's all."

Walter shook his head. "You'll make a grand entrance at the Oasis Inn when you arrive dressed like that. And by grand I mean ho-hum."

"I really don't care about making an entrance. I just want to get there and relax."

"Naturally. But unlike you, *I* dress to impress. And to impress, one must be prepared for anything. But don't you worry, we'll stop by Rudy's on Palm Canyon when we get to town and find you at least one other decent outfit. They specialize in giraffe sizes for tall galoots like you."

"Do they have clothes in stock? I don't want to wait to have things altered."

"No worries at all, most everything is off the rack and ready to wear. We'll find you something absolutely smashing."

"If you insist, but nothing too outlandish or expensive."

"Of course not, just something with a little more color. Oh, and speaking of, I just realized I forgot my favorite pocket square. Be a lamb and load my luggage while I go and fetch it, won't you?"

"Baaaa," Mason said, doing his best to imitate a sheep.

"So witty. I won't be but a minute."

"Knowing you, you'll be gone just long enough for me to wedge all of your bags into the trunk of my car."

"I resent your implication, but thank you ever so and do be careful with the garment bag. My dinner jacket wrinkles something fierce. If you don't lay it flat, it will have more lines and creases in it than your face."

Mason scowled. "I *could* just wait here on the porch until you get your pocket square, and then let you load your luggage all by yourself."

"Oh, all right, I'm sorry. It's just that you're so big and strong, unlike little old me. And don't scowl. You know, when Adrien was living here, he used to do all my heavy lifting, but now…"

"What happened to that strong, strapping lad anyway?"

"Well, as you know, he moved in with me after his parents threw him out."

"When they found out that he's a homosexual."

"Exactly. I *was* taken with him, but unfortunately, nothing came of it. He moved in with another gymnast from the team at school."

"Really?"

"Yes, though he swears they're just friends. I suppose it could be true, as Adrien usually likes them older. Me excluded, apparently."

"I keep telling you that you need to start dating men your age."

"Most of the men my age are dull or dead."

"You're not that old. You're younger than me by a few months."

"True. And I *look* younger by several years."

"Behave."

"You know I'm just pulling one of your long, skinny, oh-so-white chicken legs."

"Yeah, yeah. Get going. I'll load your stuff, and I'll handle your garment bag like a basket of eggs I just hatched."

"You're a regular Rhode Island Red!" Walter said, reaching up and pinching Mason's cheek as he turned and entered the front door of his house once more.

Mason picked up the bags two at a time and carried them to his automobile, where he fit them into his trunk without too much trouble. He laid Walter's garment bag out flat on the back seat, atop his own. As soon as he'd finished, Walter emerged, red pocket square now in place, and sashayed down the walk toward the car.

"All finished?" Walter asked.

"As if you weren't watching from the window until I was."

Walter patted his chest with his left hand. "That hurts my heart. I had trouble finding my pocket square, that's all. I hope you took good care of everything."

"I wouldn't hear the end of it if I didn't. I put all your suitcases and your hatbox in the trunk, and I laid your garment bag flat out on the back seat on top of mine."

Walter peered in the rear window. "It looks like they're mating, and I'm on top!"

"There's a first time for everything, I suppose. All set?"

"Yes, I think so. You know the way, I imagine."

"I plotted it out on my Arizona and California maps, but it's pretty straightforward. We'll take highway 60 to Wickenburg and then on to Blythe. I think that will be a good place to stop for lunch."

"Since there's not much before or after that, I would have to agree," Walter said. "Blythe is a good stopping point."

"Yes, then it's on to Palm Springs via highway 60 and 111. With stops, we should be there around three this afternoon."

"Just in time for a little catnap before we need to change for dinner."

"Let's get going, then, shall we?"

"We shall, my darling, we shall!"

CHAPTER FIVE

Tuesday afternoon, May 28, 1946
Palm Springs

The drive was uneventful. Fortunately for Mason, Walter dozed most of the way, snoring softly with his head back and mouth agape. Mason woke him up when they got to Blythe, where they ate lunch at a small diner, and once more when they stopped at a Sinclair gas station to use the restroom, but otherwise Walter was happily in dreamland.

As they approached the Palm Springs city limits on East Palm Canyon Drive, Mason slowed his Studebaker to twenty-five miles an hour.

Walter awoke at last, cracking his neck and rubbing his eyes before putting his sunglasses back on and looking about. "Are we here already?" He took out his handkerchief and wiped away a bit of drool from his chin and mustache.

"If by *already*, you mean six hours and seventeen minutes later than it was when we left your house, then yes. We're here already."

"Oh good, I'm ready for a cigarette and a cocktail or two, and I'm rather peckish."

"I could use a cocktail myself," Mason said. "My back is killing me from all this sitting, and the long drive has made me sleepy."

"The drive here *is* boring, but surprisingly I feel refreshed." He pushed in the cigarette lighter on the dash and took out a Camel from the pack in his breast pocket.

Mason gave him a side-eye. "Hardly surprising. You slept almost the entire way here, except for when we stopped for lunch and when we used the bathroom at that gas station. And speaking of, I should probably fill up again."

"Because you used the bathroom?"

"Fill up the *car*, Walter. It's low on gas, almost empty. There's a Sinclair station on that next corner."

"Fine, but I do hope their restrooms are cleaner than the last one. Now that you mention it, I feel the urge to go."

"Why don't you just wait until we get to the resort? We can't be far now."

Walter considered this briefly. "I suppose that might be better. I held my breath the entire time I was in the men's room at that last place."

"I didn't think it was that bad."

"Ugh, there was crude writing on the walls, the floor was sticky, and the sink and toilet were filthy." The cigarette lighter popped out. Walter removed it and lit up, inhaling deeply.

"I did notice the hole in the wall of the stall and the graffiti. I wonder if Tom really does all those things it said."

"I don't know, but I copied his number down just in case," Walter said, blowing out a cloud of smoke.

"Naturally."

Mason pulled into the station, driving over the rubber hose that rang a bell inside the small white brick building. He stopped the car next to the first pump, switched off the engine, and engaged the brake. Presently, a fetching young man dressed in a uniform of white pants, white shirt, white cap, black bow tie, and black cap-toe shoes emerged from the building and approached the driver's side as Mason rolled down his window.

"Good afternoon, sir. Fill 'er up?"

"Yes, please," Mason said with a smile.

"Regular or ethyl?"

"Ethyl."

"Yes, sir. Check your oil?"

"Sure, it's probably low," Mason said. "We've just driven in from Phoenix."

"Welcome to Palm Springs," the young man said cheerfully. "In that case, I'll check the air in your tires and make sure your radiator's full, too." He walked back to the pump and inserted the large gas nozzle into the car's fuel tank. While that was pumping, he proceeded to the front windshield and squirted cleanser on it from a bottle, then squeegeed it off in long, slow strokes. Mesmerized, Walter watched through the glass, a grin on his face.

"I just love Palm Springs," he said, still staring through the front windshield. "Everyone's so friendly."

"That kid can't be more than nineteen, Walter," Mason said softly so as not to be overheard through the open window.

"Closer to twenty or twenty-one, I'd say. Probably working his way through college or just home from the war."

The young man finished with the windshield and popped the hood of the Studebaker so he could check the oil and the water in the radiator.

"Maybe I should get out and ask him if he knows the way to the Oasis Inn," Walter said, grinding out his Camel in the car's ashtray.

"I have the address, and I think we can find it on our own, Walter. Behave," Mason said sternly.

The young man came over to the driver's window, holding the greasy dipstick in his hands. "You're about a quart low. Shall I put some in for you?"

"Yes, please. Thank you."

"Yes, sir," the young man said, moving away once more.

"He's delightful," Walter said.

Mason looked over at Walter. "This is going to be a long few days. Hand me the Palm Springs city map from the glove box, will you?"

"It could be a long, fun-filled few days," Walter said, opening the glove box, "if you'd stop being such a fuddy-duddy." He rummaged around a bit. "I don't see a Palm Springs map."

"It's the blue one under the California state map. I picked it up last week."

"Oh, yes, here," he said, handing it to Mason.

Mason unfolded it and held it up to his face, looking for the street the hotel was on.

"Need directions?" the attendant said, appearing at Mason's window once more.

"Yes, we do," Walter said, leaning over Mason and crushing the map. "We're looking for the Oasis Inn. We'll be staying there until Friday. Do you know Marvin Gagliardi? He owns the place, and he used to work at the Triada Hotel."

The young man bent down and peered in the window at Walter. "The Oasis Inn is that new place on the corner of South Warm Sands Drive and East Camino Parocela. Just follow Palm Canyon to Ramon and turn right. Warm Sands will be on your right. And no, sorry, I don't know a Mr. Gagliardi."

"Oh, that's too bad," Walter said. "In addition to owning the Oasis he does photography, you know. Male art portraits, mostly. He's sold a few to the muscle and fitness magazines."

"Oh, yeah?" the young man said, leaning in further.

Mason could feel his breath on his face. He smelled like he'd had tuna fish for lunch.

"Yes, he does very artistic work," Walter said. "He has a little shop on Palm Canyon here, upstairs from the hardware store. If you're interested, he pays rather well, and I think he'd enjoy taking your picture."

"Gee, I want to get into the movies eventually. You think having my photo in a muscle and fitness magazine would help?"

"It couldn't hurt," Walter said. "It might catch the eye of a movie producer or director."

"A better option would be to go to LA and find yourself an agent, young man," Mason said. "A reputable agent."

"I actually thought about hightailin' it to LA and getting a job at a filling station until I get my big break. A buddy of mine is working at one right on Hollywood Boulevard, and he says he's met a few stars there. That's the place to be, he says."

"Don't be taken in by the big city," Mason said. "And don't get starstruck."

"Don't mind my friend, Leroy, he's a fuddy-duddy," Walter said.

"How did you know my name?"

"It's embroidered on your uniform."

He glanced down at it and then nodded. "Oh, right. I forgot. Well, thanks for the tip. Maybe I'll look this Mr. Gagliardi up."

"Please do. And tell him Walter Wingate sent you."

"Sure thing, Mr. Wingate, thanks."

"My pleasure entirely. I look forward to seeing your photographs."

"How much do I owe you, Leroy?" Mason said.

"Hmm? Uh, two dollars and sixty cents for the gas and the quart of oil. I put air in all four tires for ya and added some water to your radiator. No charge for that."

"Thanks," Mason said. "Here's two seventy, keep the change."

"Golly, thanks, mister."

"You're welcome."

"I'll get your trading stamps."

"That's okay, give them to the next customer, I don't collect them. And thanks for the directions," Mason said, rolling up his window as Leroy gave him a friendly wave.

"Well, wasn't he just charming?" Walter said.

"And you were obnoxious. Here, fold this map back up and put it away."

"Grumpy, grumpy, grumpy," Walter said, attempting to fold the map as best he could.

"And you're dopey, dopey, dopey. Let's go." Mason started the engine, released the brake, and steered his Studebaker back out onto Palm Canyon Drive toward Ramon.

"I don't see what's wrong with suggesting Marvin's photo studio to him," Walter said as he struggled with the map.

"You wouldn't."

"I wouldn't and I don't. And I don't know how to fold this stupid map, either," he said, tossing it over his shoulder into the back seat.

"You're impossible, Walter."

"I'm not impossible, I'm just challenging. That *map* is impossible. Anyway, having his picture taken at Marvin's might help Leroy break into showbiz, you never know."

"Doubtful."

"But you never know. Stranger things have happened, and it would help Marvin, too. By the way, don't forget we're stopping at Rudy's before we go to the inn. It's just a few blocks past Ramon, between an art supply store and the hardware store that's below Marvin's photography studio," Walter said.

"I really don't think it's necessary. I've brought more than enough clothes for the few days we'll be here."

"But you promised you'd pick out at least one outfit that's fun and colorful."

"I already have the outfit you made me buy at Diamond's in Phoenix."

"I know, but you need at least one more. It will only take a moment, and it's just a few blocks out of our way."

"All right, fine, but only because I'm dying to get out of this car and stand up for a while. My back is killing me."

"It's because you're too tall. Cars and chairs and doors and things weren't meant for giraffes like you. And slow down a bit, we just crossed Ramon. There it is on the right, next to Palatable Art and Supply. And, look, there's a parking spot close to the shop. Our lucky day. We were meant to stop here."

Mason pulled into the spot, shut off the engine, and set the brake.

"Okay, we're here, but ten minutes, no more. I want to get to the hotel and relax."

"Ugh, you'll have two full days to relax. Let's go in and see what they have to offer."

The two of them strode into the little shop, the bell above the door tinkling.

"Good afternoon, gentlemen. How may I help you?" a middle-aged male clerk said, looking at them from behind the counter. He was dressed in a light blue suit with an orange paisley tie and a white carnation in his lapel.

"Good afternoon. Oh, is, uh, Rudy in this afternoon?" Walter said, glancing about.

"No, I'm afraid not, sir. He won't be back until the day after tomorrow. Is there something I could assist you with?"

"Hmm, yes, actually, I'm sure. We're looking for an outfit or two for my tall friend here. We're from out of town, so it has to be ready to wear, and it has to be fabulous."

The clerk looked at Mason critically and then back at Walter. "Of course. But your, uh, friend seems to dress conservatively. I'm afraid I don't have much in the muted tones."

"The uh, friend, is right here and can hear you," Mason said. "And they don't have to be muted tones, just nothing too garish or outlandish."

The clerk nodded. "Ah, I see. If you'll follow me to the rear, that's where I keep the larger and taller sizes."

Thirty minutes later, Mason was the owner of two new pairs of trousers, one baby blue gabardine, the other a yellow plaid, and two sport shirts—one a green paisley, the other one white with a navy check.

"Do come again next time you're in town, gentlemen," the clerk said, handing the bag across the counter to Mason.

"We will. And do give my best to Rudy," Walter said. "Don't forget, Walter Waverly Wingate from Phoenix. Oh, and thank you for letting me use your bathroom while Mr. Adler was trying on his new clothes."

"Of course, Mr. Wingate. Ciao."

"Ciao."

"Good day," Mason said. They pushed through the glass door and stepped out onto the sidewalk. "Sixteen dollars and eighty-nine cents for two pairs of trousers and two shirts. You may be going back there, Walter, but I certainly won't be."

"Don't be cheap. You can't find this kind of fashion at J. C. Penney."

"With good reason," Mason said. He was staring sternly at Walter as he walked toward the car, and he ran right into a woman who was leaving the art supply shop, knocking her handbag and small package to the sidewalk.

"Oh, I beg your pardon," Mason said, picking up her package and handbag from the pavement. She was well dressed, in her late thirties or early forties, and wore slightly too much makeup, giving her a severe look.

"Do watch where you're going," she snapped, adjusting her wide-brimmed hat.

"I'm so terribly sorry," he said, handing the things back to her. "My fault entirely. I hope there was nothing breakable inside."

"A few paints and art supplies, that's all. I'm sure it's fine. Thank you." Her tone was sharp and curt.

"If there is anything damaged or broken, I'd be more than glad to reimburse you. The name is Mason Adler. My friend here and I are staying at the Oasis Inn until Friday."

The woman looked surprised. "My, what a small world. My husband and I, our son, and my husband's brother are also staying there," the woman said. "We just checked in yesterday."

"It is a small world, Mrs....?"

"Mrs. Angus Pruitt. We're from Los Angeles, here for a week." Her tone had softened a bit.

"I look forward to visiting with you and your family, then, Mrs. Pruitt. We've only just gotten to town from Phoenix. Oh, this is my friend, Mr. Wingate."

"How do you do, Mrs. Pruitt?" Walter said, tipping his hat.

"How do you do?" she said. "Are the two of you here on business?"

"No, just a little getaway," Mason said. "A quick vacation."

"I see. Will your wives be joining you?"

"Wives? We're not married. Whatever gave you that idea?" Walter said huffily.

"I beg your pardon?" she said.

"Forgive my friend, Mrs. Pruitt. He's a bitter fellow, unlucky in love, you see. As for me, I'm a confirmed bachelor, set in my ways."

Mrs. Pruitt nodded sagely. "I see. I know a few confirmed bachelors in Los Angeles."

"I'm sure you do," Walter said. "I hear Los Angeles and San Francisco are just teeming with them. Perhaps you could introduce me next time I'm there."

"Introduce you?" Mrs. Pruitt looked puzzled.

"To your confirmed bachelor friends," Walter said.

"Perhaps. I don't know them well, though. Anyway, I must be going. Nice meeting you both, Mr. Adler, and, um, Mr. Wingate."

Mason and Walter both tipped their hats.

"Likewise, Mrs. Pruitt," Mason said. "I'm sure we'll see you later at the Oasis. Good day."

"Good day." She turned and walked away as Mason glowered at Walter.

"Do you always have to be so insufferable?" Mason said.

"What did I do?"

" 'Perhaps you could introduce me next time I'm there'?"

"What's wrong with that?"

"You could try being a little more discreet, Walter, though I suppose that's like asking a peacock to blend in with a herd of turkeys."

"I don't want to blend in. Certainly not with turkeys. Besides, she knew."

"Well, of course she knew with you behaving like that."

"So what?"

"So, she's staying at the same resort we're staying at. Everyone's going to know, and I don't like people knowing my business."

"Your business is as dull and gray as dirty dishwater, darling, and would bore everyone to tears, me included. Anyway, let's get going. It's almost five already, and I'm certain Marvin is wondering where we are," Walter said.

"Fine, but since we're here, let me pop into the hardware store first and pick up a picture postcard for Lydia."

"Ugh, we're only here three full days. You'll probably beat it home."

"I know, but I promised her I'd send one."

"Postcards are silly. Blah, blah, blah, having a great time, wish you were here. How droll."

"Don't be bitter just because you don't have anyone to send one to. Wait here, I'll be back in a flash."

"I'm not bitter, and I do have someone to send one to if I wanted to. I just don't want to, that's all."

"Fine. I'll give her your regards." Mason went into the hardware store and was back quickly with a penny postcard of an aerial view of the city in his hands. "Now we can go."

"Goody," Walter said.

CHAPTER SIX

Tuesday afternoon, May 28, 1946
The Oasis Inn, Palm Springs

The inn was easy enough to find—a set of three single-story light blue stucco buildings set back off Warm Sands just far enough for a couple of cars to park on either side of the entrance gate. Two L-shaped buildings to the left and right faced a long rectangular one at the rear, creating a center courtyard. Between the short ends of the two L-shaped buildings was a black metal gate with the office entrance in front of and to the left of it, marked by a red neon sign.

"Looks like the front parking area is completely full, but Marvin told me we can park along the left side of the inn, too," Walter said.

"Okay," Mason said. He put his car in reverse and turned the corner onto East Camino Parocela to the first open spot, shutting off the engine. "Let's get checked in, I'm beat."

"Sure. I'll carry your bag from Rudy's and pop into the office to see Marvin and let him know we've arrived, while you bring in the rest of the things," Walter said, opening his door and stepping out onto the pavement.

"The rest of the things being my one suitcase and garment bag and your four suitcases, train case, garment bag, and hatbox?"

Walter counted briefly on his fingertips. "That sounds right. Just bring everything to the office until we find out what room we're in."

"You could lend a hand, you know."

"Darling, I *am* lending a hand. I've got your bag from Rudy's right here. Don't be long now, and be careful with my garment bag!" Walter said as he turned and sashayed around the corner toward the office.

"Careful with my garment bag my ass," Mason said, annoyed. He opened the trunk and removed the bags, setting them on the concrete. He tucked one suitcase under his right arm, took two more by the handles, and then walked awkwardly to the office, where he noticed Walter chatting animatedly with an attractive, small-built man behind the counter. The man looked up as Mason entered and smiled.

"Ah, you must be Mr. Adler," the man said. "Welcome to the Oasis." He had reddish, wavy hair, almost curly; a clean-shaven, light complexion; and brilliant blue eyes the color of a vibrant desert bluebell. He was dressed in a pale yellow shirt with the sleeves rolled up, a red and blue tie, and navy blue suspenders holding up his navy blue pleated trousers, just visible over the top of the counter. A small gray cat was curled up next to the telephone. She lifted her head and mewed softly at Mason.

"How do you do?" Mason said. "I take it you're Mr. Gagliardi."

"The one and only if you don't count my father, and he doesn't count for much. But please call me Marvin."

"A pleasure to meet you, Marvin. So, you run this place all by yourself?" Mason said, setting down the three suitcases.

"Mostly. I have maids who come in daily and do the rooms and the laundry, and my cat Toujours here keeps the rodent population under control as well as keeping me company. She works cheap."

Mason scratched the little cat's head and was rewarded by a soft purr. "Toujours is an interesting name."

"French for *always*."

"You speak French?"

"French Canadian. I'm from Canada originally."

"Ah, nice. Lovely country, I hear. Well, I have a few more things to bring in, if you'll excuse me."

"Oh, please, let me help you," Marvin said, coming around from behind the counter.

"Thanks, but I can manage."

"Don't be silly. That's what I'm here for."

"What am I supposed to do?" Walter said, looking from one to the other.

"You could help," Mason said. "Or just stand there and chat with the cat."

"Oh, I'm sure you two big strong fellows can manage just fine without me," Walter said, lighting up a cigarette.

"You haven't changed a bit, Walter," Marvin said with a smile. He followed Mason to the car and quite ably picked up the remaining suitcases, train case, and hatbox.

"You're pretty strong," Mason said.

"For a little fellow you mean, right?"

"For any fellow. Clearly you keep in good shape."

"Thanks. Is this everything?"

"Not quite, there are two garment bags in the back seat. I can manage those," Mason said, opening the left rear door. "Oh, I forgot about this mess of a map."

Marvin glanced in at the mangled paper map Walter had tossed into the back seat earlier. "Jeepers, what happened to it?"

"Walter happened to it. He was trying to fold it back up, but he had some problems."

"So I see. Well, allow me." Marvin set the bags down, took the map out, smoothed it, and expertly refolded it before placing it back into the car's glove box. "There you go, good as new."

"Thanks."

"My pleasure," Marvin said.

Mason pulled out the two garment bags, draped them over his left arm, and shut the car door. "That's everything. Only the one suitcase and one of the garment bags belong to me. The rest are Walter's."

Marvin grinned. "Walter's never been one to pack light. Or to lift a finger if he can help it."

Mason smiled back, admiring the man's physique. He appeared to be in his early to mid-thirties and reminded Mason a lot of the movie actor Danny Kaye. He had a slight build, stood about five foot eight, and weighed around 135 pounds. "Sounds as if you know him well."

"We go back a few years. Walter's unique."

Mason laughed. "You can say that again. He told me he met you here in Palm Springs."

"That's right. I moved here in 1941 from Quebec when I was thirty-three, just before the United States got into the war. I couldn't take the Canadian winters anymore. Shortly after I arrived, I got a job at the Triada, and I met a fellow who invited me to a private house party. That's where Walter and I became acquainted. How about you?"

"I've known him since ninth grade. A long time," Mason said.

"I understand the two of you are just friends?" Marvin said.

"Yes, nothing more. I'm a confirmed bachelor."

"Same here. It's the best way to be. No strings, no commitments, no ties."

"Yup. Besides, even if I wasn't a confirmed bachelor, Walter is definitely not my type," Mason said.

"Oh? What is your type, if you don't mind my asking?"

"I like men a little less, well, a little less like Walter."

"Same here. Not that there's anything wrong with Walter."

"No, of course not. He can be a bit much, but down deep he's got a good heart, and he's a good friend."

"Good friends are like gold, maybe more so with men like us," Marvin said.

"I agree. Hard to find, important to keep."

"Yes. So, Walter tells me you're a private detective."

"I am. And he told me you do photography work on the side, selling your photos of attractive young men to muscle and fitness magazines."

Marvin sighed. "Walter talks a lot."

"He does. I hope you don't mind him sharing that with me, though."

"No, it's fine. Any friend of Walter's is a friend of mine, Mr. Adler."

"Thanks, I appreciate that, and please call me Mason."

"Thanks, Mason. The fitness photos are just to help pay the bills, actually. I also do weddings, portraits, that sort of thing. Owning the Oasis resort is a dream come true for me. Being my own boss is wonderful. I get to meet so many people, and it helps with keeping my photography studio afloat, too."

"That's terrific. Palm Springs is a pretty small town, though, only about four thousand people. Where do you find the men to photograph?"

"The winter population goes much higher, and the entire Coachella Valley is close to fifty thousand, not to mention Riverside County, which is huge. So I don't seem to ever have a shortage of eager young fellows wanting to get their picture taken."

"Speaking of that, Walter gave your name to a young man who works at a filling station on Palm Canyon today, a handsome gentleman who wants to break into show business."

"Ah, I get a lot of those."

"I suppose you do. This fellow's name is Leroy. Not sure of his last name. Any of the other guys ever make it?"

"In showbiz? There was one fellow, but honestly most of them haven't, at least not as far as I know, but anything's possible. The photos give them a lot of exposure, though. So to speak."

"So, you pay these men to take their photos, then you sell them to the magazines for a profit?"

"That's right, but I don't take just any fellow's picture. I have a pretty good eye for who will sell and who won't."

"Are they nudes?"

"No, those would never get published, not to mention they're illegal. If I were to get arrested, it would be the end of everything for me. My photography, the inn, *everything*."

"Best not to take chances," Mason said.

"Exactly. The men usually wear jocks or posing straps and the like. And I only shoot guys twenty-one or over. It's all strictly professional and strictly business."

"No funny business?" Mason said, raising a brow.

Marvin shook his head adamantly. "Not that it's any of your business, but absolutely not, not on my end. Some of the men have made a pass at me in the studio, but I don't go for that when I'm working. I keep things on the level. Besides, most of the fellows who want their pictures taken are heterosexual, or at least they claim to be. Some even pose for free, just on the hopes their pictures get published."

"Interesting and surprising."

"I guess so. Anyway, it's a living. And I make pretty good money at it now, both there and here at the Oasis."

"I'm glad to hear it's lucrative for you."

"It has been so far, though I have a lot of bills, too." Marvin shifted his weight from one foot to the other. "I suppose Walter told you about what happened at the Triada?"

"He did," Mason said, setting the garment bags on the hood of the car.

"I figured. I was the night manager, but I was working the day shift for a coworker on vacation. One of the guests, a Mr. Rich Thompson, invited me to his room early one afternoon. I stupidly agreed because he was handsome and just home from the war. I figured it was my duty to my new country to help out a veteran, you know?"

"Very patriotic of you."

"Yeah, well, he told me his wife had gone shopping and wouldn't be back until much later. We were in bed when she walked in unexpectedly. I got dressed and got the hell out of there, but Boyce

Bergman, the general manager, soon called me to his office. He told me Mrs. Thompson was threatening the hotel with a lawsuit, and she was going to file for divorce. He also said she planned on getting the police involved, but Mr. Bergman talked her into waiting until the next day, giving her a chance to calm down. Given the threat of a lawsuit, he said he had no choice but to fire me. I got my things and left the hotel about three o'clock. The next day, I discovered Mrs. Thompson had drowned in the hotel pool in the early morning hours. Apparently she couldn't sleep and went for a swim. The police listed it as an accident, but no one knows exactly what happened."

"How horrible."

"It was, but for me it was a good break, and for Mr. Thompson, too, in a way. Neither of us were arrested, and the news of her death overshadowed any rumor that may have leaked out about him and me, so there was no scandal. I think Mr. Bergman kept things quiet. Mr. Thompson went home, and I bought this place. I never heard from him again."

"The Oasis must have been expensive."

"It was, and I didn't have much. I found a silent partner, though. He supplied most of the cash in exchange for my knowledge of the business and the idea that I would do most of the work around the place. I have a small apartment on the premises, just across from the office. I'm there almost all the time."

"Lucky for you to find someone willing to invest."

"Not so lucky, as it turns out. He's not so silent anymore. I can't seem to get rid of him, and I still owe a hefty amount of money. I didn't read the loan agreement very carefully, I'm afraid. The interest amount keeps increasing."

"That puts you in a difficult position, I suppose."

"Yeah. But I probably shouldn't be talking about all this with you, Mason."

"Sorry for sticking my nose in, Marvin. Professional habit, I guess, of being a dick."

"It's okay, I understand. Well, let's get you two checked in," Marvin said, picking up the suitcases, train case, and hatbox once more.

"Sure, after you," Mason said, draping the garment bags over his arm.

The two of them walked back to the office where Walter was waiting impatiently, the little gray cat watching him from her perch.

"What took you two so long?" Walter said, as Marvin and Mason set the remaining luggage down.

"We were just talking about a mutual friend," Mason said.

"Oh?" Walter said. "Who?"

"You, of course," Marvin said with a chuckle.

"Oh. Oh! I hope it was all good things," Walter said, extinguishing his cigarette in a glass ashtray emblazoned with *The Oasis Inn* as the cat leaped down from the counter.

"More or less," Mason said.

Marvin smiled as he stepped back behind the desk. "You're in room two, second door on the left as you enter the courtyard. You have a pool view. All the rooms have pool views except numbers four and nine, which are in the corners by the side gates. Here are your keys." He slid them across the counter, and they each took one.

"Thanks," Mason said.

"I just need your signature in the register. You pay when you leave."

Mason scribbled his name into the book. "Looks like quite a few guests have checked in already."

"Mmm, yes, we're nearly at fifty percent occupancy, which isn't bad for midweek this time of year," Marvin said. "Most are the Pruitt family, they have three rooms. Two ladies from San Diego checked in Sunday, and I have another woman coming in tomorrow. Counting her and the two of you, that will make six rooms full out of twelve."

"I assume the Pruitts rode together, and so did the two women, but there are four cars out front," Mason said.

"Yes, the red one belongs to the ladies, the Ford sedan and the truck are mine, and the DeSoto belongs to the Pruitts."

"We ran into Mrs. Pruitt downtown earlier today. She mentioned she was here with her husband, their son, and her husband's brother," Mason said.

"That's right. They've stayed here before, though usually it's just been Mr. Pruitt alone or with his brother."

"The wife seemed nice enough," Mason said.

"I suppose she is. Her husband, not so much. He always finds something to complain about."

"And yet he comes here regularly?"

"I wouldn't say regularly, but he's come a few times, yes. He has a vested interest in the place."

"Ah, I see. The silent partner?" Mason said.

Marvin shook his head. "It's nothing, forget I said anything. I'm sure you'll get a chance to meet them all around the pool tomorrow, and you can form your own opinions. Everyone's getting ready for cocktails and dinner at the moment, I believe."

"As we need to do," Walter said. "It's coming six, you know."

"Honestly, I'd be happy with just a cocktail, a quick dinner, and a hot bath," Mason said.

"Oh, for heaven's sake. I don't know why you even came," Walter said. "But you'll feel better after a drink or two and some dinner. Since you are apparently so fatigued, I suppose we could dine downtown, but tomorrow the Racquet Club, and the day after that the Triada." Walter gazed at Mr. Gagliardi. "I hope you don't mind, Marvin. About us patronizing it, I mean."

"Not at all. The Triada's a nice place. I hold no grudges," Marvin said.

"That's big of you, darling," Walter said. "And thank you for everything."

"You're welcome. I hope you enjoy your stay."

"We will, I'm sure. See you in the morning," Mason said.

"Need help with your bags again?"

"Thank you, but I'm sure Mason can manage," Walter said. "I'll take my train case and the bag from Rudy's and unlock the door."

"Of course you will," Mason said, picking up four of the suitcases, one under each arm and one in each hand. "I'll have to come back for the other one, and the garment bags and hatbox."

"It's just two doors down," Marvin said, coming out from behind the counter again. "Let me help." He picked up the rest of the bags, and the three of them, followed by Toujours, left the office and went through the side door to the courtyard, the pool gleaming in the middle. Marvin led the way, stopping at room two, as the cat moved off in search of dinner. "Here you are."

Mason inserted the key and opened the door, and they all went in as Walter turned on the lights and looked around. "Well, this looks homey. Just set the bags anywhere, fellas."

"Sure," Marvin said as he and Mason set the suitcases down.

"Looks nice," Mason said. "What's that little octagonal window next to the closet?"

"It looks onto a small, narrow area between each of the buildings and the surrounding walls. If you open both it and the front window at the same time, you can get some nice cross-ventilation. We don't have conditioned air here, so that and the ceiling fan help. There's also an in-room heater built into the wall there," Marvin said. "It gets pretty chilly at night this time of year. Oh, and there's a soda pop machine and a cigarette machine down the way outside. You can get ice from the one next to the office. We have books, board games, and whatnot, too, if you like. Those are complimentary. We just ask you to return the books and board games when you're finished."

"Marvelous," Walter said.

"We serve iced tea out by the pool from eleven to three every day, and I can make you a sandwich if you get hungry. The kitchen's open from noon to one for that. Nothing special, usually just cheese sandwiches and some chips, but it tides folks over. Oh, and there's coffee and doughnuts in the office from eight to ten, or until they're gone."

"There, you see, Mason? They even serve breakfast and lunch," Walter said.

"Yes, so I hear, but somehow I think you'll be wanting to go out for your meals."

"Well, of course, but it's nice to have the option, anyway," Walter said. "Oh, by the way, I'll need to have my dinner jacket and tuxedo pressed before tomorrow night, Marvin."

"I'm afraid we don't offer that service here, Walter," Marvin said, "but I can get you an iron and ironing board if you like."

"Oh. Well, I suppose that will have to do." He looked at Mason. "Do you know how to iron?"

"I've done it when necessary."

"Excellent. Then drop the iron and the board off tomorrow morning, please, Marvin," Walter said. "But not too early. Any time after ten should be fine."

"All right. Let me know if you need anything else."

"We will," Mason said. "Thanks again." He held out a quarter to Marvin, who paused just briefly and then took it, dropping it into his pants pocket.

"Have a good night. It was a pleasure meeting you, Mr. Adler—Mason, I mean. And good seeing you again, Walter."

"Likewise," they both said, as Marvin exited and closed the door behind him.

"Well? What do you think?"

"He seems like a nice man," Mason said. "He's not at all what I expected."

"I meant what do you think about the room, but what do you mean Marvin's not what you expected? What did you expect?"

"I don't know. Someone shiftier, I guess, a little sleazier, greasy."

"Why on earth would you expect that? Because I met him at a dark, lights-out house party and because he got fired from the Triada for fooling around with a married male guest whose wife ended up dead, and he takes erotic pictures of young men for muscle magazines?"

Mason shrugged. "Yeah, I guess so."

"Well, no one's perfect, you included."

"Granted and likewise."

"Then we should all get along fine," Walter said. "You don't still think he had anything to do with the drowning of that woman, do you?"

"I honestly can't say for certain. He told me more of the details when we were getting the last of the bags. It sounded like he was telling the truth, but it's impossible to know for certain. What do you suppose is up with him and Mr. Pruitt?" Mason said.

"Oh, he means Angus Pruitt. He was telling me about it on the telephone. Mr. Pruitt invested in the Oasis and helped Marvin buy the place."

"I figured he was the silent partner Marvin mentioned who's not so silent anymore."

"My, you two did have a nice little chat, didn't you? Well, I don't know everything, of course, but I do know Mr. Pruitt has been pressuring Marvin to expand his photography business into nudes. And not just pictures, but films, and not just men, but women, too. And men and women together. He wants to shoot some of the films here at the Oasis, in the rooms and out by the pool, since it's so private."

"Really?"

"Yes, but Marvin is loath to do it for some reason. Personally I don't see why. It sounds like a good opportunity and good money to me."

"Pornography is illegal. It could get Marvin arrested."

"Pish posh. That's highly unlikely."

"Not a risk Marvin wants to take. He said if he were to be arrested, he'd lose the inn, his photography business, everything."

"Oh, well in that case he should just tell him no," Walter said.

"I don't think it's that easy. Marvin mentioned he still owes Mr. Pruitt a sizeable amount of money."

"Yes, I know. And Marvin told me Mr. Pruitt keeps increasing the amount of the interest. Apparently, the contract Mr. Pruitt had him sign has some kind of balloon payment built into it, and interest fees that increase quarterly."

"Never borrow money without reading the fine print. I suppose it's none of our business," Mason said.

"None at all, though that's never stopped you from snooping around before. So what do you think of the place?"

Mason looked about. There were two twin beds with matching blue-and-cream striped coverlets, and a single nightstand between them that held an alarm clock and a small lamp. A rattan ceiling fan rotated overhead, the floor was tiled, and there was a full-length mirror on the back wall, which was next to the little octagonal window by the closet and opposite the entrance to the blue tiled bathroom. In front of the larger, courtyard-facing window was a small combination desk and dresser, which held another lamp and a small radio. A wooden armchair was tucked under the desk portion, and a floor lamp that matched the others stood in the corner. "It's not bad. Clean and orderly, looks comfortable."

"Yes, I think it will do nicely. I'll take the bed nearest the bathroom, if you don't mind."

"And nearest the wall heater."

"Well, you know how beastly cold I get, and I only brought my silk pajamas. It's supposed to be in the forties tonight. I'm already a little chilled."

"Fine," Mason said, shaking his head. "I suppose we should unpack and get ready for dinner. I'm hungry and thirsty."

"Me too," Walter said, opening one of his suitcases and unzipping his garment bag. "I think simple suits and ties for tonight. Tomorrow and the next night will be black tie after you press everything, of course. At the Triada they do those things for you, you know."

"And at the Oasis, apparently you think *I* do those things for you." Mason walked to the window and pulled the blue and tan plaid curtains closed.

CHAPTER SEVEN

Wednesday morning, May 29, 1946
The Oasis Inn, Palm Springs

Mason woke slowly and glanced at the alarm clock. A quarter to nine. He pulled his near-naked body out of bed and padded quietly to the bathroom so as not to disturb Walter, who was still snoring softly. He used the toilet, washed and shaved, and then, with a towel around his waist, came back into the room, put the dirty underwear inside his suitcase, and peeked out the front curtains before stepping back and starting to get dressed. The nightstand light clicked on and Walter sat up, pushing his black silk sleep mask atop his head.

"What time is it?" he asked, groggily.

"Twenty after nine, sleepyhead."

"Ugh, these early mornings are just beastly."

"It's hardly early. I'm going into town for breakfast. If you get up, you can join me. My stomach's grumbling."

"I'm a bit peckish myself. I don't suppose I could persuade you to bring me back a cup of strong black coffee and a hard-boiled egg?"

"No. Come with me or do without until lunch."

"You're a mean man, Mr. Adler." Walter threw back the covers and climbed out of bed, smoothing his red silk pajamas and removing the sleep mask entirely. "What's all that racket outside?"

"Just some of the other guests staking their claims on the lounge chairs for the day."

"Already? The sun's barely up. Are they crazy?"

"It's probably just a vicious rumor, Walter, but as I said before, I've been told the sun comes up around five-twenty this time of year, and some people actually get up at seven or earlier."

"Voluntarily?"

"Yes."

"Well, they're mad, simply mad." He picked up his train case and took it into the bathroom while Mason finished getting dressed, putting on the light blue gabardine trousers he'd purchased the previous day at Rudy's along with one of the shirts, a short-sleeved white with navy knit, which he tucked in. As he was yanking on his loafers, Walter exited the bathroom, dressed in a black silk kimono and matching slippers, his pajamas now over his arm.

"Well, I did the best I could with my hair and mustache, considering you're in such a hurry," Walter said, glancing at himself in the full-length mirror.

"You packed a robe and slippers?" Mason said, staring at him.

"Of course, darling. Didn't you?"

"No. I don't even own slippers, and the only robe I have is a tattered gray terrycloth, which I left at home."

"Gray. Of course it would be gray. *And* terrycloth. But at least you're wearing some of the fabulous new clothes you bought at Rudy's, I see," Walter said, looking at him approvingly. "You look marvelous."

"Thank you."

"You're welcome, darling." Walter walked over to the dresser, put his pajamas away, and pulled out a few articles of clothing which he carried back to the bathroom. "I won't be but a minute, I promise," he said over his shoulder.

"You're going to dress in the bathroom?"

Walter turned and faced Mason. "What's wrong with that? You've never seen me naked, and I don't intend to start now. Best to keep some mystery in our relationship, you know."

"There's nothing *but* mystery in our friendship, the biggest being why I put up with you sometimes."

"Oh, Mason, you are so very droll. No wonder I adore you," Walter said, closing the bathroom door. "Sit tight, I'll be quick as a flash."

Twenty-three minutes later, he emerged dressed in pleated teal short pants, a black belt, white shirt, black leather loafers, and yellow over-the-calf socks. He set his train case on the floor of the closet and looked over at Mason. "All right, I think I'm all set now."

"Short pants?"

"Darling, we're in Palm Springs. It's a resort town. We should dress like the locals."

"Somehow, I don't think the locals dress quite like that, especially for breakfast."

"Of course they do." He walked to the window, its curtains now open, and gazed out at the courtyard. "So much sunshine, and, oh my, so much exposed skin on those people."

"It *is* a pool, Walter. I'm sure they're just dressing like the locals."

"Ha ha. Oh dear, I think I've forgotten my sunglasses in your automobile. I don't suppose you'd fetch them for me?"

"No. You can get them when we leave."

"But you know squinting causes crow's feet, and my skin is so delicate."

"Like a cactus. You'll be fine for the two-minute walk to the car."

"Well, I suppose I have no choice, so let's go. I'm simply famished, and I desperately need a cigarette." He pulled out a Camel and lit up, blowing the smoke upward. "You really should take up cigarettes. I've heard the smoke in your lungs is good for you, like smoked meat. It's a preservative, and you could certainly use that."

"Hasn't seemed to help you any."

"Droll this morning, aren't you? Now then, where shall we eat? The Racquet Club?"

"That's a bit out of my price range for breakfast. There's a little place I spotted yesterday on our way into town, the Big Cup Café."

"Sounds dreadful, but don't let it be said I'm not adventurous. What shall we do afterward?"

Mason glanced at the clock. "It's almost ten thirty. After breakfast it will be time for lunch."

"Oh, don't be a goose. We're on holiday, as they say on the Continent. I tell you what, we'll finish breakfast around noon or so, then come back here and lounge about the pool, reading and soaking up the sun and a little vodka. At three-ish, we'll change for a late lunch in town, then back here for a siesta, or nap, as you call it. It should be five thirty or so when we awake, just in time to freshen up and change for cocktails around six thirty, followed by dinner at the Racquet Club at eight. After dinner, we'll swing by the Chi Chi Club."

"What for?"

"What for? Dorothy Dandridge is performing tonight, of course, along with the Incomparable Hildegarde, not to mention all the celebrities that go there that we can rub elbows with," Walter said, taking another drag on his Camel. "There'll be drinks, music, handsome men, and dancing all night long."

"I must admit I adore Dorothy Dandridge, and Hildegarde has a lovely voice, but who will we dance with? I don't want to just sit around listening to the music, drinking all night, and watching everyone else have fun."

"Single women are always looking for dance partners, don't you worry," Walter said. "And rumor has it some of the busboys can be rather friendly. Not for dancing, of course, but perhaps in other ways after they get off work."

"Friendly if you give them a big tip."

"I *always* do, darling. I may be frugal, but I know where to spend my money wisely. Anyway, that will take us to the wee hours of the morning, when we shall tiptoe quietly back to our beds here and sleep until noon tomorrow, a much more civilized time to rise."

"I see."

"Unless I can convince one of those busboys to take me home. In that case, you're on your own," Walter said, picking up his jaunty straw boater and placing it atop his head at a rakish angle. "Remember, I brought my handcuffs."

"I don't want to know. Honestly, you're incorrigible."

"Thank you, so glad you noticed. And perhaps tomorrow afternoon we can play a game of tennis at the Racquet Club."

"I don't play very well," Mason said.

"You don't need to. Jerome is the pro there. Rumor has it he gives private lessons for a fee, and he's very, very good."

"At teaching tennis?"

"Hmm? Oh yes, that, too, I'm sure."

Mason sucked in a breath and let it out slowly. "I'm sure. Come on, Walter, I'm hungry, it's getting late, and I want to stop and mail this postcard to Lydia. I wrote it out while I was waiting for you."

"Waiting for me? Tut, tut. I've been standing here all ready for the last ten minutes."

Mason rolled his eyes as he turned off the heater, pulled open the door to the room, put his hat and sunglasses on, and walked out, Walter trailing behind shielding his eyes from the bright sun and puffing away on his cigarette.

CHAPTER EIGHT

Early Wednesday afternoon, May 29, 1946
The Oasis Inn, Palm Springs

"Welcome back," Marvin said, opening the gate for Mason and Walter as they approached. "Have a nice lunch?"

"Actually it was a late breakfast," Mason said. "But it was fine."

"It was adequate," Walter said, taking off his sunglasses and looking at Marvin. "Not to my standards, but I suppose one must make do."

"Especially when I'm paying for it," Mason said, looking at Walter sideways before turning back to Marvin. "We went to the Big Cup Café."

"I know it. It's usually pretty good."

"I had something called a Big Cup Platter," Walter said. "It wasn't Eggs Benedict, but it was satisfying, in a greasy sort of way."

"Uh-huh. Anyway, most of the other guests are out at the pool, as you can see, but there's still a couple of loungers left if you'd like to join them."

"Sounds like an excellent suggestion. Come on, Walter. We'll see you later, Marvin."

"Do let me know if there's anything else you need. I put that ironing board and iron in your room, and there are towels on the tables by the loungers. There are also metal pitchers of tea on the table by the office. Help yourself. It's there every day from eleven to three."

"I hate warm tea," Walter said. "No offense."

"Ice is available from the machine next to the side door to the office. Just let me know when you're finished with the iron and board, and I'll collect them."

"Thank you," Mason said again as he walked through the gate into the courtyard, Walter following behind.

Heads turned as they entered. Mason felt a bit uncomfortable but nodded politely as he walked toward their room. Walter, on the other hand, gave the queen's wave to them all and called out a cheery "Hello!" which was mostly not returned.

Once safely inside their room, Mason closed the door, pulled the curtains, and turned on the overhead light. The iron and board were set up near the closet, and the beds had been neatly made.

"No mints on the pillows, but I suppose I didn't really expect any at this place," Walter said, taking off his straw hat and placing it on the dresser/desk along with his sunglasses.

"You'll just have to suffer through."

"You joke, but it really is the little things, you know. Oh well, I'll have to give Marvin a list of suggestions before we leave. I'm sure he'll appreciate it. You can press my jacket and tuxedo later, darling, don't worry about that now."

"I wasn't planning to, and I wasn't worried," Mason said, removing his hat and setting it beside Walter's upside down so as not to crush the brim.

"Good, because right now we should change and make our entrance out by the pool," Walter said. "Our public awaits. Well, mine, anyway."

Mason looked critically at Walter. "Honestly, Walter, do you always have to be so…so much?"

Walter cocked his head. "So much *what*?"

"You know. So much. Sometimes it's just *too* much. Doing that little wave out there just now, calling men *darling* and *love*." Mason gestured at Walter. "And wearing those clothes."

Walter walked to the full-length mirror and studied himself. "What's wrong with what I've got on? It's fashionable and stylish, though I admit I *was* the only fellow over twelve wearing short pants at breakfast this morning. Nevertheless, someday men will wear them everywhere, mark my words, like they do in Bermuda."

"If you say so."

"I do." He turned back to Mason. "And so what if I wave and call some men *darling*?"

"Because it's all just too much, that's what's wrong with it."

"You mean it makes me look like a pansy or a fairy."

"Well, yes. Yes, it does, to be frank."

"You're always frank. I'd like to be Frank sometime, though I suppose you are better at it. All right, you be Frank, and I'll be Nancy. Oh, I love a good role play."

Mason sighed and shook his head. "That's exactly what I'm talking about. You're so far over the top as to be embarrassingly outrageous."

Walter looked indignant as he pouted. "I'm *embarrassing*?"

Mason paused, staring at him. "I don't want to hurt your feelings, Walter, but yes, you are sometimes."

"I see. And if people think *I'm* a pansy, they'll think you're one, too. Guilt by association, is that it?"

Mason sighed and rubbed his eyes. "I just think it pays to be discreet. For your own safety."

"And for yours," Walter said huffily.

"Fine, for my safety and comfort, too."

"At least you admit it, darling. Oops, sorry, I mean Mason."

"I'm just saying it wouldn't hurt to tone it down a bit. Especially around people you don't know. You know what Emil's always saying."

"Oh, he thinks like a big old policeman."

"Emil *is* a big old policeman," Mason said. "Or a police detective, at any rate."

"I know. But I'm just being me. I don't like pretending to be someone different. Or something I'm not."

"You may not like it, but I'd appreciate it if you'd make an attempt. I don't want to see you hurt."

"I've been hurt all my life. Do you think I don't know what people say about me behind my back? Or sometimes even to my face? I've always been picked on because of my size. I'm barely five foot six. In fact, five foot five last time I checked. I think I'm shrinking."

"That happens as people age."

"Well, that's just swell."

"Just a part of getting older."

"Well, besides being short, I'm also a pansy and I have a fairly high voice, so of course they're going to talk about me. And if they're going to, I'd rather give them something interesting to talk about. I'd rather be fabulous than invisible."

"You're certainly not invisible."

"Thank you, and I mean that sincerely, though I know it wasn't given as a compliment. Oh, believe it or not, there was a time when I tried to blend in, to fit in, to be masculine. I wore lifts in my shoes, and I dressed like everyone else. I also lowered my voice, as much as

I could anyway. But you know what? It didn't help, at least not much. So, now I'm the genuine me, like it or not. And I'm sorry I embarrass you. I know I *can* be a bit much sometimes."

"You can, it's true, and I admit I can sometimes be a little *too* fretful about appearances. But you have to be careful, or you could end up face down in the canal some day with a bullet or a knife in your back. Do you understand what I'm saying?"

Walter nodded. "Yes I do, I truly do. But now let me ask you something, if I may. And I want you to be honest with me *and* with yourself."

Mason looked at him suspiciously. "What?"

"You admitted you're too fretful about appearances and what other people think, and I'd like to know why. Why *are* you so tightly wound? And why are you always so concerned that I'm a little flamboyant? I certainly don't care."

"You may not, but I do."

"You've made that painfully obvious over the years, but *why*? As long as I've known you, you've been this way," Walter said, lighting up a Camel.

"Yeah, well, as long as I've known you, you've been *that* way. Maybe that's why I've kept my distance in the past. Why I never wrote or telephoned after I left home."

Walter inhaled and let out a poof of smoke. "We didn't see each other again until after your father died, fourteen years after you'd left. I remember we ran into each other downtown a few weeks after the funeral. I almost didn't recognize you."

Mason sighed. "Yes, I'm sorry for not keeping in touch. To be honest, it wasn't just you, and it still isn't. It all goes back to something that happened a long time ago. I really don't like to talk about it much."

"Talk about what? You can tell me. Something that happened in your youth? You've made vague references to your father and your childhood on occasion. I recall when we met on the street that day and you told me he'd died, you were very blasé about it all. You weren't exactly in mourning."

"No. We weren't close. I never spoke to him once I left. My only regret is that it tore my mother apart."

"Family relations can be difficult, darling. I mean Mason."

"Yeah. I think about my childhood and early years every once in a while. You know, memories are funny. Some warm your heart, and some others freeze it cold."

"So, tell me about the ones that froze it cold."

Mason stared back at Walter while he put some Vaseline on his lips. After what seemed like forever, he nodded, slowly. "Fine. But this stays between you and me, understood?"

"Scout's honor."

"You were never a Scout," Mason said.

"Then I swear on my mother's grave," Walter said, holding up his right hand, palm toward Mason.

"All right, I suppose that will have to do. When I was about eight, a neighbor girl, Lula May Armstrong, and I were playing in the backyard of our house. It was spring, close to Easter."

"Oh, I do love Easter. So many fabulous clothes..."

"Yes, well, speaking of that, Lula May had borrowed a couple of her mother's hats, a colorful silk scarf, her parasol, and a red feather boa, and we were playing Easter parade. I had on one of the beautiful hats, with light green ribbons trailing down my back and feathers all over it, and the red feather boa about my neck."

"That's all you were wearing?"

"No, of course not. I had on my usual white shirt and gray knickers, and I was barefoot. I usually was in warm weather, and so was Lula May. I remember she wore a lavender gingham dress that day, accented by a pink hat with artificial roses and red ribbons, the colorful scarf, and the pretty pink parasol."

"Sounds like you two made a lovely couple of girls."

Mason shrugged. "We were just having fun as kids do, you know? I always had more fun with the neighborhood girls than I did the boys."

"That certainly changed as you got older. Now you have much more fun with the fellows."

"Yes, but I just wanted friends at that age, and Lula May and I were the best of friends. I was leading the parade, swishing this way and that, and Lula May was behind me, pulling her wagon with her stuffed animals and her little dog Elmo, when my father came charging out of the house. He'd been at work, but when he got home he apparently saw us from the parlor window."

"Oh dear." Walter took another long drag on his cigarette and blew the smoke out sideways.

"I remember his look of utter rage and disgust, his face a frightening shade of reddish purple. He blew across the yard, snatched the hat off my head, threw it in the dust, pulled the boa off my neck, almost choking me in the process, and grabbed me by one arm, lifting me off the ground. As he carried me to the house, still by one arm, I looked back at Lula May, who was just standing there crying as Elmo started barking, and I started to cry, too."

"Of course you did. It's only natural. How terrifying."

"It *was* terrifying. I didn't know why he was so angry. When we got in the house he spanked me so hard, I had welts on my bum, and when I cried even more, he slapped me across the face and gave me a fat lip. He told me that boys don't wear women's clothes or act like that, and that I had embarrassed and humiliated myself and the entire family in front of Lula May and the neighborhood."

"I see. And you were only eight years old. A manly man, your father," Walter said quietly.

"He was strict but a good provider for us. With him, it was all appearances and propriety. What other people thought of him was important, and first impressions were critical. He always said that to disgrace oneself or one's family is the worst thing a person could do, and that once you're disgraced, there's no turning back."

"Well, dare I say, he was wrong on nearly everything," Walter said. "What other people think isn't important in the least, and there are worse things one could do than disgrace himself or his family."

"Not in his opinion."

"What happened to you and Lula May after that incident?"

"I still saw her at school, but my father forbade me from playing with her anymore. I hated him for that."

"I would, too."

"Yes. I hated hating him, but I couldn't let it go. It festered inside me like a wound that never properly healed. He insisted I learn to do manly things, and he took me to sporting games, boxing matches, and on hunting trips, all of which I found brutal and appalling."

"What did your mother think of all that?"

"She deferred to him, as she always did except when it came to my education. She put her foot down about sending me to Wharton Academy."

"What did your father want?"

"I was the oldest son, and he expected me to become a carpenter like he was. Adler and Son, that was his dream. But it wasn't mine. He didn't see the need to waste money on Wharton when he could teach me everything I needed to know about carpentry and about being a man, or his version of it, anyway. Fortunately, my mother insisted on a formal education."

"Yes, if it wasn't for her, we might never have met. I was a year behind you at Wharton," Walter said. "Things never got any better with your father?"

"No. They got worse. I failed at most everything he wanted me to try, partly because I was angry with him. We butted heads constantly. I knew he would never accept me as I was, as I am, so I left home when I graduated from Wharton. I was just eighteen years old. It broke my mother's heart, but I couldn't stand him anymore. I don't think he could stand me, either."

"I remember that, though I didn't know all the details."

"No one did outside of the family. I was young, headstrong, and full of myself, but I was also scared out of my wits, with no real clear idea of what I was going to do or where I was going to go. I took job after job, moving from place to place, town to town, and man to man, I must admit. I found out early on that some men, especially older men, were not all like my father. Some were kind to me, took care of me, and actually even loved me for a while."

"In exchange for certain favors?"

Mason blushed. "Yes. It was a fair trade, and I didn't mind. Not really."

"I'm sure they didn't, either."

"They didn't seem to. One portly old fellow in particular, Oliver Walker, took quite a liking to me when I was in my mid-twenties and had settled back in Phoenix. He was a private investigator and did pretty well for himself. After a time, I got my private investigator license too, with his help, and we went into business together, Walker and Adler, Private Investigations."

"Just business?"

"No, we had an arrangement. I lived with him and shared his bed. He told people I was his nephew. I had my own room for appearance's sake. He was kind and generous and showed me the ropes. He also taught me that it was best to keep a low profile and be inconspicuous as a private investigator, which went along with what my father had always said. Ollie told me to carry myself with confidence and to make a good first impression. He said clients wouldn't hire a nelly private detective. They wouldn't trust him."

"I would."

"Yes, but not most people."

"I suppose," Walter said. "So, what happened to Mr. Walker?"

"Oliver passed away when I was just thirty, and he left me

everything—the house, the business, and a considerable amount of money. I was his only heir."

"That was kind of him. What became of your siblings? You don't speak of them much."

"We're not close, though I hear from them now and then— Christmas and birthday cards, an occasional letter, that sort of thing. Ray ended up becoming a carpenter, so Dad finally got his wish of a son for Adler and Son. He seems to be doing well. Both he and Clara got married and now have families of their own. Even though I never spoke to Dad again after I moved out of the house, my mother and I kept in touch through telegrams, letters, and the occasional telephone call. I was thirty-two when the old man had a stroke and dropped dead. For my mother's sake, I went to the funeral. Ray and Clara were there, of course. Our father would have been proud of them. He *was* proud of them, especially Ray."

"But not of you?"

Mason swallowed and stared down at his shoes. "I don't know. I think he'd be proud that I'm a successful private detective. I sometimes regret cutting off all ties with him, but I was stubborn and so was he. I know he suspected I was a homosexual, but it was never discussed. Not with him, not with my mother, not even with Clara or Ray. No one ever knew for sure. No one still does, I don't think, though I suppose they must wonder why I've never married."

"Your father sounds beastly. Not that mine was a cupcake. My old man believed in the old adage 'Spare the rod, spoil the child.' Let me tell you, I was never spoiled as a child. That's why I spoil and indulge myself as an adult. In some ways, I do it just to spite the old bastard's ghost. Frankly, Mason, I'm surprised you're still so afraid of your father and what he thinks. He's been dead for a long time."

"Yes, he has. I can't say I miss him, but I do think about him from time to time, and I still hear his voice in my head. I know my mother misses him. At least I think she does. Maybe she's just lonely. I know she was angry with me for not talking to him and for not coming back to visit all those years."

"That had to have been difficult for you."

Mason looked at Walter. "It was, probably more so for her. I'm sorry, I shouldn't have brought this all up, but I wanted to explain why I react to you the way I do sometimes."

"I'm glad you did. I'm surprised you never told me all this before, but I understand."

"Thanks. Family secrets. I suppose we all have them."

"Sadly, yes," Walter said. "You know, I think it's time to let go of those demons and live your life. Well past time, I must say."

Mason shrugged. "Sure, I agree, though it's not as easy as it sounds. Believe me, I've tried. And I still believe what Oliver and even my father said all those years ago. Appearances, first impressions, and people's opinions are important to me and for my business."

"Fair enough. That makes sense, I must admit."

"Good. And please promise me you'll be a bit more discreet in public. Your flamboyant personality, I mean."

"I'll try my best, but you must also promise to take me as I am when I do get a little carried away, or at least make more of an effort."

"I will, Walter. You drive me dopey sometimes, but I promise."

"Swell. I'm so glad we've had this little chat."

"Me too. Now, let's get our suits on and get some sun, shall we?"

"Yes, let's." Walter ground out his cigarette in the ashtray, pulled out his swimming suit, which was a pair of red trunks with white stripes on the sides and a matching button-up cabana jacket, and disappeared into the bathroom while Mason stripped down in the room and put on his own bathing suit, a solid navy blue number.

When he'd finished, he opened the curtains once more, took a quick glance at himself in the mirror, and shuddered. "You're right, Walter, I am far too pale. And you can come out when you're ready, I'm dressed."

Walter opened the bathroom door and stepped into the room, gazing at Mason. "Oh, how I wish I had your figure and your height. But you definitely do need some color. It's like looking at a tall, skinny ghost in a swimming suit. Well, don't worry, we'll soak up the sun and take care of that in an instant. And later tonight, we can both forget our troubles and be a little decadent."

"You're decadent enough for the two of us. Come on, let's get some towels and grab a couple of lounge chairs," Mason said, picking up his book as Walter grabbed a few fashion magazines and a brown bottle of coconut oil. "It's already almost two."

CHAPTER NINE

Later Wednesday afternoon, May 29, 1946
The Oasis Inn, Palm Springs

They stepped out into the courtyard, where half a dozen or so people were lounging about both sides of the pool. The air was still, the sun fierce in the clear blue sky. A solitary woman sat at one of the round metal tables reading a book beneath a gaily striped umbrella. Or rather, Mason noticed, she held the book in her hands, looking everywhere but at the pages as she watched the other guests.

"Doesn't anyone actually swim? There's no one in the pool," Mason said.

"Not me," Walter said. "I paid far too much for my ensemble to ever get it wet. Besides, the water's cold and would muss my hair and make my mustache droop."

"Only you, Walter, would buy a swimsuit you had no intention of swimming in."

"My *intention* is to be stylish and look marvelous. Besides, that pool is at least four feet deep in the shallow end, practically over my head, and I don't know how to swim. You giraffe types can wade wherever you want."

"You're a goof," Mason said with a laugh as he looked around. "There's a couple of empty loungers there on the left." He pointed toward the diving board end of the pool as he picked up some towels from a nearby table and handed one to Walter. "Next to those two ladies. Looks like Marvin hasn't put all the loungers out yet, probably since they're not at full occupancy."

"He'll get them all out in time for the weekend, I'm sure."

"Probably. Want some tea?"

"No, not now, thank you. Perhaps later. I left the vodka in the room, and I can't stand plain tea."

"I thought it was warm tea you didn't like. I could get us some ice."

"It needs ice *and* vodka. I'll pass for now. Maybe after a nap."

"Fine, I can wait, too."

Walter took the end lounger while Mason settled on the one next to him, beside one of the women. Walter slipped off his cabana jacket and folded it carefully before placing it on the table and sitting down.

The buxom woman next to Mason had her long, bleached blond hair pulled into a ponytail, and she was dressed in a tight, revealing bright red swimming suit with lipstick to match. She lowered her sunglasses and turned her head toward him with a broad grin. "Well, hello there!"

"Hello," Mason said. "I'm assuming these two loungers are available?"

"Why yes, absolutely, welcome. You two just check in?"

"Yes, last night. We're staying until Friday morning."

"Oh, gee, that's swell. My friend and I are here until Sunday. Just two single girls looking for a little fun," she said, giving Mason an even bigger smile that revealed yellowed teeth between her vivid red lips. "We're from San Diego. That's here in California, you know." She sat up straight and arched her back, thrusting out her ample chest.

"Yes, I know," he said, trying not to stare below her chin.

She laughed rather loudly, her large breasts bouncing up and down. "Oh, wasn't that silly of me? Of course you know where San Diego is, probably everybody does. My friends all say I'm such a silly girl. Where are you from?"

"We're from Phoenix. That's in Arizona."

She laughed again. "Don't tease me! You're terrible!"

"My apologies, miss."

"Don't worry about it, honey. I've never been to Arizona, but I hear it's nice and all, I'm sure. I'm Miss Campbell—Ermengarde Campbell—and this is my friend, Miss Myrtle Schultz," she said, nodding at the woman on the other side of her, who, at the sound of her name, raised the brim of her oversized straw hat and smiled more or less politely. The two women were roughly the same age, but Miss Schultz was a little simpler in her appearance, with less obvious makeup, a full figure, and short brunette hair.

"How do you do, Miss Campbell, Miss Schultz? I'm Mr. Adler, Mason T. Adler, and this is my friend, Mr. Wingate," Mason said as Walter nodded.

"How do you do? About time you two showed up," Miss Schultz said dryly. "Ermengarde saw you earlier today when you went out. She was watching through the window of our room. That's why she left those loungers next to her open. And we saw you come back from lunch."

"It was a late breakfast," Mason said.

"Oh, sure. Anyway, Erm figured you'd change clothes and come out here to the pool. She was hoping you'd settle in by us."

"Myrtle!"

Myrtle yawned and reclined herself, putting the hat over her face again. "You know it's true, Ermengarde, and you got what you wanted. Now leave me alone. I just want to nap."

"Don't mind her," Ermengarde said huffily to Mason. "She gets cranky when she's on a diet."

"I'm *not* on a diet. I happen to like the way I look, and I'm happy with my weight. But I do get cranky when you talk too much," Myrtle said from beneath the hat. "So, I'm usually cranky."

"You *should* be on a diet. You won't find a man with your brains," Ermengarde said, looking back at Mason. "Myrtle's really smart, but I keep telling her men don't care about that."

"I happen to like intelligent people," Mason said. "And I think you look just fine the way you are, Miss Schultz."

"Thanks, Mr. Adler," Myrtle said. She raised the brim of the hat briefly and looked at Ermengarde. "Maybe I don't want to find a man, Erm, did you ever think of that? And you should try using *your* mind sometime instead of acting like a giggling idiot. You're not as stupid as you pretend. In fact, you're quite smart, but you feel the need to hide it for some reason."

"Honestly!" Ermengarde said, turning to Mason once more. "You'll have to excuse her. You know how friends are sometimes."

Mason glanced at Walter and then back at Ermengarde. "Yes, I do. How was the drive over from San Diego?"

"My poor old Mercury, I didn't think she'd make it. Overheated twice on the way here," Miss Campbell said.

"Ah, yes, the red 1940 coupe out front," Mason said.

"That's right, gee, you sure know your cars. Anyway, we're in room three," Ermengarde said to Mason as she motioned with her left hand over her shoulder. Her long fingernails matched her lips, blood red.

"We're staying in number two, right next to you, it seems," Mason said.

"How about that? How nice and neighborly. Maybe I'll have to borrow a cup of sugar, sugar."

"I'm afraid I didn't bring any sugar along, Miss Campbell. No room in the suitcase."

She laughed again, even louder this time, sounding more like a riotous giggle. "Aren't you a kidder? Have you been here before?"

"To Palm Springs, yes, but not to the Oasis," Mason said.

"No, I suppose not. It's almost brand new, you know. It's nice to have some fresh faces around here, especially men's. The others," she glanced about the courtyard, "well, they keep to themselves. They're all traveling together."

"So I understand. The Pruitt family," Mason said.

"That's right. Have you met them?"

"Only Mrs. Pruitt. We ran into her downtown yesterday afternoon."

"Oh yeah? She told me Regina is her given name. She's all right, I guess, kinda fancy and proper, though. Stuck up, if you know what I mean. I was chatting with her and her husband for a while earlier. He seemed kinda rude and didn't say much. That's him across from me, third lounger from the left, the one with that awful tattoo on his chest, snoring away like a freight train. I couldn't resist taking a photograph, he looks so ridiculous," she said, lowering her voice so as not to be overheard.

Mason and Walter looked at the people assembled on the opposite side of the pool. On the far left, closest to the diving board, was a man of about forty or forty-five. He was talking quietly with the woman next to him, who Mason recognized as Mrs. Pruitt. She was wearing a solid raspberry-colored swimsuit with thin straps. On the other side of her was the man Miss Campbell had indicated, also in his middle forties or perhaps slightly older. The tattoo on his chest was red with a black arrow going through it from right to left on a diagonal, pointing down and away from the diving board. The lines were shaky and rough. Mason looked back at Ermengarde. "It is a bit on the amateurish side."

"Ain't it, though? His wife told me he got it when he was in the Navy. Looks to me like whoever did it must have had a shaky hand or been under the influence of somethin'."

"I would have to agree. He's certainly a sound sleeper," Mason said. Mr. Pruitt was sitting upright, his head back, and he was snoring quite loudly.

"Yes, he sure is. I don't know how his wife stands that racket," Ermengarde said. "Oh look, he's just woken up."

They gazed back at the man, who looked over at them blankly, shielding his eyes. He had awakened suddenly with a snort and a shake of his head. He got slowly to his feet, glanced at his wife and the other man, and went inside.

"Probably needs a bathroom break," Mason said.

"Who's the young man on the right?" Walter said, lowering his dark sunglasses briefly. "That deeply bronzed fellow in those tight plaid trunks."

"Walter," Mason said quietly.

"What? I'm just making conversation, that's all."

"Uh, that's Granville Pruitt," Ermengarde said. "I believe he's Mr. and Mrs. Pruitt's son. He's kinda cute but not very friendly, either. I tried talking with him earlier, and he only grunted, just like his dad," Miss Campbell said, raising her sunglasses back up. "He's the only one of the men not all pasty white, though."

"Oh yes, he's quite tan indeed," Walter said, staring at Granville.

"Yeah, but like I said, he's kinda stuck up," Ermengarde said. "He clearly sees us here, but he won't come over and say hello. None of them are too cordial. Me, I like to be friendly."

"Er, yes, I'm sure," Mason said.

Ermengarde took a pack of cigarettes from her clutch bag and pulled one out. "Have a light, honey?"

"I'm afraid I don't smoke, but Mr. Wingate does. Get the lady a light, won't you, Walter?"

"Sure," Walter grumbled as he grudgingly got to his feet, took a book of matches out of the pocket of his cabana jacket, and lit her cigarette.

"Thanks ever so," she said, inhaling deeply.

"You're welcome." He handed her the book of matches. "I have more, so you can keep them."

"Oh, thanks," she said, dropping the matches into her bag.

"You smoke Old Golds?" Walter said. "I'm a Camel man myself."

"Old Golds are milder, more ladylike. Smoking promotes weight loss, you know. Probably a good thing you don't smoke, Mr. Adler. You're too thin as it is," Ermengarde said with a laugh.

"Yes, I don't seem to gain weight easily. Ah, I see Mr. Pruitt has returned," Mason said. He had come back to the pool area and said something to his wife that seemed to annoy her. She didn't reply but picked up her book and scowled, glancing briefly over to the woman at the table. The man Mrs. Pruitt had been talking to turned away and lay down as Mr. Pruitt, also frowning, settled back into his lounger again, this time flat on his back.

"That's curious," Mason said. "I wonder what that was all about."

"He's just an old grump," Ermengarde said.

"Who was the man talking to Mrs. Pruitt?" Mason said.

"Oh, that's his brother. Arlo, I think his given name is."

"That makes sense," Mason said. "I can see the family resemblance."

"Yeah, they both have the same thinning hair, heavyset build, and pasty complexion. It must run in the family. Young Granville better be careful or he'll go from a bronzed god to a fat, balding old man just like they are," Miss Campbell said.

"It's hard to fight family traits," Walter said. "Believe me, I know. My father was only five foot four."

"Oh yeah? *Your* father must have been a tall, skinny one, Mr. Adler," Ermengarde said.

"In some ways, he was actually a very small man," Mason said.

"Really? Gee, that's funny. Anyways, that's the lot of them," Ermengarde said.

"What about that woman over at the table there, with the book?" Mason said.

Ermengarde followed his gaze. "I don't know her. She got in a little while ago, just after lunch. She went straight to her room, unpacked, I'm guessing, changed, and came out here. She tried to take one of the loungers you two are in, but I told her they were reserved, so she plopped herself down at that table with a book, her cigarettes, and a drink and hasn't moved since."

"Curious," Mason said. "She's all alone?"

"As far as I know," Miss Campbell said. "But gee, who cares about her or any of them?"

"I'm just interested in my fellow guests," Mason said.

"Well, I'm a fellow guest, too, you know. Aren't you interested in me?"

"Oh, uh, yes, yes, of course. I'm sure you're quite beguiling, Miss Campbell."

"Be what now?"

"Beguiling. It means fascinating, interesting."

"Oh. Well, why didn't you say so, you big silly!"

"You know full well what beguiling means," Myrtle said, annoyed.

"Hush, Myrtle! So, you two fellas traveling alone?"

"Yes," Mason said. "My lady friend, Miss Lydia Dettling, had to stay behind. She works at J. C. Penney and couldn't get the time off. And Mr. Wingate here is a confirmed bachelor."

"Geez, you have a lady friend?" Ermengarde said, pouting again.

"Yes, she's a lovely woman."

"Your lady friend," Walter said with a smirk. "Rub some coconut oil on my back, won't you, Mason?" He turned over onto his stomach, removed his sunglasses, and closed his eyes.

"Sure," Mason said.

"Oh, would you do my back next, Mr. Adler?" Miss Campbell said. "My front is just about done, don't you think?"

"Ah, you are looking a little pink," Mason said, glancing over at her as he started rubbing the oil on Walter's back.

"Pooh, that's what I thought. I hope your lady friend won't mind, and I hope you don't mind my asking you to do it. Myrtle always misses a spot or two when she does it, and I end up looking like Swiss cheese."

"Well, excuse me," Myrtle said from beneath the straw hat.

"You know you do, Myrtle," Ermengarde said, and then turned her head back to Mason. "So, you and your lady friend aren't married?"

"No, miss. I don't think we're that serious at this point."

Walter chuckled and Mason jabbed him in the side with a finger, causing him to squeal.

"Sorry, Walter, my hand slipped. What about you, Miss Campbell? No fellow in your life at the moment?"

"I was engaged, but my fiancé was killed in the war," Ermengarde said quietly. "Just before it ended, actually."

"Oh, I'm so sorry," Mason said.

"Your fiancé," Myrtle said to her with a snicker, raising her straw hat to the top of her head and sitting up. "He was your third cousin, and your mother and his mother set the two of you up because you were both over thirty and still single. The two of you only met in person a handful of times before he shipped off overseas."

"So?" Ermengarde said sharply, looking at her friend again with a cross look on her face. "We were still engaged, unlike you, still single at thirty-four."

"Happily single, Ermengarde."

"Don't be silly, no one is happily single."

"I am. I don't need a man telling me what to do, and I *don't* want to get married."

"Pooh, every woman wants to get married. But you act like you don't even like men. You were more upset when that Katie girl you were rooming with moved out than when Don broke up with you, and after I went to all that trouble to fix you and him up."

"Katie was fun. He was boring, and *I* dumped *him*."

"Don was handsome, and he had a good job. Honestly, Myrtle, I don't know what's wrong with you."

"Nothing's wrong with me, but you seem to think so."

"I do think so. Say, I have an idea," she said, turning her head once more toward Mason. "Why don't I trade places with your friend Mr. Wingate there? That way it will be girl, boy, girl, boy, and Mr. Wingate and Myrtle can get to know each other while you and I get to know each other."

"Actually that would be girl, boy, boy, girl," Mason said.

Ermengarde considered this briefly. "Oh, silly me, you're right!"

"Silly you," Myrtle said, rolling her eyes.

"Hush. Oh, I know, I'll move to where Mr. Wingate is now, he can go where Myrtle is, and Myrtle can take my old spot. Then it will be me, Mr. Adler, Myrtle, and Mr. Wingate."

"Now see what you've done?" Walter said to Mason out of the corner of his mouth.

"That sounds like a splendid idea, doesn't it, Walter?" Mason said with a wry smile, giving him a hard slap on the behind as he set the bottle of coconut oil on the table. "Get up."

"Ouch!" Walter said, glaring at Mason over his shoulder. "Oh, I'll get up, and I'll get you for this. Why are you the only person who doesn't have to move?" Walter got to his feet, rubbing his ass with one hand as he picked up his magazines, towel, and jacket with the other and put his sunglasses back on.

"Oh goody!" Ermengarde said. She got to her feet, picking up her towel and sandals. "Come on, Myrtle, take my lounger while I take Mr. Wingate's and he takes yours."

Myrtle glared at Ermengarde. "Aren't we a little old for musical chairs? And I don't want to move. I'm perfectly happy right here."

"Don't be rude. Mr. Wingate will think you don't like him. He's single, you know."

Myrtle looked over at Walter, who was staring back at her, his mustache drooping in the heat as he clutched his magazines, his little cabana jacket over his arm, and his towel about his shoulders. "Good for him. But what are we supposed to talk about? The joys of being single?"

"I'm perfectly happy to stay where I am if Miss Schultz would prefer not to move," Walter said indignantly.

"Don't be silly. Myrtle wants to, don't you, dear? After all, you still owe me fifty cents from our cribbage game. If you do this for me, I may forget about the bet."

Myrtle got slowly to her feet and picked up her towel and sandals. "Fine. I suppose I'll never hear the end of it if I don't." She glanced at the periodicals in Walter's arms. "*Collier's, Charm, Glamour,* and *Good Housekeeping?* Interesting selection. For a fella, I mean."

"I'm an interior decorator. I need to keep up with the latest trends in fashion, the movies, and what not."

"Oh, that's *swell.* I think I would have rather paid the fifty cents and stayed where I was. I could care less about decorating."

"It's 'I *couldn't* care less,' and I'll have you know I'm quite successful," Walter said. "What do *you* do, Miss Schultz?"

"I work at a machine shop, wise guy. I started during the war and decided to keep at it. Ermengarde's a waitress."

"Charmed, I'm sure," Walter said.

"Charmed," Myrtle said. "Anyway, I guess it doesn't matter where I nap, but I don't want to chat, Mr. Wingate."

"Okay by me. I just want to read my magazines," Walter said.

"Fine. Well, let's get this over with then, shall we?" Myrtle said resignedly.

"Might as well." They settled into their new spots, but neither Walter nor Myrtle looked particularly happy about it.

"Now, isn't this better?" Ermengarde said with a satisfied smile. She ground out her cigarette in the metal ashtray. Her rouged cheeks were glowing in the sunlight like two red beach balls, and her sunglasses were on top of her head.

"I hope your friend doesn't mind too much," Mason said.

"Oh, she's fine. She's just a little shy, that's all," Ermengarde said.

"I'm not shy, you're just aggressive," Myrtle said.

"I'm assertive. There's a difference."

"And you cheat at cribbage," Myrtle said.

"Don't believe a word she says, Mr. Adler. Would you mind

terribly doing my back now?" She rolled on her stomach and flicked her ponytail to the side so that it just kissed the cement as she slid her shoulder straps down a little lower than necessary.

"Yes, certainly." He picked up the bottle once more and began rubbing the lotion on Ermengarde's back, which, he noticed, was surprisingly soft but not as soft as Walter's.

"Mmm, that feels nice. The sun's made the lotion so nice and warm, and you sure have big, strong hands."

"Thank you. Hopefully, I won't miss a spot."

"I'm sure you won't, and thanks ever so, truly," she said. "I'd be happy to return the favor if you like."

"Uh, thanks for the offer, but I'm fairly flexible. If I need some, I think I can manage on my own." He did one more pass over her shoulder blades. "I think you're done," Mason said, putting the top back on the bottle and setting it on the table again. He wiped his hands on his towel before making himself comfortable once more in his lounger. "Don't forget to pull your shoulder straps back up."

That giggle again. "Wouldn't that be something? If I'd sat up and forgotten? Can you imagine?" she said, tugging the straps up as she turned over.

"I'm trying not to," Mason said.

"You're so naughty, Mr. Adler! I'm going to have to keep my eye on you. Oh, pooh, I've forgotten my camera. I set it under the table next to where Myrtle was lying to keep it out of the sun. Would you mind getting it for me, Mr. Wingate?" Ermengarde said, lifting herself up on her forearms and looking across Myrtle at Walter.

"Of course not." Walter reached down and retrieved the Brownie camera wrapped in a black leather case. He handed it to Myrtle, who handed it to Mason, who in turn gave it to Ermengarde.

"Thanks ever so," she said, sitting up. She removed the lens cap. "Everyone look this way and smile."

"I'm not in the mood to smile," Myrtle said, lying back down on her chaise lounge and placing her straw hat atop her face once more. "I'm in the mood for a nap if you'd ever shut up."

"You're such a party pooper, Myrtle." Click, click. "There, I got you two fellas, anyways," she said.

"Into photography, Miss Campbell?" Mason said. "I remember you saying you took a photo of Mr. Pruitt earlier."

"Yes, I love taking pictures, but just as a hobby. I do it for fun. Lots of candids, scenery, that sort of thing."

"Lots of fingers in front of the lens and blurry landscapes, more like it," Myrtle said from beneath her straw hat.

"I'm told Mr. Gagliardi is into photography too, and he has a studio downtown," Mason said.

"Who?" Ermengarde said.

"The man who works here, Marvin Gagliardi. He actually owns the place."

"Oh yes, he's kinda cute," Ermengarde said. "He reminds me of Danny Kaye."

"Yes, I thought so, too. I can see the resemblance," Mason said.

"Yeah, but he says he's not allowed to mingle with the guests, unfortunately. Which I don't understand if he owns the place."

"Maybe it's just his policy," Mason said.

"At least with certain guests," Walter said under his breath.

"Say, what do you do, Mr. Adler?" Ermengarde said, putting her camera away once more in the shade under her lounger.

"I'm a private detective."

"Ooh, really? Ain't that exciting! I've never met a private eye before."

"It's really not all that exciting, Miss Campbell. Most of my cases are boring. Long hours spent on surveillance, missing persons, fraud, that sort of thing."

"He's just being modest," Walter said. "He's really quite clever, and he's solved more than a few murders."

"Thanks, Walter, that's kind of you. Say, it looks like the lady with the book is on the move," Mason said, nodding in her direction. Walter and Ermengarde turned and watched as she got up from the table, set her book down, and walked to the cigarette machine against the wall. She rummaged in her bag, deposited a coin, yanked a lever, and then banged her fist against the glass as no cigarettes dropped, a look of frustration on her face.

"Hello," Mason called out to her.

She turned and glanced at him and the others, shielding her eyes as she began to walk over to them. "Hello, there."

"Good Lord, another annoying woman," Walter said.

"Be nice," Mason said as he got to his feet. "And get up."

Walter grudgingly stood, slipping on his sandals to protect his feet from the hot pavement and stepping over to Mason's side.

"Having a problem, miss?" Mason said as the woman stopped in front of him and Walter. She was dressed in a one-piece black tank suit, belted at the waist. She was fairly petite, with a short torso, small bosom, shapely legs, and black high heels that made her appear taller than she was. She wore her rich, light brown hair up and swept back, and her features were delicate and well proportioned.

"Yes. I'm out of cigarettes, and I can't get that blasted machine to work," she said.

"So what are we supposed to do about it?" Ermengarde said curtly. "The fella who works here is in the office, I think. Go tell him."

"What brand do you smoke?" Mason said.

"Old Gold, why?" the woman said.

"You're in luck. This lady here smokes those, too. I'm sure she'd be more than happy to give you one, wouldn't you, miss?"

"Huh? Oh, uh, sure, I guess so," Ermengarde said, clearly annoyed.

The woman looked down at her. "I'd appreciate that, if you don't mind."

Ermengarde gave her a sickly sweet smile. "Not at all, dearie." She reached into her bag and handed the pack to the woman, who took one out, lit it, and handed the pack back to her.

"Thanks," she said, taking a deep puff on the cigarette. "I hope I didn't bother you folks."

"No, not all," Mason said. "We were just chatting."

"And *I* was trying to nap," Myrtle said, sitting up once more and placing her straw hat atop her head. Her face softened as she saw the woman close up.

"Sorry to disturb you," the woman said.

"You didn't," Myrtle said quickly. "Not at all. I'm awake now."

"Good. Well, thanks for the cigarette, miss, and for your kindness, sir. I should be getting back to my table."

"Bye now," Ermengarde said. "Don't feel the need to come over again soon. It looks like you're having a nice time at the table with your book."

"Don't be rude to the pretty lady, Erm," Myrtle said.

"I'm not. I gave her one of my cigarettes, didn't I?"

"Yes, well, thanks again, both of you," the woman said.

Mason smiled. "You're welcome. I'm Mason Adler, by the way, and this is my friend, Mr. Wingate."

"How do you do?" the woman said to Mason and Walter. "I'm Miss Atwater, Cornelia Atwater. I just checked in today."

"How do you do? Oh, and this is…uh, oh dear, I'm afraid I can't remember your last names," Walter said, gesturing to the two young women.

"I'm Miss Campbell," Ermengarde said, "and this is my friend, Miss Schultz."

"Hello," Miss Atwater said.

"Hello, there," Myrtle said with a friendly smile. "So, you're not married?"

"No, I'm a career woman."

"Meaning you haven't found a man yet," Ermengarde said.

"I don't need a man in my life. I'm quite happy being single."

"Spoken like a true spinster," Ermengarde said.

"I don't need a man in my life, either," Myrtle said with a toothy grin.

"Quiet, Myrtle."

"Where are you from?" Miss Atwater said as she took another drag on the cigarette.

"San Diego," Ermengarde said.

"Hmm, yes, obviously."

"What do you mean by that?" Miss Campbell said, staring at her.

"I'm from Vancouver, Canada," the woman said. "Where I come from, ladies don't paint their faces and nails so garishly or wear such revealing swimming attire. You ought to be careful. That suit can barely contain you."

"At least I have something to contain," Ermengarde said. "And *I* don't wear heels to the pool. You're the one who should be careful, dearie, or you'll break your neck if you step in a crack in those shoes."

"You're a long way from home, Miss Atwater," Mason said, interrupting them.

She looked at him. "I came to California to attend my brother's funeral in Los Angeles and decided to extend my trip with a visit to Palm Springs to, uh, take my mind off things. Burying him in the U.S. was easier and more affordable than transporting his body back to Canada. I would have gotten here sooner, but I took the train to Los Angeles and had to take a Greyhound bus out here. My car is still in Vancouver."

"That must make it difficult to get around. The Oasis isn't exactly within walking distance of much, especially in the heat of the day."

"I'm not here to sightsee, just to relax. Mr. Gagliardi was kind enough to make me a cheese sandwich and some iced tea for lunch when I arrived."

"He's a good host. I'm so sorry to hear about your brother," Mason said.

"Thank you. He was my only sibling, and he was murdered in cold blood."

"Murdered? How awful. Did they find out who did it and why?" Mason said.

"No. The police say it was a random shooting. They said he was just in the wrong place at the wrong time, but I'm not so sure I believe it."

"Why was he in Los Angeles?" Walter said.

"He moved there a couple years ago during the war because he got a job as a bookkeeper for a large firm." She glanced about the pool area, but no one seemed to be paying her any attention as they relaxed in the sun. All was quiet except for the soft rumble of Mr. Pruitt's snoring. Still, she kept her voice low. "Something fishy about it all, if you ask me. About my brother's death, I mean."

"If you ask *me*, if the police think it was a random shooting, that's probably what it was," Ermengarde said.

"Clearly you don't know how the police operate, Miss Campbell. And you certainly didn't know my brother. Ralph was not the type to be in the wrong place at the wrong time." She inhaled again and let out a delicate cloud of smoke through her full lips.

"Have you thought about hiring a private investigator?" Mason said.

"That would be a waste of money, no doubt. Private dicks are just glorified cops. They're good for divorce cases, but that's about it," Miss Atwater said.

Ermengarde snickered. "Careful, honey, you're talking to a big, tall private dick right now."

"At your service," Mason said with a smile.

Miss Atwater looked embarrassed. "*You're* a private eye? Oh, I'm so sorry. I meant no offense."

"None taken, but I do think a private investigator could do you some good, if you really think something is off about your brother's death."

"Well, maybe I'll look into it."

"I think you should. What do you do in Vancouver, by the way?" Mason said. "You mentioned you're a career woman."

"That's right. I'm a reporter for a newspaper. I do some investigative journalism, write human interest stories, and specialize in exposés that uncover the sometimes ugly truths of the world. I brought my typewriter along so I could get some work done while I'm away."

"You always travel with a typewriter?" Mason said.

"Usually. My penmanship is atrocious, so most of the time I type what I want to say. Actually, my being a reporter is what started all this, more or less. Ralph, my brother, contacted me a couple months ago. He said a woman who worked with him in the bookkeeping department had died in an accident. Ralph urged me to come to Los Angeles because he said things weren't adding up with the company's books, and he wanted me to investigate. He said he also had reason to believe the woman's death was intentional. I agreed to come, though I initially thought he was just letting his imagination run away with him. But before I could get to Los Angeles, I got word he'd been killed, too."

"Curious," Mason said.

"Yes. Two employees of Baylis and Ivy dead within three months of each other, both from the bookkeeping department."

"How did the woman die?" Mason said.

"An automobile accident, supposedly."

"Not really that unusual, honestly. People are killed in car crashes all the time," Walter said.

"I admit that's what I thought at first. It's partly why I thought Ralph was imagining things. But now that he's dead, too, I'm beginning to wonder. He wanted me to do an investigative story, and now I'm even more determined to write it. I've actually gotten a pretty good start, and I'm not afraid to name names."

Myrtle stared up at the woman. "Say, Baylis and Ivy rings a bell. I've heard that name somewhere recently." She turned to her friend. "Wasn't that the company Mrs. Pruitt was talking about earlier, Erm?"

"Yes, she told me her husband owns it," Miss Campbell said. "He bought it a few years ago from Mr. Baylis."

Mason looked at Miss Atwater. "That's interesting. It's quite a coincidence that the man who owns the company your brother worked for also happens to be staying here at the Oasis, isn't it?"

"Why yes, it is. Such a small world. I didn't realize you all knew the Pruitt family," Miss Atwater said, gazing sideways across the pool.

"We only just met them. Mostly Mrs. Pruitt. She was a bit hoity-toity, all uppity with her nose in the air. She reminds me of you, Miss Atwater," Ermengarde said.

"Does she? Well, his tattoo reminds me of you, Miss Campbell. Crude and rough around the edges. And you probably snore like him, too."

"You're hilarious," Ermengarde said dryly as Myrtle chuckled.

"Have you met Mr. Pruitt?" Mason said.

"No, but I know of him, naturally."

"Then how did you know that man over there was him?" Mason said, eyeing her critically.

She appeared momentarily flustered. "Hmm? Mr. Gagliardi mentioned the Pruitts were staying here, and I just assumed one of those men must be him, that's all."

"And you assumed it was the snoring man with the tattoo, which you can't even see at the moment since he's flat on his back."

"Just a lucky guess. I noticed the tattoo earlier. It had to be either him or the man next to him. The other fellow is too young."

"Or none of them," Mason said. "Just because he's staying here doesn't necessarily mean he'd be at the pool. Does he know you're here?"

"I doubt it. As I said, we've never met, and as you said, it's just a coincidence. He didn't even attend Ralph's funeral. It was a small service. Everything happened so suddenly, the rest of our family didn't have time to get all the way to Los Angeles, and my brother didn't seem to have many friends. A couple people he worked with in the bookkeeping department showed up, though. And the Pruitt family sent a wreath. It looked cheap."

"Still, I suppose it was a nice gesture," Walter said.

She gazed at him. "Ordered by a secretary, no doubt, and paid for by the company, Mr. Wingate. So, I gather the four of you aren't all that well acquainted, considering you couldn't remember these women's names."

"We certainly are not," Walter said.

"Mr. Wingate and I are friends rooming together, as are Miss Campbell and Miss Schultz, but Mr. Wingate and I only just met the two ladies moments ago."

"I see. And yet when I asked earlier if I could use one of these loungers, Miss Campbell told me she was saving them for two gentlemen."

Myrtle chuckled. "She was, even though they didn't know it yet."

"Quiet, Myrtle. We were all getting to know each other real nice like before you came along bumming a cigarette and yakking it up," Ermengarde said, staring up at Miss Atwater through narrowed eyes.

"I didn't bum it off you, to use your colorful expression. It was offered to me." She took another drag on the cigarette, which was almost finished.

"And you took it," Ermengarde said.

"Won't you join us, Miss Atwater?" Mason said. "You could take my lounger. I don't mind sitting in a chair."

"Thank you, but I don't wish to intrude."

"Too late for that," Ermengarde said.

Miss Atwater looked at her. "Besides, the sun is too harsh for my delicate skin, unlike Miss Campbell's. I actually prefer to be under the shade of the umbrella, so it's just as well the lounger wasn't available."

"Was that a crack against me?" Ermengarde said.

"No offense, dear. It's just that your skin is so obviously used to the sun, like oil-rubbed cowhide, whereas mine is soft, pale, and delicate like a sheet of tissue paper."

"You don't say," Ermengarde said. "Then perhaps you had better get out of the sun before you shrivel up like an old prune. You have to protect what little bloom you have left, you know. What are you, forty?"

"A lady would never insinuate another lady's age," Miss Atwater said, "but of course *you* would. I'm only thirty-five."

"I find that hard to believe," Ermengarde said.

"How do you like Vancouver, Miss Atwater? I've never been," Walter said.

She gazed at him and clucked her tongue. "It's a lovely city, full of history and culture. The people of Vancouver, unlike *some* people in the United States, are well bred and well groomed."

"So are horses," Ermengarde said. "Some of them, anyway."

Miss Atwater drew in a sharp breath through her nose and glared at Ermengarde. "Certainly nothing wrong with being a thoroughbred."

"I suppose not, but you look more like you belong behind a plow than on a racetrack."

"And you, Miss Campbell, look like you've been rode hard and put away wet. Several times. By several different jockeys." She turned her attention back to Walter as she ground out her cigarette in an ashtray on one of the tables. "So, are you two single?"

"That's right," Walter said, glancing over at Mason. "More or less."

"Careful, sweetie. We saw them first," Ermengarde said, almost growling.

"I was merely making conversation, Miss Campbell, unlike you, who is obviously desperate for male attention."

"*I'm* not the one wearing high heels with a swimming suit. I'm sure you think they make your legs look more shapely, but honestly, they're just ridiculous. What are you, competing for Miss Palm Springs 1946?"

"If I were, I'd certainly win over you. And rudeness is always a sign of a lack of good breeding, Miss Campbell."

"Just calling it as I see it."

Miss Atwater scowled fiercely. "*My* good breeding and manners prevent me from calling you what I would like to amongst mixed company."

"That hasn't stopped you so far," Ermengarde said.

"Don't mind my friend, Miss Atwater," Myrtle said. "She gets territorial about men."

"I *don't* get territorial over men, Myrtle."

"Sure you don't. Like when Millie Porter started flirting with that handsome customer of yours at the restaurant, and you broke her nose in two places."

"That was an accident," Ermengarde said.

"Right. You swung that beer stein just a little too far. Such a pity. Poor Millie," Myrtle said.

"By the way, are you enjoying your book, Miss Atwater?" Mason said.

She looked puzzled. "My book? Oh, my book. Uh, yes, fascinating."

"What's the title?"

"I don't recall, honestly. It was on the shelf in the office of the Oasis, and I just picked it up when I checked in. I thought the cover looked interesting."

"What's it about?" Mason said.

"A man and a woman find true love or something like that."

"That does indeed sound fascinating," Mason said.

"Not to me," Walter said, stifling a yawn.

"Nor me," Myrtle said.

"I'll let you borrow it when I'm finished, Mr. Adler. Just return it to the office when you're done. My, I really must get out of this beastly sun."

"Of course," Ermengarde said. "I'm sure you have to get back to your coffin. Don't let us keep you."

"I'm sorry you have to rush off," Myrtle said.

"It's fine. It was a pleasure meeting you and your friend, Mr. Adler, and Miss Schultz. As for you, Miss Campbell, good day." She turned and walked back to the corner table with the center umbrella and made herself comfortable as she picked up her book again, once more peering over the top of it at the other guests.

"I'm not quite sure what to make of that woman," Mason said.

"She's a crackpot from Canada," Ermengarde said. "A bitter old spinster."

"Or perhaps a savvy single woman with a secret or two," Mason said. "Well, I'll let you relax, Miss Campbell, Miss Schultz. I think I'll do a little reading."

"Oh, okay. What time is it, anyway?" Ermengarde said.

Mason glanced at his wristwatch. "Twenty after three."

"That late already? We should go in and start getting ready for tonight, Myrtle. I have to do my nails and wash my hair and all."

Myrtle yawned. "Sure, I guess, since you so rudely chased Miss Atwater away."

"Good riddance to bad rubbish, I say." She turned to Mason. "What are you two gents doing this evening?"

"I promised Walter we'd go for drinks and dinner, just the two of us."

"Oh, really? Well, if you want some feminine company, you know where to find us. We're just next door."

"Yes," Mason said as the two women got to their feet. "It was a pleasure meeting you both. I'm sure we'll be seeing more of you."

Ermengarde tittered. "Mr. Adler, you are so naughty! I shall have to keep our draperies closed!"

Mason blushed. "I only meant we'd see you around the resort."

"I'm just pulling your leg, silly. Well, toodle-oo. See you later." She giggled again and winked at Mason, and then she and Myrtle picked up their things and went inside.

"They certainly were something," Mason said, sitting down once more on the lounger as Walter did the same, shifting back to the one he had previously occupied.

"To say the least. Now, if only Mr. Pruitt over there would stop snoring, I could get some peace and quiet."

"I'm sure they'll be going in soon, too. As we should before long."

"Don't forget you promised to press my tuxedo and dinner jacket before we go out," Walter said.

Mason looked over at him. "I don't recall making such a promise, but since you'll probably set the resort on fire if you attempt it, I'll do them when we get back to the room."

"Oh, goody, thanks."

"You're welcome. By the way, did you want to get a late lunch?"

"Yes, I am rather hungry. I'll see if Marvin would be willing to make us something like he did for Miss Atwater," Walter said.

"He told us sandwiches and chips were available from noon to one. It's well past that."

"I know, but I'm sure he'd make an exception for us. I'm an old friend."

"Okay, if you're sure he wouldn't mind."

"He'll be delighted. And after we eat, we'll take a brief nap, then around five thirty or so we can freshen up and change for cocktails at six thirty and dinner at eight. Now then, let me just go see what Marvin can throw together." Walter got to his feet again, put on his cabana jacket and sandals, and sauntered away.

The rest of the afternoon passed uneventfully. Mason and Walter ate their sandwiches and chips, washed down with iced tea, Walter finished his magazines and dozed off, and Mason, unable to concentrate on his book, did a few laps in the pool, and then finally just sat and contemplated the mysterious woman from Canada, the two from San Diego, and the intriguing Pruitt family until it was time to freshen up and change for cocktails and dinner.

CHAPTER TEN

Wednesday evening, May 29, 1946
Outside the Racquet Club, Palm Springs

"That meal was excellent, I must say," Walter said as they stepped out into the cool desert air and Walter put his top hat back on. "The Racquet Club never disappoints."

"It was good, but it should be *more* than excellent for the prices they charged. Two dollars and twenty-five cents plus tip for a turkey dinner? I could get that same dinner in Phoenix for a dollar sixty."

"But we're not in Phoenix, that's the point. And straighten your tie, it's all cockeyed."

"But *I'm* footing the bill," Mason said, adjusting his bow tie. "And that was on top of a dollar twenty-five for a glass of Johnnie Walker, and seventy-five cents for your martini at the Triada before dinner."

"Well, they *did* put three olives in it, you know, and olives don't grow on trees," Walter said, gazing around the crowded parking lot. "Wherever did you park? I can't recall."

"Over by that crooked palm, I think," Mason said, pointing. "And olives *do* grow on trees."

"Really? Whatever will they think of next?"

"I can't imagine what you'd imagine," Mason said. "Yes, that's my car over there, I see it now."

"You know, if you'd use the valet service, you wouldn't have to remember where you parked, and it's so much more civilized."

"And more expensive," Mason said, starting out toward his car, Walter following along.

"Darling, the valet parking is complimentary at the Racquet Club *and* the Triada."

"I don't mind parking my own car, Walter. Every time I let someone else do it, I have to readjust my mirrors and the seat."

"They can't help it if you're overly tall."

"I can't help it, either. By the way, why did you insist I leave such a big tip at dinner tonight?"

"Because Charles was *so* attentive and so good looking, didn't you think?"

"He certainly was, and all of twenty-two years old. I can't believe you asked him his age."

"I was just making polite conversation."

"*And* you asked him if he was seeing anyone, not to mention what his shoe size was. Honestly."

"Well, he's not seeing anyone, and he wears a size ten. It was important to know those things before I gave him our room number at the Oasis."

"You *didn't*," Mason said, shooting him a severe look over his shoulder.

"I may have jotted it down and slipped it to him discreetly."

Mason took in a deep breath and sighed heavily. "And what are you going to do if he happens to come knocking in the middle of the night? You may recall we're sharing a room."

"Oh, please, there's little chance of him stopping over. I was just being flirtatious. Waiters love that."

"I don't think waiters love that."

"Don't be silly, of course they do. And even if by some slim chance he did come knocking, you could always pretend to be asleep."

Mason shook his head slowly. "You are something else."

"Thank you for noticing. And speaking of noticing, you still haven't said a word about my tuxedo this evening."

Mason paused and gave him a long, appraising look. "The one I pressed for you? I must say it fits you well. Smart choice going with the single button."

"Yes, *you* can get away with the double-breasted because you're so tall and lean, but not me. However, what do you think of the color?"

"I think you're the only man I've ever known who owns a light plum tuxedo jacket," Mason said as they started walking again, weaving in and out amongst the many cars in the lot.

"Oh, good, I'm so glad. I just love it. And thank you again for pressing my things tonight."

"You're welcome. Marvin said he'd pick up the board and iron while we're out this evening."

"That poor man, he works like a dog. He never had to do those things at the Triada, I'm sure."

"Yes, but he did other things at the Triada he really shouldn't have," Mason said.

"Sleeping with that woman's husband, you mean? The hotel overreacted, if you ask me, but what is one to do?"

"I'm sorry he lost his job, but he should have known better. And as I said before, he's lucky he wasn't arrested on top of being fired."

"It sounds like he would have been if the wife hadn't drowned the next day."

"Yes. It still seems suspicious. That poor woman. The whole thing with Marvin and her husband must have been a shock to her."

"True. Maybe it was a suicide."

"That's possible, I suppose, though we'll probably never know for sure. Anyway, your jacket looks nice," Mason said.

"Thanks ever so. I adore the color, and it pairs well with the black trousers and makes the white shirt, purple studs, cufflinks, and black tie just really stand out, don't you think?"

"It certainly does, not to mention all your rings."

Walter held up his hands and admired his jewelry. "Thank you. One for each finger except the thumbs."

"I noticed. Why wear one when you can wear eight? And the top hat is something you don't see much of outside of jolly old England, or at least without white tie and tails."

"I think it adds a little height and sophistication. Like I said, it makes me stand out from the crowd."

"I'm content to blend in."

"Obviously. *You're* wearing a black double-breasted jacket, matching trousers, black shoes, black socks, black bow tie, and a white shirt with black studs and links. Ho hum," Walter said, feigning a yawn.

"Ho hum, ho hum, it's off to the club we go," Mason said as they reached his car. "Come on, and try to behave yourself in there. We don't need a plethora of waiters and busboys knocking on our door in the middle of the night."

"Maybe *you* don't, but I wouldn't object. But for your sake, I will try to be on my best behavior, I promise. Oh, by the way," Walter said offhandedly as he removed his top hat and slid into the front seat of

Mason's 1939 Studebaker Champion, "the Chi Chi Club does charge a small cover."

Mason got in behind the wheel and slammed his door with a loud *thunk*. "Why am I not surprised?"

CHAPTER ELEVEN

Wednesday evening, May 29, 1946
The Chi Chi Club, Palm Springs

Mason started the engine, put the car in gear, and steered due south on Indian Canyon, taking a right on East Amado Road, then left a few blocks later, arriving at 217 Palm Canyon Drive, where the Chi Chi Club was located. Mason got out and walked around the car to join Walter on the sidewalk.

"We should hurry," Walter said. "Hildegarde comes on at midnight, but Miss Dandridge's show starts at nine, and it's almost that now."

Mason nodded. "Yes, let's go."

Together they walked to the corner, where the windowless Chi Chi Club wrapped around to East Andreas Road, hugging the sidewalk.

A large brute of a man, dressed in an ill-fitting tuxedo, his collar open beneath his bow tie, was at the door. "Good evenin', gentlemen," he said dully. Clearly he'd said that same thing, or a variation of it, at least a hundred times tonight and probably every other night that week. "A dollar cover each, exact change appreciated."

"Good evening," Mason said, handing over two dollar bills.

The man put the money into a small metal box, from which he took two slips of paper. "Here's two drink tickets, good on any beer or rail drink. The first show starts at nine, the second one at midnight. Enjoy yourselves, fellas." He handed the tickets to Mason and stepped aside as they entered the club. It was dark, smoky, and loud, with music and voices assaulting their eardrums. Near the front door was a small counter with a young girl behind it, resting her elbows on top, her chin in one hand as she flipped through a movie magazine with the other.

"Check your hat, sir?" she said, standing upright. She looked as bored as the big brute out front.

"Yes, please," Walter said as he handed over his top hat. "Please take good care of that and be careful not to crush it, young lady."

She cracked her gum. "Sure thing, mister." The girl placed his hat on a shelf above a long rack of fur coats of every type and description. All crammed together, the furs looked to Mason like a giant, dead wooly caterpillar.

"Here ya go," she said, turning back to Walter and handing him a claim check. "It's complimentary, but feel free to contribute to my tip jar on your way out, if you like."

"Thank you," Walter said. "We'll do that, provided no harm has come to my chapeau."

"Your what?"

"My hat. Chapeau is French for *hat*, you know."

"Oh. Sure. Merci." She adjusted her bosom and turned back to the magazine she'd been perusing.

Walter shrugged, put the claim check in his pocket, and turned to look about the small, dark main room as Mason did the same.

"Gee, it's awfully crowded," Mason said.

Walter lit a Camel and stood on tiptoe so he could see better. "Yes, I don't see any empty tables. I *told* you we should have gotten here sooner."

"You didn't tell me anything of the sort," Mason said, annoyed. "Come on. Maybe if we walk around a bit, we'll spot some place to sit. I don't want to spend the night standing at the bar."

"I'll follow you. You're taller and can see better than I can."

They walked into the tiny room amidst the sea of small, round tables, all covered in fresh, starched white tablecloths, with emerald-green shaded lamps glowing in the centers. The tables were surrounded by gold-painted armless chairs, their seats upholstered in a soft green velvet. Mason and Walter zigged and zagged as the seven-piece orchestra played a rendition of "Let Yourself Go." The tiny dance floor was crowded, and the people at the tables were chatting and laughing as they popped champagne corks, toasted, and clinked glasses incessantly.

The men were mostly all in black tuxedos with very little variation, but the women were resplendent in long, beautiful gowns of every possible color and style and glittering jewelry that hung about slender and not-so-slender necks. The air was thick with cigar and cigarette smoke mixed with the various aromas of different perfumes that wafted from the hair and clothing of the ladies.

Mason turned to make sure Walter was still following along, and when he moved forward again, he bumped into a woman who was returning to her table.

"Oh, excuse me, madam," he said.

The woman turned and stared up at him, annoyed. "Please watch where you're going, mister," she snapped, and then an expression of recognition crossed her face. "Oh, it's Mr. Adler, isn't it? We seem to keep bumping into each other."

"Mrs. Pruitt! This is a surprise. I do beg your pardon," Mason said.

"Hmph, it's all right, I suppose, though you really should be more careful. I was just coming back from powdering my nose."

"You know this guy?" Mr. Pruitt said, a cigar in his mouth.

Regina turned briefly and looked at her husband. "I literally ran into him downtown yesterday afternoon, dear." She looked back at Mason. "I don't believe you've met my husband, his brother, and our son?" she said, motioning toward the table she was standing next to. The three men had gotten to their feet and were all staring at them. "This is Mr. Adler and, uh, Mr. Wingate, isn't it?"

"That's right. How do you do?" Walter said.

"How do you do, gentlemen?" Mason said. "Yes, I bumped into Mrs. Pruitt here as she was leaving the art supply store, and I'm afraid I knocked her package and handbag to the ground. I do hope nothing was broken," Mason said.

"No, everything was fine, thank you. No harm done," Mrs. Pruitt said.

"What in the hell were you doing in an art supply store, Regina?" Angus Pruitt said.

"Just buying a few things, that's all."

"You've never had any interest in that stuff before," Angus said. "You're not exactly the artistic type."

"I can be clever and creative when I want to, Angus. It's so pretty out here with the mountains, the desert, and all, I thought I'd try my hand at painting something."

Angus Pruitt shook his head as he looked at Mason and Walter and chewed on his cigar. "Women. One crazy idea or harebrained scheme after the other. Say, I've seen you two before. You're staying at the Oasis, ain't ya?"

"Yes, sir, that's right. I recall seeing you all at the pool earlier this afternoon, but I didn't get a chance to introduce myself," Mason said.

"Mr. Adler and Mr. Wingate are from Phoenix, Arizona," Mrs. Pruitt said, sitting down as her husband held her chair. She was wearing a low-cut, short-sleeved chartreuse silk gown, with elbow-length raspberry-colored gloves. About each of her wrists were gold bracelets that jangled when she gestured. Her auburn hair was swept up and held in place by a small gold leaf clip.

Angus nodded. "Yeah, I remember you two, all right. You and the little fella came in from lunch, and he was waving and carrying on, wearing short pants. Then later you were with those two dames. I fell asleep but saw you when I woke up to use the can."

"It was a late breakfast," Walter said.

"What was?" Angus said.

"We came back from a late breakfast, not lunch," Mason said.

"Who cares? Where are your lady friends tonight?"

"Our lady friends? Oh, you mean Miss Campbell and Miss Schultz. We actually only just met them this afternoon. They're from San Diego. I'm sure they had other plans for the evening," Mason said.

"They're probably off annoying two other gentlemen," Walter said, looking at the three men still standing at the other side of the table. "Oh my, Mr. Pruitt, Mr. Pruitt, and Mr. Pruitt? That's a bit confusing, isn't it?"

"Call me Granville," the youngest Pruitt said, turning his head slightly. "My father here is Mr. Pruitt."

"All right, thank you, Granville," Walter said, smiling at the handsome young man.

"And you might as well call me Arlo," his brother said with a slight slur. "For clarity's sake."

"Thank you," Mason said. "That will make it a little easier."

The emcee, a middle-aged bald man sporting a white dinner jacket, took the stage as the orchestra finished. "Good evening, ladies and gentlemen. Tonight, for your pleasure, the Chi Chi Club brings you the lovely songstress Miss Dorothy Dandridge. Please return to your tables, order your drinks, and make yourselves comfortable, as the show will be starting momentarily. And stick around for the midnight show with the Incomparable Hildegarde." The dance floor slowly cleared, and the waitresses scurried about taking last-minute drink orders as the lights began to grow even dimmer.

"You really should take your seats, gentlemen," Mrs. Pruitt said to Mason and Walter.

Mason shrugged. "We'd love to, but I'm afraid there aren't any more open tables."

"Why don't you join us, then? We have a six-top, and it's just the four of us."

"Well, if you're sure we're not intruding," Mason said.

"Not at all. Please, you're more than welcome," Mrs. Pruitt said, motioning to the two empty chairs.

"Thank you, that's most kind," Mason said, sitting down along with Walter as the three male Pruitts took their seats as well.

Mr. Pruitt took the cigar out of his mouth, looked about, and then barked loudly, "Over here, girlie. We need drinks all around." A harried-looking cocktail waitress stepped over to them.

"Yes, sir?" she said.

"Another bottle of champagne for the table, little lady, on my bill. Say, you're a pretty little thing. What's your name?"

"Ida Claire," she said.

"Ida Claire? That's a riot," Angus said with a guffaw. "Your folks must have a real sense of humor."

"Sure, they're regular comedians. I'll get that bottle for you right away, sir."

"And I declare, Ida Claire, bring two more glasses. We got company," Angus said, slapping the table and guffawing again.

"Yes sir, right away," the waitress said, rolling her eyes as she walked off.

"Thank you for the offer to share your champagne, Mr. Pruitt," Mason said, "but that's not necessary. We have drink coupons to use."

Mr. Pruitt put the cigar back between his teeth and stared at Mason. "Save 'em and shut your mouth, the show's going to start."

"And now, I take great pleasure in introducing Miss Dorothy Dandridge!" the emcee announced as he stepped offstage. The audience broke out into polite applause as Miss Dandridge took the stage in a shimmering floor-length white gown with matching elbow-length white gloves. A solitary ruby hung about her neck from a simple gold chain. She stepped to the microphone, bowed, and began to sing "My Baby Just Cares for Me."

Mason and Walter moved their chairs to see the stage better, only turning back briefly when the waitress brought the champagne and two extra coupes. Mr. Pruitt tucked a dollar bill in the front of her dress and raised his glass. "I declare, Ida Claire, here's a nice tip for you, and keep the bubbly coming."

"Yes, sir, thank you." She stepped hurriedly away, putting the dollar into her apron pocket.

"Drink up, folks," Mr. Pruitt said, pouring out the champagne. Everyone took their glasses and focused once more on Dorothy Dandridge, who made performing in front of a rowdy crowd look effortless. She was mesmerizing, holding the audience captive with her soft, silky voice and elegant beauty. When she sang "Somebody," Mason thought his heart would melt, but then she brought them all back to earth with "You Do Something to Me" along with a host of other songs until all too soon, she concluded with "Chattanooga Choo Choo."

"My, she was marvelous," Walter said, clapping enthusiastically along with everyone else in the room. After two curtain calls, the orchestra started up by itself once more with a lively foxtrot, and the house lights came up a little bit as couples began to move out onto the small dance floor again.

"Not bad," Mr. Pruitt said, refilling his coupe from the bottle on the table. "For a singer."

"Not bad? She was outstanding!" Walter gushed. "And did you see that gown she was wearing? Simply stunning. That ruby around her neck matched her earrings perfectly, too."

Mr. Pruitt chewed on his cigar and growled at Walter. "What the hell are you, some kind of a little fairy in a pink coat?"

"I admire a well-dressed woman," Walter said evasively, suddenly quiet. "And my coat is plum, not pink."

"I admire a well *un*dressed woman," Mr. Pruitt said with a booming laugh. He somehow managed to drink his champagne while continuing to chew on his cigar, which was burning down rapidly.

"I'm not at all surprised," Walter said, flicking the ashes from his cigarette into the ashtray, annoyed but also noticeably subdued.

"You're embarrassing, Angus," Regina Pruitt said.

"*I'm* embarrassing? I'm not the one in a pink jacket drinking champagne with my pinkie out."

"Walter's a friend of mine, Mr. Pruitt. I don't appreciate you being rude to him," Mason said.

"I call 'em as I see 'em. You know, Mr. Adler," Mr. Pruitt said, taking the glowing cigar stub out of his mouth and pointing it at Mason for emphasis, "you really should be more selective about the people you associate with."

"What do you mean by that?" Mason said.

"Oh, you know, birds stick around in a flock and all that. People might start to wonder about you." He ground out the remains of the cigar in the glass ashtray and removed a silver cigar case from his breast pocket to get a fresh one, but found it empty.

"I'm sorry?" Mason said. "I'm not quite following you."

"He means, birds of a feather stick together," Granville said. He did not look happy.

"My brother likes to murder a phrase or a figure of speech," Arlo said, still slurring his words, "among other things."

"Shut up, Arlo. You're drunk," Angus said.

Mason nodded at Angus. "Ah, right, I see what you're implying, Mr. Pruitt. Well, Walter and I do stick together, and I happen to like it like that."

"Thank you, Mason," Walter said, his voice soft.

"And what do you mean by that, Adler?" Pruitt growled. "You two the same bird?"

"Yes. We're both men," Mason said.

Mr. Pruitt stared at Mason and Walter, but then he laughed, taking everyone else by surprise. "I sure as hell hope so!" His mood seemed to have instantly improved. "I think I like you, Adler. You're a cheeky bastard."

"Cigars, cigarettes?" a young peroxide-blond woman called out as she maneuvered amongst the crowded tables. She was wearing a very short, low-cut black dress with fishnet stockings and black high heels. A large four-sided tray emblazoned with *Chi Chi Club* on its sides hung from a thick leather strap about her neck.

Mr. Pruitt raised his right hand. "Over here, girlie."

The blonde stepped over to him. "How can I help you, sir?"

"Have any Cubans, little lady?"

"Yes, sir, straight from Havana, ten cents each."

Mr. Pruitt reached into his pants pocket and extracted a fifty-cent piece. "I'll take four, keep a dime for yourself."

"Gee, thanks, mister," she said, taking the fifty-cent piece and handing over four individually wrapped cigars.

"Say," Mr. Pruitt said to her with a sly grin as he put three of the cigars into his silver case, "did you know I've got a dog back home with no legs?"

"You do?" she said.

"Yeah, I call him cigarette because I take him out for a drag every day," Mr. Pruitt said, snorting and thumping the table again with his free hand.

"Oh, that poor dog," she said, horrified.

"It's a joke, girlie," Pruitt said, unwrapping and lighting the cigar he had kept out.

"A joke? I don't get it." She looked confused.

Pruitt looked annoyed as he took a couple of puffs and stared up at her. "What are you, stupid? He has no legs, so I take him out for a drag, like a cigarette."

"Oh. Oh! Yeah, gee, that's funny," she said, though she clearly didn't think so. "Anyway, thanks for the tip. Let me know if you need anything else." She moved off, calling out, "Cigars, cigarettes," once more as the orchestra started playing "Moonlight Serenade.'"

"That joke's older than you are," Arlo said, finishing his champagne.

"I've had about enough out of you, Arlo," Angus said.

"What else is new? Order more bubbly, my dear brother," Arlo said.

"Yes, do," Granville said.

"I think you've had enough, both of you," Angus said, glaring at his son and younger brother.

"Would you like to dance, Mr. Adler?" Mrs. Pruitt said from across the table.

"I don't think that would be a good idea," Mr. Pruitt said as he placed one of his large, powerful hands firmly on her wrist. "If you want to dance, you can dance with your grumpy son or the short, funny fella, Mr. Windbag."

"That's Wingate," Walter said indignantly. "And I don't dance, as a rule."

"Oh no? You look like a prancer to me," Pruitt said with a snort.

"I'd be happy to dance with you, Mrs. Pruitt," Mason said.

"I *said* I don't think that would be a good idea, Adler. Cheek only goes so far," Angus said.

"Thank you, Mr. Adler, but I think I'm a bit tired after all," Mrs. Pruitt said as she pried her wrist free.

"Another time, then," Mason said.

"If you're not going to order another bottle for the table, Angus, I will," Arlo said.

"How? You don't have any money," Angus said, turning to his brother.

"Of course not, because I work for you."

"Which is a good thing for you, since you're lazy and stupid. No one else would hire you."

"I'm not as stupid as you think I am."

"No one could be as stupid as I think you are."

"Yet I'm the one with a college education," Arlo said.

"Yeah, an English degree that I paid for. I got a poet for a kid brother. Big waste of my money."

"I told you I'd repay you," Arlo said.

"When exactly? Like I said, you never have a dime to your name."

"Not on the salary you pay me, but maybe I can do other things that make money."

"That's a laugh. You don't know the first thing about business."

"Maybe, maybe not, big brother, but I'm not stupid. Or lazy."

"Oh yeah?" Angus growled. "All right, wise guy with a college degree, what things can you do that could possibly make any money?"

"Arlo, please. And Angus, this is not the time or place to discuss business or argue about money," Regina said.

Arlo glanced at her, then back at his brother. "Eh, I don't know why I bother sometimes. You'll never change. Are you going to order another bottle of champagne or not, Angus?" He loosened his tie.

"No, I'm not. You drink too much, and it's fattened you up. You've put on a lot of weight recently, you know."

"He's no heavier than you are, Father," Granville said.

"Shut up, Gran. Here's two dollars, Arlo. Call yourself a taxi and get the hell out of here," Angus said. "Though if you're really making money, you shouldn't need mine."

"I'll take yours any day," Arlo said as he scooped up the bills and stuffed them into his pocket, getting to his feet. "And I'll take it with pleasure. I happen to have a bottle of very good scotch in my room that will be much better company than you, my dear brother, so I bid you all a good night." He walked somewhat unsteadily toward the exit.

"Really, Angus. Why do you pick on him so?" Regina said.

"Because he's an idiot."

Regina pursed her lips. "Dance with me, Angus. I'm tired of just sitting here, and you won't let me dance with Mr. Adler."

"I don't like other men dancing with you unless it's your son or the little fairy."

"Then you dance with me. Please."

"All right, quit your whining. I'll dance with ya," Mr. Pruitt said, getting slowly to his feet and clenching down on the fresh cigar with his teeth. "In fact, I'll do two dances in a row, that ought to satisfy you the rest of the night."

Mrs. Pruitt got up, and together they stepped out onto the small, crowded dance floor. Mason sat back and watched the lovely couples gliding by, wishing not for the first time there was someplace like this for men like him, where men could dance with men in each other's arms and no one would care.

"Having a nice evening, Granville?" Walter said to the handsome young man.

"What?" Gran said, turning his head slightly.

"I asked if you were having a nice time."

"Oh. I'm deaf in my right ear. I have trouble hearing sometimes."

"I didn't know, I'm sorry," Walter said.

"S'okay. Kept me out of the war, for better or worse. If I could have served, I gladly would have just to get away from my old man. Sorry about him calling you a fairy." He had finished his champagne and refilled his glass from the bottle on the table, draining it completely of what little was left.

"That's all right, but thank you. By the way, I'm surprised you're not here with a date," Walter said. "You're certainly a fine-looking man. You obviously didn't get your looks from your father."

"Thanks. And my not being with a date tonight is a sore subject, Mr. Wingate," Granville said. "I'd rather not discuss it."

"Sorry to have mentioned it," Walter said.

"Uh, do you also work at Baylis and Ivy?" Mason said.

Granville shrugged. "More or less. Like my uncle Arlo, I just do what my father tells me to do, and he pays me."

"Interesting," Mason said.

"Not really. In fact, it's pretty boring, but he runs the show since he owns the company, which he basically stole from Mr. Baylis after Mr. Ivy died."

"I see. I understand he has also invested heavily in the Oasis," Mason said. "At least that's what Mr. Gagliardi told me."

"Yeah. I noticed him and my old man talking earlier today in the hotel office when I went by. The door was closed, but I could see them through the window."

"What were they talking about?" Mason said.

Granville lit a cigarette. "Beats me. Business, I'm sure. Neither one of them looked too happy. I know Dad's trying to force him to do a few things that would probably make the old man a lot of money, but Gagliardi isn't very agreeable."

"So I understand," Mason said.

"Yeah, that's how he operates. He puts the screws to folks and gets 'em over a barrel, just like Mr. Baylis. Me and the rest of the family included. If he *is* my family. Frankly I wouldn't be surprised if he's not my real father. In fact, I'd be delighted if I wasn't related to that oaf. I'm just biding my time until he croaks, which probably won't be long, the way he eats and drinks."

"What then?" Walter said.

Gran shrugged. "I don't know, but if I was in charge, if the old man was out of the way, I'd do things differently."

"Such as?" Mason said.

"Just differently. I wouldn't force people to do things they don't want to do or keep them from doing things they do want to do, for one. And I wouldn't screw people in the rear, pardon my French."

"Have you worked for your father a long time?" Walter said.

"I guess. Since I got out of high school, anyway. I tried college, but it didn't suit me. The old man likes to keep me nearby and under his thumb, anyway. We don't exactly see eye to eye on a lot of things. My uncle Arlo is more of a partner in the, uh, businesses my father owns or is invested in, but as you could see, they don't exactly get along, either."

"Yes, I noticed. What was all that about?" Mason said.

Granville exhaled a cloud of smoke. "You ask a lot of questions, Mr. Adler."

"Just making conversation. Why don't your father and your uncle get along?"

Granville chuckled. "You're persistent, I'll give you that. Eh, what do I care? They butt heads like two old rams, I guess. Sometimes I think my uncle resents Dad, but who wouldn't? Uncle Arlo does a lot of Dad's dirty work for him, and my father treats him like a child, or worse, and I don't fare much better."

"So, what brought you all to Palm Springs?" Mason asked.

"Business, mostly. The old man comes out here a lot on his own or with Uncle Arlo. He's not home very often, which is fine by me. He and my uncle had planned to come out here a while ago to talk to Gagliardi about the photography stuff. But this time he wanted me to tag along at the last minute. I'm sure he thought it would take my mind off my troubles and make me forget about her."

"Her being your sore subject, I take it," Walter said, lighting a cigarette of his own.

"Yeah, that's right. He doesn't like my fiancée because he's a bigot. He's been pushing other women on me ever since we got here. I'm glad you two came along this afternoon out at the pool, or he would have tried to force those girls you were talking to on me."

"That would have been most horrible for you," Walter said.

"I agree. The blonde one with the ponytail can be annoying," Granville said.

"She is rather persistent. So, your father brought you and your mother along on this trip?" Mason said.

"Yeah. She'd been bugging him for a long time about getting out of LA and coming here. She said she was tired of being left behind and wanted a little holiday of her own."

"Ooh, a holiday! That's what they call a vacation on the Continent," Walter said, suddenly taking an interest in the conversation again.

"Do they?" Granville said, taking another drag on his cigarette. He still looked bored and grumpy.

"They do," Walter said, leaning in closer, his elbows resting on the tabletop.

"That's funny," Granville said, getting to his feet. "Excuse me, gents, but I'm going to go see a man about a horse."

"Of course," Mason said. "I think I saw the men's room near the coat check."

"Thanks," he said, moving off.

"My, he's a handsome fellow," Walter said, staring after him. "I'd steer clear of that one."

"Oh, don't worry, I intend to. He's clearly only interested in women, anyway. But he's still nice to look at."

"I suppose. There's something about him that bothers me, though."

"Stop being so detectivy, Mason, at least for tonight, and just enjoy yourself."

"I don't think *detectivy* is a word, but all right, fair enough."

Mason took a sip of his champagne and glanced about. "Say, isn't that Miss Atwater from the Oasis?" Mason said, pointing across the room where a woman sat at a small table for two along with a redheaded man.

Walter sat up straight and followed Mason's gaze. "Yes, you're right. It is. Oh, and look," Walter said. "She's with Marvin Gagliardi. How peculiar. I almost didn't recognize him in his penguin attire. You men all look alike, you know, when you're dressed like that. Oh, different ages, heights, and sizes, but otherwise exactly the same, like a herd of penguins."

"I think the proper term is a waddle of penguins. And personally I fancy a man in a classic tuxedo. Where you see a waddle of penguins, I see a dazzle of zebras."

"You giraffe types *would* see zebras, I suppose."

"Yes, we all go to the same watering hole. I think I'll go say hello."

"Suit yourself," Walter said. "I'm going to have another drink and keep Granville company once he comes back."

"Behave. And here, use the drink coupons." Mason stood up, handed the coupons to Walter, straightened his tie and jacket, and then walked around the perimeter of the dance floor to a small table for two, where Miss Atwater and Mr. Gagliardi were sitting in silence, staring out at the dancing couples and nursing their cocktails.

"Good evening, Miss Atwater, Mr. Gagliardi," Mason said.

"Mr. Adler, good evening," Miss Atwater said, looking up at him.

"Good evening, Mason," Marvin said.

"I didn't know you two were that well acquainted," Mason said.

"We're not, but I felt like going out tonight, and Mr. Gagliardi here was gracious enough to offer to escort me."

"The Oasis is a full-service resort indeed," Mason said with a smile.

"Well, I enjoy going out, too," Marvin said. "I don't get a chance to do it very much these days. Besides, it's nice to talk with a fellow Canadian. I don't get the opportunity that often."

"That's right, you're both from Canada," Mason said.

"Yes. Different provinces, of course, but same country. And you're here with Walter?" Marvin said.

"Yes, I am. We ran into Mr. and Mrs. Pruitt, and they were kind enough to ask us to join them."

"Yes, I noticed you two sitting with that rat and his family," Marvin said.

"We only sat there because the show was about to start and there were no other available tables," Mason said.

"I'd watch your back around him if I were you. And your front. And both sides. Did you enjoy the show?" Marvin said.

"Very much so. Miss Dandridge is top-notch in every sense of the word."

"I agree," Marvin said as the orchestra finished one song and struck up another, this one a waltz.

"Would you care to dance, Miss Atwater? That is, if you don't mind, Marvin."

"I don't mind at all, but it's up to Miss Atwater."

She got to her feet, smoothing out her dress as Marvin got up as well. "I'd be delighted."

Mason took her in his arms as Marvin sat back down, and together he and Miss Atwater began a slow waltz around the floor, Mason expertly guiding her to avoid bumping into anyone. As he looked down at her, he noticed her eyes darting about the dance floor.

"Looking for someone?"

"Hmm? Oh, just admiring the other couples, that's all," she said, craning her neck around Mason's broad shoulders.

"One in particular, if I'm not mistaken."

She looked up at him briefly before turning her attention away once more. "Whatever do you mean?"

"I mean you seem to be keeping an eye on Mr. and Mrs. Pruitt. Especially Mr. Pruitt. Your table tonight is directly across from theirs."

"It's a small club."

"True, but you were also watching him back at the resort out by the pool while you pretended to read your book."

"Hmm?" She glanced back at him again briefly. "Oh, all right, fine. I suppose I am keeping an eye on him. He's an interesting man."

"Rather crude, unattractive, and boorish, in my opinion. Perhaps what you find so interesting is that he owns Baylis and Ivy."

"My, you're very observant and astute, Mr. Adler."

"I'm guessing you followed him to Palm Springs and checked in at the same resort, unbeknownst to him. I figured that was too big a coincidence."

"That's right, except he drove, and I was on the overnight bus. I got here a few days after he did."

"And tonight? You followed him here, too, I imagine."

"Yes, I did. Earlier today, I happened to overhear him ask Mr. Gagliardi to make his dinner and show reservations for this evening. So I asked Mr. Gagliardi if he'd be so kind as to escort me, and here we all are."

"You said before you'd never met Pruitt, and yet you knew he was the one with the crude tattoo on his chest. Were you telling the truth about not knowing him?"

"I was, and we still haven't met face-to-face. But after I got to California, I started asking around and learned that Angus Pruitt owns Baylis and Ivy. I found out what he looked like, and after the funeral I started following him."

"For what purpose, may I ask?"

"Because I don't trust him. As I said out by the pool, my brother asked me to come to Los Angeles to write a story on Baylis and Ivy because he felt something funny was going on. But before I could do that, he was murdered by an unknown assailant. And that other bookkeeper was killed in a car accident."

"That does seem suspicious, I must admit."

"Yes, it does. I intend to continue my investigation and finish writing that column. There's a story in all of it, I'm sure."

"But do you have any proof?"

"Only that my brother, Ralph, found out something or suspected something, and Angus Pruitt had him killed."

"That's a theory, but not proof Mr. Pruitt is guilty."

"I'll get the proof I need. It stands to reason if something funny was going on, Pruitt would know about it. The more I learned about him, the more I believed he not only knew about it but was the cause of it. So, I sent him a note saying I knew what he did and what he was up to. I had hoped he would meet with me, confront me, and then I'd have my proof, or at least more fodder for my column."

"Did he respond to your note?"

"No, unfortunately. But I figured it was worth a try. I sent a few others, too. If nothing else, I hoped I could get him riled up enough to say something incriminating or do something that would prove his guilt. I also tried to figure out what exactly was going on at the company. I got in friendly with one of the stenographers there, but she didn't seem to know much."

"If something was going on, I'm sure it was kept pretty hush-hush, not something discussed around the steno pool."

"True, but you'd be surprised what the secretaries know."

"I imagine you're correct. So, what happened to your brother, exactly?"

"I'm told he was standing on a dark street corner, waiting for a bus so he could go home after work one night. Someone came by and shot him dead."

"A robbery?"

She shook her head. "Nothing was taken. I was given the possessions he had on his person—his wallet, watch, penknife, a lighter, cigarettes, a bus pass, and a key to his flat. There was six dollars in his wallet, untouched."

"And the police investigated and found nothing?"

"Correct, if you can call it an investigation."

"Do you think Mr. Pruitt shot him?"

She laughed cynically. "I doubt that. He wouldn't have the nerve. But it wouldn't surprise me if he arranged to have someone else do it, perhaps his brother. I noticed he carries a gun."

"Lots of people do, Miss Atwater, and you said earlier the police think your brother was just in the wrong place at the wrong time. Perhaps it was some kind of a gang shooting, a case of mistaken identity."

"I don't believe it. I told the police what my brother had said about everything, but they dismissed it. They said Angus Pruitt is a fine, upstanding, tax-paying citizen who doesn't go around killing his employees."

"Maybe he is."

She laughed again. "You have met him, haven't you? You're sitting at his table. And you did say he was crude, unattractive, and boorish."

"True, but that doesn't make him a murderer."

"Doesn't mean he's not, either. I kept running into dead ends in my investigation, though. When the stenographer told me he was leaving town for a few days and coming to Palm Springs, I did a little checking."

"Apparently he's invested in the Oasis Inn."

"So I gathered from what Mr. Gagliardi said. He also mentioned Mr. Pruitt wants him to do some sordid things regarding his photography. It sounds crooked and illegal."

"I'm surprised he would share that with you."

"I told him about my brother and my suspicions, and he volunteered what he knows. Mr. Pruitt is a despicable man. Mr. Gagliardi is quite angry with him, as am I."

"Understandably, it seems."

"I agree. I think he's guilty, even if the police don't. Pruitt probably paid them off, so he's guilty of that and of a variety of other heinous crimes, I'm sure, including whatever he's doing with his company."

"And you seek revenge?"

"Revenge? In a fashion, I suppose. I certainly want him to get what's coming to him. And as a plus, it will be a great story."

"And then what?"

"My, Mr. Adler, you do ask a lot of questions."

"You're the second person tonight who's told me that. Guilty as charged, I suppose."

"Well, I guess I haven't thought it that far through."

"If I may offer some advice, I would suggest you be very careful. Angus Pruitt strikes me as a fierce and potentially dangerous man."

"I can take care of myself. Thanks for your concern, though. Even though I don't know all the facts yet, I figure Pruitt doesn't know that. He's not going to do anything to me until he knows for certain what I know and who I may have told."

"Nonetheless, proceed with extreme caution. Better yet, forget all about it and go home."

"I'm not going anywhere until Angus Pruitt gets his just desserts and my column is written and printed. By the way, do you know Mr. Gagliardi well?"

"I only just met him when we checked in. Why?"

"Just that from the things he's told me or alluded to, there may be more to him than he lets on. I think perhaps there may be a story in that, too."

"In what?"

"His photography, the Oasis, and himself, but I have more digging to do."

"As I said before, Miss Atwater, please proceed with caution."

"I always do, more or less. He's certainly attractive, don't you think?"

"Mr. Gagliardi? I hadn't really thought about it."

"Hmm. Well, I think so, but he's been a perfect gentleman all evening. I wonder, and I think I know just how to find out the answer to what I'm wondering."

"Why do you care?"

"I'm a journalist, first and foremost. It's nothing personal, just business."

"I see," Mason said as the song ended. He escorted her back to the table as Marvin once more got to his feet. "Thank you for the dance, Miss Atwater. I should be getting back to Walter and the others."

"Of course."

"I think we'll be leaving soon," Marvin said as he held Miss Atwater's chair for her. "I have an early morning tomorrow at the inn and then a late afternoon at my photography studio."

"Yes, I'm ready to go, too. I'm a bit tired, and I think I've seen all I need to see here," Miss Atwater said.

"Then I bid a good evening to you both," Mason said. "Oh, by the way, Marvin, might I have a brief word? Privately?"

"Let's talk tomorrow, Mason, if you don't mind. I'm all talked out tonight."

Mason looked from Miss Atwater to Marvin. "All right, I suppose it can wait. But do be careful."

"I haven't had that much to drink, but I'll be careful, don't worry," Marvin said.

"Please do. And watch what you say," Mason said. He turned and walked around the perimeter of the room back to the six-top. Mr. Pruitt and his wife had also returned, as had Granville.

"Who was that you were dancing with, Adler?" Angus Pruitt said as Mason took his own seat once more, opposite Mr. and Mrs. Pruitt. "She kept staring at me and Regina."

"That was Miss Atwater. She's also staying at the Oasis."

"Cornelia Atwater?" Angus said.

"Er, yes, that's right."

"Jeez, what a pain in the ass. So, that's what she looks like. She's a tiny little wisp of a thing, but not bad looking. She certainly doesn't look anything like her big oaf of a brother. Ralph Atwater worked for me, you know."

"Yes, so I understand," Mason said.

"What do you understand, exactly?" Angus said, scowling.

"Just that her brother worked at your company, like you said, and that he was murdered."

"She tell you all that?"

"More or less."

"I'm guessing more. So, she's staying at the Oasis, huh? What the hell is she doing in Palm Springs? She must have followed me," Mr. Pruitt said.

"Probably just a coincidence," Mason said.

"Hardly. I don't like it. She seems to think she's got something on me, from those notes she's been sending to my office."

"Forget about her, Angus," Regina said. "She's only trying to get you riled. She just sat at the pool and watched us all afternoon."

"Whaddya mean? Did you know she was at the Oasis?" Mr. Pruitt said, glaring at her.

"Well, yes, but I didn't say anything because I didn't want to upset you. I saw her check in, and I asked Mr. Gagliardi who she was."

"You shoulda told me, for Christ's sake," Mr. Pruitt said, looking back at Mason. "What else did she say?"

"Nothing much. Just small talk, why?"

"Small talk my fat ass."

"Angus, language," Regina said.

"That dame's like a pesky fly, but I know just where to get my hands on some flypaper."

"What kind of notes has she been sending you?" Mason said.

"Typewritten, threatening, demanding notes. If she thinks she's going to get even one thin dime out of me, she's mistaken."

"Is she trying to blackmail you about something?" Mason said.

"Angus, you've had too much to drink," Regina said.

"The hell I have. Who's she here with?" Mr. Pruitt said, ignoring Mason's question.

"Marvin Gagliardi, from the Oasis also," Walter said.

"That figures. They're in cahoots, most likely," Angus Pruitt said. "Him and I had words, too. He seems to forget who helped him by loaning him a big sum of cash. And he seems to have forgotten what he owes me."

"Really, Father, so what if they are in cahoots?" Granville said, lighting another cigarette as he finished his third glass of champagne from a fresh bottle he'd obviously ordered while the others were away. "You're the big, bad Angus Pruitt, afraid of nothing and no one, isn't that what you always say?"

"Shut up, Gran," Angus said.

"Did Ralph Atwater work for you for some time?" Mason said.

Angus stared hard at him, not saying a word. Slowly he took out another cigar, unwrapped it, and lit it. He took three solid puffs and blew the smoke across the table before speaking, the cigar clenched between his teeth. "You know, I didn't even know he had a sister until after he died. I'm told she started snooping around and asking questions after the funeral, so I had Arlo do some checking. Ralph Atwater listed her, an aunt, and a cousin in Ottawa, Canada, as his next of kin, and what little he had when he died, he left to the cousin and the aunt."

"I admit that surprises me," Mason said. "So, Miss Atwater got nothing?"

"Apparently not. And now she's trying to get something. What's it to you, anyway, Adler? Why all the questions?"

"Miss Atwater said her brother asked her to come to LA to do an investigative column on Baylis and Ivy," Mason said. "A company you own, and the one Ralph Atwater worked for. And for the record, that's not a question, just a statement."

Angus laughed loudly, causing those at nearby tables to turn and stare. "You're something else, Adler. You a cop?"

"A private detective, but I'm on vacation. I'm not working for anyone at the moment, just curious."

"Curiosity killed the dog," Angus said.

"Cat," Gran said.

"What?"

"Curiosity killed the cat," Granville said.

"That's what I said, ain't it? And Adler here is one curious cat."

"I'm only on my second life," Mason said. "I can afford to be curious."

"Huh?" Angus said.

"He's talking about cats having nine lives, Dad."

Angus glared at Granville. "Stop explaining things to me like I'm stupid. You're my son, and you work for me. Without me you're nothin', and don't you forget it."

"I don't forget much," Granville said, blowing out a cloud of smoke.

"What's that supposed to mean?" Angus said. "You've been in a mood all night. All day, actually. In fact, ever since we got here to Palm Springs. You still sore about that dizzy dame back in LA?"

"That dame is Annabelle Abrams, and we're in love."

"The hell you are. Our kind don't mix with her kind. I thought I made myself clear on that," Angus said.

"Crystal clear, Father. If I continue to see Annabelle, you'll ruin her father's business, sully her reputation, and disinherit me."

"That's right."

"Like I said, I don't forget much," Granville said.

"Angus, please," Regina Pruitt said. "Let's not start this again."

"He's the one who brought it up. All the broads in the world, and he's got to go and get mixed up with the likes of her."

"I'm an adult, and I should be able to make my own decisions about who I choose to date," Granville said.

Angus snorted as he puffed on his cigar. "An adult. There's a laugh. You're twenty-four years old and have never held a job except in one of my companies or doing odd jobs for me. You couldn't get into the military because of your bum ear, and you flunked out of college after not even a year. You spend all your free time laying out by the pool, drinking, and carousing with that dame until all hours of the night while spending my money. You got no ambition, and when that dame realizes you'll be disinherited if you keep seeing her, she won't want you anyway."

"I've already told her that's a possibility, and she doesn't care. We plan to marry."

"Like hell you are. I forbid it."

"We'll see about that," Gran said, grinding out his cigarette and sinking low into his chair as he poured himself another glass, emptying the bottle.

"Jeez, you finished that whole bottle on your own. You're drunk," Angus said.

"Not drunk enough."

"Don't come crying to me when you're puking it up at three in the morning," Angus said.

"I won't, don't worry."

"Stupid kid." Angus snapped his head around and spotted a waitress nearby. "Girlie, another bottle of champagne for the table."

"Yes, sir," she said, moving away quickly.

"I wish you wouldn't call waitresses *girlie*," Granville said, slurring his *s*'s together.

"What should I call them, *fella*?" He laughed at that, guffawing actually.

"You could try being a little more refined, Angus," Regina said.

"What, like Arlo? Or Granville? Or these two? A big dick and a fairy? Refined my ass."

"Angus, please," Regina said. "Mr. Wingate and Mr. Adler are our guests. And Arlo's your younger brother. He doesn't deserve to be treated like a lackey by you, and neither does your son. You're always criticizing and insulting both of them."

"Because they *both* act like spoiled children. By the way, I saw you and Arlo talking this afternoon out at the pool when I woke up and went in to use the can. What was that all about? I don't like the two of you yakking it up while I'm sleeping."

"So I can't even talk to him without you getting upset?"

"I bet you do more than talk. I bet you're sweet on each other. Well, I'll be damned if I'm going to give you a divorce. Wouldn't I look like the big dope if my wife ran off with my idiot baby brother? Though it would serve you both right. He'd have to get a real job, and you'd have to give up all your pretty gowns and furs."

"Honestly, I don't know why you think this way. I've given you no reason to believe it, and neither has he."

"That's because you two are too clever, but you'll slip up one of these days, I know you will. And then I'll have my proof. And if it ain't him you're fooling around with, I'm willing to bet it's some other guy. I'll find out who it is sooner or later."

"And what if you did find this proof you think exists?" Regina said. "You just said you'd never divorce me."

"You're right about that, Regina, but if and when I find out for sure, I'll enjoy giving both of you a nice hard smack."

"Mr. Pruitt, I don't think threatening to hit your wife is a good idea, and I certainly don't think it's wise under any circumstances," Mason said.

Angus glared at him. "I don't give a crap what you think. Or your little fairy friend, for that matter."

"Now, wait a minute, Mr. Pruitt, I've had enough of you insulting my friend," Mason said, rising quickly to his feet.

"Oh yeah? What are you gonna do, wise guy? Hit me?"

Walter got angrily to his feet also. "You are a fathead. Insult me all you want, but Mason is my friend, and I'll not tolerate you berating him. If you care to step outside, we can settle this like gentlemen."

Pruitt guffawed again. "And what would we do outside, little fairy? Would you hit me with your purse? Or slap me and throw your drink in my face?" Mr. Pruitt snorted loudly as heads at nearby tables turned and stared once again. "Besides, I ain't no gentleman, Windbag."

"*That* is obvious," Walter said. "And it's Wingate."

Mason put his hand on Walter's shoulder. "Come on, I think it's time we call it a night."

"I agree," Walter said. "I've had more than enough of this."

"Good night, Mrs. Pruitt, Granville," Mason said.

"I apologize for Angus," Regina said, looking up with a pained smile.

"Shut your mouth, woman. Nobody apologizes for me, and I ain't got nothin' to apologize for. And stop flirting with the big dick. What is it with you two, anyway? Maybe you met him before this trip, huh? Maybe it's him you like."

"Good night, gentlemen," Granville said, staring into his glass and avoiding eye contact.

"Please stop, Angus," Mason heard Mrs. Pruitt say as he and Walter maneuvered their way to the front of the club as quickly as they could. Walter retrieved his hat, dropping a dime in the girl's tip jar, and they hurried outside to Mason's car. The cold air and silence of the night felt refreshing.

"I was going to suggest we have a nightcap somewhere," Walter said. "But I think I'm done after all that."

"Likewise," Mason said as he got behind the wheel and Walter slid in beside him. "And we didn't get to see Hildegarde, either."

"Unfortunately. The only saving grace of the evening was Miss Dandridge," Walter said as they pulled away from the curb. "She's lovely and talented."

"And Angus Pruitt is rude and contemptible," Mason said, holding the steering wheel in a death grip. "A bully, a thug, and thoroughly obnoxious."

"I feel sorry for his entire family."

"Me too. Thanks for sticking up for me back there, by the way," Mason said.

"Of course, and thank you for sticking up for me. It's what friends do."

Mason glanced over at Walter and gave him a smile. "You're right, friend. But what would you have done if Mr. Pruitt had taken you up on your offer to step outside?"

"Well, since I don't have a purse to hit him with, and I'd finished my drink so I couldn't throw it in his face, I suppose I would have given him a roundhouse with my left fist to his balls. Then when he was doubled over in pain, I'd have punched him straight in the kisser with my right."

"Really?" Mason said, surprised.

"Absolutely. If he's Goliath, I'm David. Never underestimate the little fellows. I've had to protect myself more times than I care to remember, and I'm tougher than I look. Besides, I don't wear all these rings just for fashion, you know."

"I'm sorry you went through all that when you were younger," Mason said.

"People can be cruel. I'm used to it. And sadly it will happen again, no doubt."

"I truly hope not. Speaking of cruel, I wonder if Mr. Pruitt did, in fact, have something to do with Ralph Atwater's death, not to mention the other bookkeeper."

"It wouldn't surprise me in the least," Walter said, lighting a Camel.

"Nor me."

"Knowing you, you'll find out. But Miss Atwater ought to be careful stirring up trouble with Angus Pruitt. He's not trustworthy, and I think he's capable of anything."

"That's pretty much what I told her while we were dancing. What is she hoping to accomplish by sending him threatening notes?"

"To frighten him, perhaps?" Walter said. "Or irritate him?"

"If it's the latter, she's certainly accomplished her goal. I wonder if she's not resorting to some sort of blackmail."

"Oh my, you really think she would?"

"Hard to say, but that's certainly a possibility, and Pruitt hinted at it. He suggested that maybe she feels entitled to some sort of payment, seeing as how her brother didn't leave her anything in his will."

"And she wants that payment from Pruitt?"

"Could be, but she's playing with fire, and I'm afraid she may get burned."

"Or do the burning," Walter said.

"That's possible, I suppose. And then there's Granville."

"Quite a handsome fellow," Walter said.

"Quite a troubled fellow. He has a difficult relationship with his father."

"Who doesn't?"

"But Mr. Pruitt is threatening to ruin Granville's fiancée's reputation and her father's business and disinherit Granville if he marries the girl he loves. Gran understandably seemed quite angry."

"Yes. Angus Pruitt is a two-bit thug. The way he treats his family is atrocious," Walter said. "And he is clearly paranoid and possessive. He thinks his brother and his wife may be sweet on each other."

"Maybe they are," Mason said.

"Why dump one rat for another?"

"Maybe Mrs. Pruitt likes rats. Or perhaps there's someone else."

"Like you," Walter said, chuckling. "He's certainly barking up the wrong tree there."

"Obviously, but who knows? Maybe she does have someone on the side. I can't say I'd blame her."

"Nor I."

"I also wonder about Marvin and Miss Atwater. Maybe they're both out for something," Mason said.

"You really think they're in cahoots, as Pruitt said?"

"No idea, honestly. But Miss Atwater mentioned she thinks she may have a story to write about Marvin as well as the one on Baylis and Ivy."

"What kind of a story?"

"She mentioned his photography, the inn, and Marvin himself. I didn't like what she was insinuating. It didn't seem friendly."

"How would she know anything about all that?"

"Apparently, the two of them were comparing notes about Mr. Pruitt, and I think Marvin may have said too much."

"Oh, I don't like the sound of that."

"I don't either. I wanted to warn Marvin about what she'd said, but I couldn't get him alone easily. Perhaps I'm overreacting."

"I hope so, for Marvin's sake. He doesn't need any bad publicity."

"No, he doesn't. I plan to talk to him about it in the morning. Regardless, Mr. Pruitt should watch his step. He's making a lot of enemies."

"And Miss Atwater should watch her step, too."

"I hope she heeds my warning. Anyway, here we are," Mason said, parking the car right in front of the Oasis, as most of the other guests were obviously still out for the evening.

They got out and Walter put his top hat back on, shivering as they walked to the gate. Toujours was lurking in the shadows, watching as they passed.

"There's that cat again," Walter said.

"Looks like she's caught something, a big roof rat, most likely."

"Speaking of rats, maybe we should sic her on Pruitt. Come on, let's get inside, I'm freezing," Walter said.

"All right, hold your horses." They walked quickly to the door of their room, unlocked it, and stepped in, Mason flicking on the overhead light as Walter closed and locked the door behind them.

"Turn the heater on," Walter said.

"Okay." Mason stepped over to the unit built into the wall and turned it on high as it crackled to life. "Shouldn't be too long before it's nice and toasty in here."

Chapter Twelve

Thursday afternoon, May 30, 1946
The Oasis Inn, Palm Springs

"Well, this has been a quiet day," Walter said, lying back in his lounger with a sigh. "And that darling Charles, the handsome waiter from the Racquet Club, never did come knocking on our door last night."

"Did you really expect him to?" Mason said.

"It's been known to happen. At least once."

"Well, I, for one, am glad he didn't. By the way, I stopped in the office this morning and spoke to Marvin about Miss Atwater, but I'm afraid I was too late."

"Why? What did he say?"

"He said the drive home with her from the club was uncomfortable. She was blatantly flirting with him, and he let it slip that he prefers the company of men, which I believe she already suspected."

"Oh dear, was that wise of him?"

"Personally, I don't think so. But I think Marvin felt she was an ally in his hatred of Angus Pruitt, and the fact that they're both from Canada. He hadn't counted on her being a reporter, though. He told her more about what Mr. Pruitt was trying to force him to do with his photography, too. Things she can and will use against him in her article."

"Oh, I imagine he was quite upset. Poor Marvin," Walter said.

"Yes. He's worried he may get arrested or deported. He'd lose everything."

"Why would she do that? Marvin's never done anything to her."

"She's a journalist. To her, it's strictly business," Mason said.

"Well, it's distasteful and cruel. I still think we should have checked out of here this morning and gone to the Triada. I really don't want to be at the same place as all these nasty people."

"I don't either, believe me, but the Triada's full this week. Besides, Angus Pruitt is behaving himself today, more or less."

Walter gazed across the pool, where the obnoxious man with the tacky tattoo sat next to his wife. His son was a few loungers down, flat on his back. "Yes, so far. I suppose that's something. But then we also have to contend with Miss Campbell and Miss Schultz, not to mention Miss Atwater."

"Oh, I don't think Miss Campbell and Miss Schultz are all that terrible," Mason said, glancing up their side of the pool to where the two women were apparently asleep or at least dozing. "And as for Miss Atwater, I admit I don't care for her much, especially after hearing what Marvin said, but she's back at her table, keeping watch. I don't know if Mr. Pruitt has noticed her or not today. She's staying in the shadows and hiding behind sunglasses and a big straw hat."

"So I see." Walter fiddled with his mustache and yawned. "I'm getting a little restless."

"If you're bored, there are books to read in the office, you know. It looked like they had a nice selection, including some of the classics."

"Ugh, no thanks. Far too many words."

"Suit yourself. Iced tea?" Mason said, pouring himself a second glass.

"Good Lord, no. I should go get the vodka from our room. Honestly, if this were the Triada…"

"I know, there would be handsome waiters in white jackets serving us drinks. But it's not the Triada, and please don't bring it up again."

"Sorry, sorry. My, you're in a mood."

Mason sighed. "I suppose I am. If you want the bottle of vodka, go get it. Our room's only a few steps away. But be careful, we're not supposed to have glass out here."

"Maybe I will in a bit. Ugh, this is all so dull."

"Then do something."

"Like what? And how can you not be bored, too? We're just lying here. We could be doing that in Phoenix," Walter said.

"True, but if we *were* in Phoenix, we wouldn't be relaxing poolside. I'd be working on a case, most likely, and you'd be trying to scare up some decorating business. So, just sit back and enjoy yourself."

"But the day is slipping away from us. We slept in, had breakfast, came back, changed, walked around downtown, had lunch, and now we're back here just lounging about. I've finished all my magazines, and there's nothing else to do."

"Why don't you people-watch? That's one of your favorite hobbies," Mason said.

Walter glanced about. "It is, usually, but no one's doing anything interesting. They're all just lying there sleeping or reading. Oh, pooh. Now it looks like Granville is going inside, so I won't even have him to admire."

Mason gazed at him as he got up from his lounger, stretched provocatively, and picked up his towel. He stopped and said something to his parents that Mason and Walter couldn't quite hear, then walked to his room, closing the door behind him.

"Maybe he'll be out later," Mason said.

"I certainly hope so."

"He has quite a hangover, I'm sure, and he was in direct sun, so he probably just wanted to go inside for a bit, cool off, and lie down."

"The sun can be beastly. And speaking of that, you're looking a little pink."

Mason glanced down at his chest and legs. "Am I? Well, good thing this side of the pool is mostly in shade now."

"Yes. You're not the bronzed god Granville is, darling. I should have asked him to come join us over here on the dark side."

"I doubt he would have accepted, Walter."

Walter sighed. "You're probably right. His loss."

"He's pretty to look at, I admit, but spoiled, don't you think? I'm sure he's been cossetted his whole life."

"I hardly think he wears a corset," Walter said. "He's got a stunning figure."

"Not corset, *cosset*. It means *to care for overindulgently*."

"Oh, I suppose he has been that in some ways, by his mother, anyway. Though I think his father treats him quite harshly. And I'm still bored."

"Well, perhaps this will spark your interest."

"What?"

"Take a look across the pool," Mason said, his voice low. "Mrs. Pruitt has gotten up, and it looks like she is going over to Miss Atwater's table."

Walter sat up and lowered his sunglasses as he gazed across the water. "Ooh, yes she is. That's unexpected."

"I wonder if Mr. Pruitt sent her or if she's going over on her own."

"Indeed. Hmm, oh that's disappointing," Walter said, after Mrs. Pruitt had reached Miss Atwater's table. "They're just chatting. I was hoping for a catfight. Still, it doesn't look exactly friendly."

"I wish I knew what they were saying to each other."

"Me too. Oh, wait, now Miss Atwater's on her feet. I bet she throws Mrs. Pruitt in the pool."

"No such luck, Walter. The two of them are going back over to where Mr. Pruitt is."

"Oh, my, yes they are. And Miss Atwater's carrying her drink. Maybe she'll throw it in his face! Perhaps she's going to confront him. Oh, I wish I had popcorn."

"Keep quiet, Walter. Maybe we'll be able to hear something."

Miss Atwater and Regina approached Angus, who was sitting up in his lounger. Miss Atwater said something to Angus that neither Mason nor Walter could make out, but it obviously agitated him.

"She does like to stir up trouble," Walter said. "I wonder what she hopes to accomplish. And what Mrs. Pruitt hopes."

"I'm not sure. Miss Atwater's kept her distance so far, but I suppose there's no point now. I suspect Mrs. Pruitt got tired of all the notes and accusations and wanted to bring them face-to-face once and for all, since they hadn't actually met until today."

"Well, they're meeting now," Walter said, "thanks to you spilling the beans about her being here. Even Mrs. Pruitt kept her mouth shut about it."

"I feel bad about that. It was a slip of the tongue."

"Loose lips sink ships, as they say."

Walter and Mason watched the scene, entranced. Angus was scowling, and Regina was standing between the two of them, her arms crossed. Cornelia set her drink down on the table next to theirs and started to move around Regina toward Angus, but Regina cut her off. Angus got to his feet, his voice booming across the water.

"Shut the hell up," he said. "I'll sue you, or worse."

"Go ahead and try. I'd be happy to see you in court," Cornelia said, almost as loudly.

"Anytime, girlie, anytime," Angus said.

"You can't ignore me, Mr. Pruitt. I know what you did."

"I didn't do nothin', but I bet you don't know what I'm about to do to you if you don't shut up and leave me alone," Angus said.

"You're contemptible, and I feel sorry for your wife and family, though it's going to make an excellent newspaper story. I'm going to go lie down. You've given me a headache," Cornelia said. She picked up her glass and strode off in a fury toward her room. Mason noticed she wasn't wearing her heels this time.

"My goodness, I wonder what that was all about?" Walter said, still looking across the pool at Mr. Pruitt, who had sat back down and was taking a drink from his own cup. "I don't think that went the way Mrs. Pruitt expected it to."

"No, definitely not. Curious behavior on Miss Atwater's part, though. If she really is blackmailing or threatening him, why make such a public scene and then storm off?"

"Maybe she's angry because he refuses to give in to her demands."

"She certainly is, but we don't know she's making demands," Mason said.

"Well, she's gone back to her room now, and good riddance. I notice Mr. Pruitt's brother isn't around this afternoon, either. He's probably hungover, too."

"Yes, most likely. He and Granville were both pretty intoxicated last night."

"True. And may I say," Walter said, lowering his voice, "thank God Miss Schultz and Miss Campbell chose to relax on the far end of the pool today."

"If I recall correctly, and I do, they were already out here when we got back from lunch, and they were dozing in the sun. You chose loungers as far away from them as possible on purpose," Mason said, "now that Marvin's put them all out."

"Guilty, but I just couldn't subject either one of us to another afternoon of mindless flirtation and idle chatter."

"Thanks, I guess." Mason said. He glanced once more down the row of loungers to the two women. Myrtle was still recumbent, but Ermengarde was sitting up now and clicking away with her camera, the little argument probably having disturbed her. She seemed to be focused on Mr. and Mrs. Pruitt for the moment and apparently had not yet noticed Mason and Walter.

"Looks like Miss Campbell was awakened by the ruckus," Mason said.

"Ugh, yes, and she's at it again with that camera. Click, click, click."

"And it looks like Mr. and Mrs. Pruitt are going inside now," Mason said.

Walter looked across the pool again. Angus and Regina had indeed gotten up and were going into their room. "He looks a bit unsteady. I bet he had more than iced tea in his glass."

"It wouldn't surprise me in the least. They've already been to lunch and back, as has most everyone, I think. I wonder why they're going in," Mason said.

"Certainly not an afternoon romp, not those two," Walter said as Mr. and Mrs. Pruitt went in and closed the door.

"No, but they have drawn the curtains," Mason said.

"Just to keep the heat out, I'm sure. Perhaps Miss Atwater upset him more than he let on. Or maybe *they've* had enough of Miss Campbell and her camera, too. Oh, and look, Mr. Pruitt's brother Arlo has finally emerged from his room," Walter said.

"So I see. He doesn't look too well. I would say he's definitely hungover."

"Amateur," Walter said.

Arlo Pruitt, wearing a striped green button-down shirt and a khaki swimsuit, walked slowly toward the office, shading his eyes from the glaring sun, only to return to the pool area a short while later, stopping at Angus's room. He knocked softly and Regina opened the door, letting him in.

"What was he doing in the office? And why is he knocking on his brother's door now? How curious," Mason said.

Walter yawned. "Mildly curious, if that. For a moment, I thought things might get interesting again."

"Perhaps they've called a family meeting to discuss last night. Maybe Arlo is getting a dressing-down from Mr. Pruitt, and Mrs. Pruitt is acting as referee. Maybe she's hoping to call a truce and that's why they went in. Because they were expecting Arlo. Or maybe they're discussing what to do about Miss Atwater."

"Don't know, don't care," Walter said, lowering his sunglasses once more. "Not if they're going to do it behind closed doors, anyway. Say, why don't we take a drive by the Kaufmann House? Everyone's talking about it, you know, and then we can go to the Racquet Club. I think things would be far more interesting there. And don't forget, Jerome gives excellent tennis lessons, and we can have drinks after."

Mason glanced over at him. "I can't afford tennis lessons or drinks at the Racquet Club, Walter, so unless you're buying, I think we should stay here for the afternoon."

"Oh, cheese and crackers. It's always about money with you."

"It is when I'm paying for both of us."

"Fine. How about I pay for drinks at the Racquet Club, and we skip the tennis lesson?"

"Goodness, you really must be bored."

"I am. And restless. How about it?"

"I don't know, Walter, I'm actually kind of comfortable here now, and I'm enjoying myself, just relaxing. Tell you what, we can head to dinner early and stop by the Racquet Club for drinks on the way."

"Oh, I guess that will have to do. And to show what a good sport I am, I'll still pick up the bill for the drinks."

"Thanks."

"It's the least I can do, I suppose. Well, if we're both going to just sit here for the next hour or so, we might as well gossip about the fellow guests and try to guess what they're up to. And speaking of curious, I say, there's Marvin, pushing that housekeeping cart, and he's going into Arlo Pruitt's room. Rather late in the day to make up the beds, isn't it?" Walter said.

"Hmm, yes, it is. And I thought Marvin had to be at his photography studio this afternoon."

"That's what he said, yes. Arlo probably went to the office to ask Marvin to clean something in his room. I'm sure Marvin's not happy about all this."

"I'm sure not. And Arlo probably won't even tip him," Mason said.

"Doubtful. Dreadful people, all of them. Well, except perhaps for Granville."

"Really, Walter? He's not dreadful just because he's handsome and bronzed?"

"Well, it doesn't hurt. Besides, I'm giving him the benefit of the doubt. He hasn't said all that much."

"Fine, but handsome and bronzed people can be just as dreadful as those that aren't. Sometimes more so because they think they can get away with it."

"I suppose, but I can still enjoy looking at him, can't I?"

"Of course. That's about all you can do with that one. Oh, look, Mr. and Mrs. Pruitt have returned poolside."

Angus and Regina came out once more to the pool deck, Angus still sporting his bright red trunks, sunglasses, and a wide-brimmed straw hat, and Regina still in her raspberry-colored suit, though now partially covered with a trim white cabana jacket. The two of them sat back in their lounge chairs at the shallow end of the pool, and Regina took out her book to read while Angus lay down and dozed, his hat over his face.

"Mr. Pruitt still looks a bit wobbly, and Mrs. Pruitt looks a bit frazzled," Mason said.

"Can't say I blame her. I can only imagine what was said between those three behind the closed door."

"Nothing good, I'm sure. And Arlo is still inside. That seems odd."

"Must have something to do with Marvin going into his room with that housekeeping cart."

"Most likely." Mason glanced at his watch. "Mr. and Mrs. Pruitt and Arlo were only in the Pruitts' room about fifteen minutes or so."

"Enough time to talk about the problem of Miss Atwater or for Mr. Pruitt to give Arlo a dressing-down or whatever it is they did in there."

"I suppose so. Well, I'm going to get some reading done. How about you, Walter?"

"Oh, ho hum. Are we finished chatting and being curious already? Well, perhaps I'll just take a little catnap, then, though I want to be in the sun." He shifted his lounger closer to the pool where there was still some sunlight, then looked back at Mason. "Wake me in half an hour, won't you?"

"Sure," Mason said, making a note of the current time as Walter reclined in his lounger, crossed his hands over his belly, and closed his eyes. "And we can drive by the Kaufmann House on our way out of town when we head back to Phoenix. I do want to see that."

It was almost exactly thirty minutes later when Mason got up and gave Walter a gentle nudge.

"Has it been thirty minutes already?" Walter said, awaking with a start and a snort.

"Yes, and I don't want you to burn. If you're going to continue napping, you'd best turn over."

"Naturally. Most of the boys like me face down, you know."

"Walter."

"Sorry, it just slipped out," Walter said, sitting up. "Have I missed anything on the gossip front? It's so quiet out here, you could hear a pin drop. Not a sound from anyone." Walter gazed about the pool area, shading his eyes. "Oh, wait, look who's coming our way."

Regina Pruitt had put her book down and was walking around the shallow end of the pool to where Mason and Walter were. "Hello, Mr. Adler, Mr. Wingate. I wanted to take the opportunity to apologize for my husband's behavior last night. It's just that Angus isn't feeling too well."

"Oh, I'm sorry to hear that, Mrs. Pruitt," Mason said. "Nothing serious, I hope."

"I don't think so. He's just overtired, he works too much. And today he has a headache and indigestion. He's finally fallen sound asleep, as you can see."

"It might do him well to get out of the sun," Walter said.

Mason looked at Angus across the pool, reclining in his lounger with his hat worn low, the arrow in the heart tattoo pointing rather comically toward the diving board at the deep end. "I agree. Perhaps he should lie down in your room with a cool compress and the overhead fan on."

"Yes, that would be a good idea, and I wanted him to do just that, but then Arlo showed up at our door."

"I saw him going into your room earlier, and I noticed you and your husband came out, but he did not."

Regina inhaled and exhaled deeply. "Yes. Arlo has a bit of a drinking problem in that he spills more than he drinks. Earlier today, he managed to knock over an entire bottle of scotch onto his bed, apparently, and it soaked right through to the mattress. The maids have all gone home for the day, so Mr. Gagliardi is in his room now, trying to dry it out so he can put on fresh linens."

"Dear me," Mason said. "I imagine Mr. Gagliardi's not too happy about that."

"Well, he is the help, you know, and it is his job to take care of us. My brother-in-law was careless, but it was an accident."

"Yes, of course, but I know Marvin had hoped to be at his photography studio this afternoon."

"That's unfortunate, but this incident shouldn't delay him too long. Arlo's napping in our room now, or more accurately, sleeping it off until Mr. Gagliardi finishes and he can go back to his own room. Arlo claims to have a headache, and I bet he does. Our son has one, too. They both drink too much."

"Such a pity about the scotch," Walter said. "I'm a vodka and gin man myself, but I hate to see any liquor go to waste."

"My husband was furious about it."

"He seems to be furious about a lot of things," Mason said. "Including you and your brother-in-law just talking to each other."

"Angus is and always has been jealous and possessive, with a wild imagination. As you saw, he even suspected you and I had met before and suggested we were having an affair. It got ugly after you two left last night."

"I'm sorry to hear it," Mason said.

"It's hard to believe it could have gotten uglier," Walter said.

"And yet it did," Regina said. "He's so angry all the time. He only grudgingly let Arlo use our room temporarily because we were coming back out here. I wanted Angus to stay and lie down out of the sun, but he refused, and I've learned you can't make him do anything he doesn't want to."

"So it would seem," Mason said.

"Believe me, when Arlo came knocking and told us what had happened, I thought Angus was going to strike him." She shook her head slowly. "I get so tired of trying to keep the peace in the family. It's just sometimes too much."

"I can't even imagine," Mason said.

"Ahh, It looks like Mr. Gagliardi is finished in your brother-in-law's room now," Walter said, pointing toward Marvin as he exited Arlo's room and hurriedly pushed his cart back toward the office.

Regina and Mason both followed his gaze. "Good. Then I think it's time to wake Angus up and get out of the sun and time for Arlo to go back to his own room, and I'm going to see to it one way or the other." Regina turned and walked back around the pool to Angus. She gave him a shake, and he slowly got to his feet, putting the straw hat back upright on his head, his dark sunglasses still shading his eyes. They talked together for a couple of minutes, then Regina took a seat in her lounger and Angus walked to their room, unlocked the door, and went in, leaving the door open. Arlo came out less than a minute later, still looking groggy and tired, wearing his khaki swimsuit and slightly rumpled green striped, short-sleeved shirt. He turned and said something to Angus that Mason and Walter couldn't make out, then closed the door and strolled slowly back to his own room.

"Well, Arlo doesn't look like his brother punched him," Walter said.

"No, apparently not. Arlo must have been awake and ready to come out when Mr. Pruitt entered. Good thing, too, I suppose."

"Yes. Still, I was hoping for at least another argument, with maybe Arlo throwing Mr. Pruitt through the front window or perhaps punching him in the kisser."

"Honestly, Walter. Violence isn't going to solve their problem."

"I guess not, but it would be entertaining. I don't like Angus Pruitt in the least."

"A common consensus, I think."

"Yes. Well, since the floor show's over and we're now almost in complete shade over here, I'm going to go in and use the bathroom and see if I can't find something to snack on. I'll be back in a bit. With the bottle of vodka."

"All right," Mason said, returning to his own lounger. He read a few more pages in his book, then set it aside and dozed for a while. When he awoke, he sat up, looking around the pool area as he rubbed his eyes. Ermengarde, Mason noticed, had put her camera away but had gotten to her feet. To his dismay, she turned his way and waved. He half-heartedly returned the wave as Walter finally returned nearly an hour later, the bottle of vodka in hand.

"Where have you been, Walter?"

"I told you, I went to use the bathroom, then I got a sandwich and some chips from the office. Actually not bad when washed down with alcohol, and there's still some left to mix in with the iced tea if you want."

"We just had lunch less than two hours ago, how can you be hungry?"

"I'm *not* hungry anymore. I told you, I had a cheese sandwich and some chips, and I brought us the vodka."

"Fine, but the pitcher of tea is empty now."

"I'm sure if you asked, Marvin would bring us some more."

"I can make do," Mason said. "Marvin's overworked as it is, and he's probably already left for his studio."

"Oh well, I can drink the vodka straight. I don't imagine there's been any more fights or arguments out here?"

Mason shook his head slowly. "No, not really. It's all been pretty quiet. Mr. Pruitt, Granville, and Arlo are still in their rooms, but one of our friends down at the other end is stirring."

"God, she's annoying," Walter said, staring at Ermengarde as he sat down and poured himself a drink. "Click, click, click with that camera. I think I shall call her the click click woman. And the other one, Myrtle, I think I shall call her the turtle. All she does is lie motionless with her hat over her face. And how much film does Click Click have in that camera? It seems she's taken dozens of photos already."

"It's her hobby, and I'm sure she's changed rolls a few times."

"Ugh. I'm not a fan of candid photography. I want to be prepared so I can look my best."

"There's something to be said for unposed shots, Walter. For capturing people in their natural state."

"Not in my opinion. I hate photos of myself as it is. I always look dreadful."

"Everyone hates looking at photographs of themselves. Well, almost everyone."

"Yes, I have a theory about that," Walter said.

"Do tell."

"It's because few people's faces are truly symmetrical. And we're used to seeing ourselves in the mirror, the opposite of how others see us. When we see a photograph of ourselves, we're seeing ourselves as others do, and it's off-putting."

"That actually makes sense," Mason said.

"Don't sound so surprised."

"Sorry."

"God, could this get any more boring? The only thing worse than doing nothing is being subjected to that Ermengarde Campbell woman."

"Well, prepare yourself, Walter, because she's headed this way," Mason said, nodding toward the blonde as she strode in their direction, her ponytail swinging from side to side. Mason got to his feet, standing next to Walter, who looked annoyed.

"Hey there, gents," Ermengarde said as she approached. "You must have snuck in when Myrtle and I were napping."

"Yes, we got in just after lunch, and we didn't want to disturb you two."

"Oh, I wouldn't have minded, it was just a little catnap. And then when I woke up, I noticed *you* were sleeping and Mr. Wingate was gone. But we're all back and awake now, so I thought I'd come over and say hello. You fellas go out last night after dinner?"

"Yes, to the Chi Chi Club," Walter said. "Dorothy Dandridge was performing."

"Gee, she's swell. I wish I'd known you were goin'. We would have went along, just to keep you company, of course. I looked for you before dinner, even knocked on your door, but you must have gone out already. I know you said it was going to be just the two of you for cocktails and dinner, but I thought maybe afterward we could join you."

"Sorry about that, Miss Campbell," Mason said.

"It's okay. Myrtle and I had cocktails and dinner downtown. But maybe we can all go out tonight, huh? Make it a foursome. I bought a new dress just for this trip that I think you'd like to see me in, and Myrtle's got a darling new outfit, too, just darling. I helped her pick it out."

"How darling," Walter said, fiddling with the ends of his mustache.

"Oh, I can't wait to wear my new dress. It's red, you know, and low cut."

"Sounds lovely," Mason said.

"Thanks. Just wait and see. Gee, it's quiet today. Looks like even Mrs. Pruitt is going in," Ermengarde said.

They looked across the pool in time to see Regina disappearing through the door.

"Probably to check on her husband," Mason said.

At that moment, just after the words left his lips, a scream came from across the pool, and all eyes turned. Regina Pruitt was standing in the doorway of their room, facing out, looking pale and shaken.

CHAPTER THIRTEEN

Later Thursday afternoon, May 30, 1946
The Oasis Inn, Palm Springs

Mason sprang to his feet and rushed around the shallow end of the pool to where Mrs. Pruitt was standing, not even bothering to put his sandals on first. "What's happened, Mrs. Pruitt? What's wrong?" he asked, his voice calm and direct.

"Something's the matter with Angus. I think he's…I think he's dead!" Her voice was shaky as she spoke, and Mason thought she looked as if she might faint.

"Stay here and try to remain calm while I have a look." He stepped into the room, noting the curtains were still closed, but the overhead light and one of the bedside lamps were on. Angus was on his back in the bed. His skin was a pale shade of blue, the thin coverlet pulled up to his waist. Mason checked his body for vital signs as Regina watched from the doorway, but Angus was clearly deceased and had been for at least an hour or so. Mason saw no obvious signs of foul play, no blood, no visible wounds or trauma, but he did a quick check of the room anyway. No one in the closet, under the bed, or in the bathroom. The small octagonal window at the back of the unit was open, though. He walked over to it and peered outside, noting a patio chair sitting beneath it. Curious. Without touching anything besides Angus, he went back outside, closing the door behind him. Walter and Ermengarde, now joined by Myrtle, were still standing on the other side of the pool, staring at him anxiously. Arlo never came back out of his room, nor did Miss Atwater or Granville, and Marvin was nowhere to be seen.

"Is he...is he really..." Regina said.

"Yes, I'm afraid he is. I'm sorry."

She looked to be in shock. "I knew it. I knew the minute I opened the door something was wrong. It was terribly quiet, and I could see Angus in the bed, on his back, his eyes closed. I turned on the lights and called out to him, but he didn't answer. I knew he wasn't asleep because he wasn't snoring, and yet he clearly wasn't awake, either." Her whole body was trembling.

Walter came over to them, carrying Mason's sandals. "Here, you're going to burn your feet if you don't put these on. The pavement must be over 100 degrees."

"Thanks," Mason said, taking them and slipping them on.

"What's happened?" Walter said, looking from Regina to Mason.

"Mr. Pruitt is dead," Mason said. "Would you be so kind as to get Mrs. Pruitt some water, Walter?"

"Dead? Are you sure? How?" Walter said.

"Yes, he's dead, and yes, I'm sure. I don't know how. Get her some water from the office, would you?"

"Hmm? Oh, yes, certainly, dar...Mason. I'll be right back." Walter turned and hurried away, his sandals slapping the pavement.

"I can't believe it," Mrs. Pruitt said, her voice still shaky. "Angus and I were just talking out here only an hour ago or so."

"Death can sometimes be quite sudden. Did he seem to be okay before he went in?"

"Okay? I don't know, I guess so. He was complaining of a headache and some chest pain. He also seemed a bit unsteady when he got up. I figured he just had too much sun. I wanted him to go in and lie down."

"And so he did," Mason said.

Walter, followed closely by Marvin, returned quickly with a tall glass of ice water and handed it to Mrs. Pruitt. "Here you go."

"Thank you," she said.

"You're welcome," Walter said, turning to Mason. "Miss Campbell and Miss Schultz were bombarding me with questions. I told them to go back to their room and stay out of the way."

"Thanks, you've got a good head on your shoulders," Mason said. He looked at Marvin. "Didn't you have an appointment downtown today?"

"Oh, yes, but he, uh, canceled on me at the last minute," Marvin said. "Walter told me what happened when he came to get the water. Heart attack, I imagine."

"I don't know for certain yet," Mason said. "What makes you think so?"

"Well, it makes sense given his age, weight, lifestyle, and such."

"Hmm, yes, possibly," Mason said. "Mrs. Pruitt, sip that slowly and please sit down. Walter, stay with her, won't you? And don't let anyone in the room. Marvin, I'm going to go telephone the police, will you let me into the office?"

"Of course, but why are you calling them if it was a heart attack?"

"It was a sudden and unexpected death. They have to determine exactly what happened and what the cause was for certain, and the body will have to be removed."

"Oh, okay," Marvin said.

"Yes, that makes sense," Regina said quietly. She sank into a chair by the door, clutching the tumbler of water.

"I'm so sorry," Mason said to Regina, and then he and Marvin hurried away.

A few minutes later, a black-and-white cruiser and two unmarked cars parked out front. Two uniformed officers, a handsome middle-aged man in a dark suit, and a much older-looking man stepped into the office a short while later.

"Afternoon," the middle-aged man said, not bothering to remove his hat. "I'm looking for a Mr. Adler."

"That's me," Mason said. "I placed the telephone call. This is Mr. Gagliardi, he owns the place."

"How do you do? I'm Detective Branchford of the Palm Springs police. This is Mr. Silas Drake, the county coroner, and this is Officers Blondine and Call. Who found the body?"

"His wife. She's waiting outside the room where he died," Mason said.

"It's pretty warm out. Would you mind asking her to come to the office? I think she may be more comfortable."

"I'll get her," Marvin said, stepping around the counter.

"Thanks."

Marvin went out, closing the door behind him.

"Are you a guest here, Mr. Adler?" the detective said.

"That's right. I'm from Phoenix." He couldn't help but notice the detective's green eyes, bright and piercing, looking him over.

"And you were acquainted with the deceased?"

"I only met him the other day, and then just briefly. We also shared a table at the Chi Chi Club last night, along with his brother, his wife, and their son. I was out at the pool when I heard Mrs. Pruitt scream."

"I assumed you must have been at the pool," Detective Branchford said, looking him up and down. Mason realized he was still in his swimming suit, bare chested.

"I didn't have time to dress. I ran over to see what had happened, and then I went into their room where the body was. I checked for vital signs, but I really didn't expect to find any given the way he looked. It appeared he'd been dead for some time."

The office door opened, and Marvin entered, followed by Mrs. Pruitt, Granville, and Arlo.

"This is Mrs. Pruitt, the deceased's wife, their son, Granville, and the deceased's brother, Arlo Pruitt," Marvin said. "This is Detective Branchford, Mr. Drake, and Officers Blondine and Call."

"How do you do, gentlemen, ma'am? Sorry to hear about your husband, ma'am," Detective Branchford said.

"Thank you," Regina said. "I asked Mr. Gagliardi to get my son and Arlo, too. They wanted to come with me when they heard what happened. I hope you don't mind. This is all such a terrible shock." A little color had returned to her cheeks. Arlo was still wearing his green striped, short-sleeved shirt and khaki swimsuit, and Granville was in his tight plaid swimming trunks, bare chested, as Mason was. While Mason appreciated the view, he couldn't help but feel a bit intimidated. Gran was trim, fit, and athletic, and damned attractive even hungover. He wasn't sure, but Detective Branchford also seemed to be admiring Gran's bronzed body.

"Um," the detective said, averting his eyes from Gran to focus on Regina. "No, I don't mind. It's important to have family near you at times like these. I understand you found your husband, Mrs. Pruitt."

She bit her lip nervously. "Yes, I did. It was just awful."

Detective Branchford consulted his notebook. "It says Mr. Adler indicated on the telephone that there didn't appear to be any signs of foul play. What exactly happened?"

"I don't really know," Regina said. "We were both out at the pool. Arlo here, he's my husband's brother, was in our room napping while his own room was being cleaned. When I saw Mr. Gagliardi had finished Arlo's room, I woke my husband and told him he should get out of the sun. He agreed, saying he had a headache, some indigestion, and an aching sensation in his chest. He went inside, and Arlo came out less than a minute later."

"That's right," Arlo said. "I had just gotten up from a nap when Angus came in, not looking too well. He said my room was ready, so I walked out. Before I shut the door, I said I'd see him later and he said okay. I still can't believe it."

"Neither can I," Regina said. "After Arlo went to his own room, I settled into my lounger, but after an hour or so I thought I'd better check on Angus. That's when I found him dead."

"Okay. I'll be wanting to get a full statement from each of you, but right now, if someone would show us where the, uh, body is?"

"Certainly, I can do that," Marvin said.

"You'll need to man the office, Marvin. I can show them. Walter's been guarding the door," Mason said.

"All right," Marvin said.

"If the family wouldn't mind waiting here for the time being," Detective Branchford said.

"Of course," Arlo said, turning to Marvin, who was back behind the counter. "Mrs. Pruitt will need another room for tonight, Gagliardi."

"Certainly. She can move into room twelve. I'll make sure it's cleaned and ready to go."

"Thank you," Mrs. Pruitt said. "I'll need to get my things."

"Of course. Once the uh, body, has been removed and we've finished, I see no reason why you can't retrieve your belongings. I imagine you'll want to pack your husband's things, too," Detective Branchford said.

"Oh. I hadn't thought of that. Yes, I suppose I will."

"I'll help you, Mother. We can pack his suitcases and put them in the DeSoto until we're ready to leave."

"Yes, we'll need to make funeral arrangements back in LA. We should probably head home tomorrow," Arlo said. "There's lots to do."

"I just can't think about all this right now," Regina said, sitting in a small chair near the side door.

"Of course not," Arlo said, "and you don't have to. Just rely on me and Gran."

"Thanks, I appreciate it."

"Well, Mr. Adler, if you'd be so kind as to show us where the body is located, then," Detective Branchford said.

"Yes, certainly. This way, gentlemen." The detective, Mason, Mr.

Drake, and the two police officers stepped out of the office and closed the door. "He's in room eleven, just down the way here."

As they approached, Walter, who had retrieved his cabana jacket and was leaning against the door frame, stood upright, extinguishing a cigarette.

"This is Mr. Wingate," Mason said. "Walter, this is Detective Branchford, Mr. Drake, and Officers Call and Blondine."

"How do you do?" Walter said.

"Mr. Wingate's a friend of mine and has been watching the door to ensure nothing was disturbed."

"Good thinking," the detective said.

"Mason's a top-notch private investigator," Walter said.

"Oh? A private eye, eh?"

"That's right. In Phoenix, of course."

"Nice. We'll have to compare notes sometime," he said, giving Mason a soft smile. "Is the door unlocked?"

"It is," Mason said.

Detective Branchford turned the knob and pushed the door open. "Officers Call and Blondine, stay out here in case I need you. Mr. Wingate, you can go back to your room if you like."

"Thank you, but I'd rather not be alone just now. Maybe I should go see how Granville's doing."

"I think you should leave them be for now, Walter," Mason said.

"I have to agree, Mr. Wingate," Detective Branchford said. "Best to give them some time alone. They've all had quite a shock."

Walter looked annoyed but nodded just the same. "Fine, I'll just go back to my lounger for the time being until you're all finished. It looks like Miss Campbell and Miss Schultz are still in their room."

"Good, see you in a bit," Mason said.

Mason, Detective Branchford, and Mr. Drake entered Angus Pruitt's room, closing the door behind them. Mr. Drake walked over to the body and turned on the other bedside lamp so he could see better. He put on a pair of thick glasses and opened his medical bag, extracting a stethoscope and some other instruments. He drew the thin coverlet back, exposing Angus's nude body completely. It wasn't a pretty sight, and both Branchford and Mason looked away.

"Are those his red swimming trunks and straw hat in the corner?" Branchford said.

"Yes," Mason said. "He was wearing them when he came in here to lie down."

"Mrs. Pruitt said Arlo Pruitt was resting in here while his room was being cleaned, is that correct?"

"Yes, something about a bottle of scotch being spilled on his mattress. He was in here when Mr. Pruitt entered, but he left only a minute or so after. I was watching the whole thing from my lounger on the other side of the pool."

"Okay. When Angus Pruitt came in, did he close the door behind him?"

"No, he left it open. As I say, it was only a minute or less before Arlo came out."

"All right. So, as soon as the door was closed, and Arlo was gone, Mr. Pruitt here probably stripped and got into bed. And then an hour or so later, his wife came in to check on him and found him like this," Branchford said. "And no one else came or went during that time?"

"No, sir. I definitely would have seen."

"Where was everyone else when it happened?"

"Mr. Wingate and I were standing talking to one of the other guests, Miss Campbell, on the other side of the pool. Granville Pruitt was in a lounger just down the way, but at some point he went into his room and didn't return. Miss Campbell was with us, as I mentioned, and her roommate, Miss Schultz, was in a lounger just up from us. That's everyone, I think."

"So Arlo and Granville Pruitt were both in their rooms?"

"Yes, that's correct. Neither of them came out when Mrs. Pruitt screamed, but if they were dozing, showering, or otherwise engaged, they may not have heard. Granville's deaf in his right ear, so he may have been sleeping on his left."

"Okay," Branchford said, making a few more notes in his notebook. He walked slowly around the room, stepped in and out of the bathroom, and gazed at the small back window. "Was this open when you got here the first time?"

"Yes. It's a small window designed for cross-ventilation."

"Yet the front one is closed, and the drapes are drawn."

"Probably so Mr. Pruitt could nap without being disturbed by pool noise or light."

"I suppose that makes sense." Branchford got on tiptoe and craned his neck out. "There's a patio chair under here. That's a bit odd."

Mason walked over and joined him, noting he smelled like a hint of cedar and musk. "I noticed that, too, just after I checked for vital signs. There was no indication of foul play that I could immediately discern, and no sign of a struggle, but I just wanted to make sure no one was hiding in the room. I saw the open window and peeked out, as you just did."

"Impressive. I can tell you're a good detective," Branchford said.

"Thanks and likewise. The chair seems odd to me."

"Almost as if someone used it to climb in or out. Except it's a pretty small window and oddly shaped. It would have to be someone diminutive."

"I agree. And for what purpose would anyone want to come or go that way?" Mason said. "Assuming foul play's not involved."

"Good question," Branchford said, turning to Mr. Drake. "Find anything, Silas?"

"Eh, probably cardiac arrest based on what I'm seeing and what his wife told us," he said. "No signs of marks, bruises, or puncture wounds anywhere on the body that would indicate foul play, no vomit in the mouth or on the lips that may suggest poison, and no indications of any kind of a struggle in the room here, as Mr. Adler said earlier. His urine and excrement were released upon death, which is what that smell is. I took a small sample of the excrement for analysis, but I don't think it will be necessary."

"So, you're saying it was a heart attack?" Mason said.

"Yes. His wife said he had indigestion, a headache, and pain in his chest when he came inside. Worst possible thing to do in those situations is to lie down, which is exactly what he did. It's what most folks do, unfortunately, and then they die."

Mason studied Silas Drake. He appeared to be in his seventies but was probably much younger. His skin was dark, thin, spotted, and leathery from years of being in the sun, and what little hair he had left was stark white. He stood about five foot nine and had a slender build, his green checked suit ill fitting.

Detective Branchford nodded. "Okay. I'll talk with Mrs. Pruitt and see if she wants an official autopsy done, but she probably won't if you're certain the cause of death was cardiac arrest."

"It does look like a heart attack," Mason said. "But what about the chair beneath the window? As far as I know, the only access to that walkway is either from the small octagonal windows in each room or from the openings at either end of the buildings. It's too narrow to be of much use and not likely someone would just sit out there."

Branchford shrugged. "I'll walk back and take a closer look, and I'll ask Mrs. Pruitt and Mr. Gagliardi if they know anything about it.

But chances are it's been there a while, maybe left by a previous guest or a short Peeping Tom."

"I suppose. But it seems odd."

"Heart attacks happen all the time, Mr. Adler, especially in men his age and physical condition," Silas Drake said, getting to his feet and removing his spectacles as he began packing up his bag.

"Yes, but couldn't someone have smothered him in his sleep?" Mason said.

Detective Branchford shrugged and gave Mason a quizzical look. "I suppose that's possible. But why are you so unwilling to accept he died of natural causes?"

"I don't know, exactly. It's just that he had a lot of enemies, including several here at the inn. His death is convenient. I must say a lot of folks will be happy he's dead."

"Well, you'll have to give me a full statement regarding that, of course. But even if he did have enemies, it's unclear how anyone could have smothered him to death. Mr. Pruitt appears to have been a fairly large, strong man. Even if he'd been asleep, surely he would have wakened if someone tried to smother him. And it would have taken an equally large, strong person to subdue him. Anyone coming through that window would have to be small in stature, as I said before."

"What about the brother?" Mason said.

"He's hardly a small man, from what I saw," Branchford said. "He's just as big as the deceased."

"Yes, but he was in this room alone when Mr. Pruitt entered and was the last person to see him alive, apparently. And he and his brother didn't get along very well."

"But you, Mr. Wingate, and Mrs. Pruitt all swear Arlo Pruitt was only in the room with his brother less than a minute before he came back out. Even if the brother had been lying in wait and jumped him the moment Angus Pruitt opened the door and stepped inside, he wouldn't have had time to suffocate him, strip him naked, haul the body into the bed, cover him up, and casually make his exit in less than sixty seconds. Plus, you stated the door was left open during that brief time. Surely you, Mrs. Pruitt, or someone else would have heard the struggle, but nothing has been tipped over or broken or is out of place."

Mason sighed, knowing what Branchford said made sense. "That's true. I guess if he *was* lying in wait, he would have closed the door after Mr. Pruitt entered and then jumped him, and there would have been a fight. But my mind keeps going back to that small window and the chair."

"All right, I like to be open to suggestion. I suppose it's possible someone could have gotten in that way and smothered him in his sleep, but didn't you say all the other guests were at the pool except the brother and the son? And both of them are too large to fit through."

"Yes, but Miss Atwater was also in her room, and she *is* small in stature."

"Who's Miss Atwater?"

"A guest from Canada. Didn't I mention her before? She was out at the pool earlier but went to her room and hasn't been out since, as far as I know. She's in number four."

"No, you didn't mention her, but I'll speak to her along with everyone else. Fair enough?"

Mason nodded. "Fair enough."

Branchford turned to Silas, who had finished packing up and was standing near the door. "Finished?"

"Yes, Detective. Like I said, pretty straightforward in my opinion. Cardiac arrest. I've seen hundreds of 'em."

"Okay, go ahead and make arrangements to have the body taken downtown, then. I imagine Mrs. Pruitt will want it shipped back to LA for interment."

"Will do," Silas said.

"Is there some place private the two of us can talk?" the detective said.

"Talk? We can use my room, if that's okay. I'm just on the other side of the pool."

"Lead the way," Branchford said, ushering Mason out. "Guard the door until the fellows from the morgue show up, boys."

"Yes, sir," Officer Blondine said.

Mason and Branchford walked around the shallow end of the pool as Walter watched from his lounger, cigarette in hand and the bottle of vodka on the ground by his side. Mason shot Walter a look and shook his head slightly, as if to indicate *stay where you are.* He unlocked the door to his and Walter's room and stepped inside, the detective following.

"Can't get much more private around here than this," Mason said, picking up the shirt he'd been wearing earlier and putting it on. He also turned the deadbolt just in case Walter decided to intrude. "So, how can I help you?"

"Well, Mr. Adler," Branchford said, opening his notebook to a fresh page and wetting the tip of his pencil with his tongue, "why don't you tell me about these enemies?"

"Oh. Of course," Mason said. "Well, first there's Miss Cornelia Atwater, the woman from Canada. She believes Angus Pruitt had something to do with her brother Ralph's death. He worked for a company Mr. Pruitt owned and operated in LA, Baylis and Ivy."

"Does she have any proof? Never mind, I'll discuss that with her. Who else?"

"Arlo Pruitt, Angus Pruitt's brother, whom you met earlier in the office. They seemed to dislike each other. Angus Pruitt also believed Arlo and Mrs. Pruitt may have been sweet on each other, so to speak."

"Interesting," Branchford said, making scribbles in his notebook.

"When we were all at the club, Mr. Pruitt said he'd relish punching Arlo and his wife, if he ever found proof the two of them were having an affair, and that he'd never divorce her."

Branchford looked at Mason briefly. "What a swell guy. Anyone else?"

"Yes, Granville Pruitt, Angus Pruitt's son, whom you also met. According to him, his father was forbidding his potential marriage with a certain young lady, threatening to sully her reputation, disinherit him, and ruin her father's business if Granville continued to see her. He seemed to despise his father and even doubted he was really his son."

"Can't say I blame the kid. Mr. Pruitt sounds like a real gem," Branchford said.

"Yes. To be completely honest, I didn't like him much myself. Except I didn't kill him. I barely knew him."

"Okay," Branchford said, a slight smile on his full lips. "Is that everyone?"

"Well, no. There's also Marvin Gagliardi, the fellow at the front desk. As I believe I mentioned, he owns the Oasis, and Pruitt had invested in the place at perfidious terms."

"Such as?"

"Interest rates that increase quarterly, a balloon payment at the end, that sort of thing."

"Mr. Gagliardi sounds like he was foolish in accepting those terms," Branchford said.

"I agree, but many folks don't always read the fine print. I'm sure he tried the normal venues for loans at first, but he was without steady employment at the time except for his photography studio downtown."

"So, Pruitt took advantage of Gagliardi's desperation to buy the place."

"Yes, and apparently Pruitt was using the loan to try to force him to do a few things he didn't want to do with his photography, things that were immoral and illegal."

"Interesting. What kinds of things?"

"I don't know all the details, but it sounds like nude films and photographs and pretty graphic sex stuff."

Branchford raised his eyebrows. "And I take it Mr. Gagliardi didn't want to do those things?"

"Correct."

"Hmm, I also noticed Mr. Gagliardi is small and slim," Branchford said, making a notation before looking at Mason again. "What about the dead man's wife?"

"I can't say she seemed to be in love with her husband, which is understandable. But I'm not sure she had a clear reason to kill him."

Branchford raised his eyebrows. "Other than the fact that he was contemptable, and she may have had a thing for his brother. So, Angus Pruitt was an all-around swell fellow. Think there was anything to his accusations regarding the brother and his wife?"

"I don't know. I should tell you it wasn't just Arlo that Mr. Pruitt suspected. He thought it could possibly be some other man, too. He even suggested she and I had met before and were having an affair. Mr. Pruitt seemed to have a jealous and possessive streak, and I suspect all of his suspicions regarding his wife may have been unfounded."

"Okay. Thanks for the information. I'll let you know if I have any further questions. In the meantime, I need to go speak with the rest of the guests. For the record, though, most likely nothing will come of it. Just because the man sounds like he was a genuine ass and he had a lot of enemies doesn't mean he was murdered. Guys like that have heart attacks just like anyone else does."

"Of course, but I appreciate you asking around nonetheless."

"My pleasure, it's all part of the job. Have a good rest of the day, Mr. Adler."

"Likewise, Detective."

CHAPTER FOURTEEN

Early Thursday evening, May 30, 1946
The Oasis Inn, Palm Springs

"That was an unsatisfying meal, I must say. I thought we were done with the Big Cup Café," Walter said as the two of them drove back to the inn. "And did you notice we were the only men there wearing neckties and coats?"

"I guess it's a more casual place, even in the evening. Anyway, it's quick and easy. *And* affordable."

"Why do we need quick and easy? What else do we have to do? They took the body away hours ago, those two adorable policemen left along with the coroner, and I don't think that Detective Branchford you're so obviously interested in is coming back anytime soon."

"I'm *not* interested in him."

"I've known you a long time, darling. Don't try and kid me."

"Fine, he's attractive and smart and a good age. But he's probably married with three kids."

"He wasn't wearing a wedding ring."

"I noticed. But that doesn't always mean anything. Lots of married men don't wear rings."

"True, but I just got the feeling he had his eye on you."

Mason looked thoughtful. "Gee, ya really think so?"

"It certainly appeared that way to me. I think he plays for our team," Walter said.

"He did seem to be awfully appreciative of Granville Pruitt earlier, when he was was standing in the office all shirtless, handsome, sweaty, and hungover."

Walter looked annoyed. "Yes, I *know* Granville was all shirtless and sweaty. Marvin got Mrs. Pruitt, and then they got Arlo and Granville from their rooms. I saw the four of them walk down the other side of the pool to the office where you and Detective Branchford were waiting. And there I was left standing in the hot sun guarding the door to Angus Pruitt's room."

"Sorry, I didn't plan it that way."

"Sure you didn't."

"I *didn't*, honestly. I guess when he heard about his father's death, he didn't think about putting on a shirt. He came just as he was to the office, in his swimming suit."

"You could have called *me* to the office."

"You were standing guard at the door to Mr. Pruitt's room."

"I *know*. And you were in the office, in close quarters with that beautiful, sweaty, shirtless young man. And then, when I wanted to go check on him afterward, you and that Branchwood both told me not to."

"Branch*ford*, and it would have been awkward having you fawn all over Granville with everyone else in the office and his father lying dead a short distance away. Gran's too young, anyway."

"For you, but certainly not for me. I believe I heard he's twenty-four."

"Honestly, Walter. Find someone your own age. You're nearly fifty."

"I've told you before, men my age are of no interest to me. They're all old and dull."

"I'll try not to take offense at that statement."

"Fine. By the way, what were you and Branchford doing all alone in our room this afternoon?"

"I told you, he just wanted to ask me some more questions."

"Uh-huh. In the privacy of our room. Just the two of you."

"There was no other place, Walter. The Pruitts were in the office, we couldn't stand out in the courtyard where we could have been overheard, and neither of us wanted to talk in the Pruitts' room with him lying on the bed dead."

"Still, it seems suspicious."

"Well, it's not. Anyway, here we are back at the inn," Mason said, parking his car in one of the end spots.

"So I see. And now what shall we do, may I ask? It's only seven thirty. We *should* be just finishing cocktails at this point in the evening and heading to dinner soon, but here we are, already fed and back at our hotel. I feel like an old man. What's next, a game of checkers?"

"Sorry, I'm just not in the mood to go out tonight," Mason said.

"Why not, for heaven's sake? Because Angus Pruitt had a heart attack and died? He was a despicable person."

"He was, I agree. But I still feel his death may not have been natural," Mason said as the two of them walked toward the gate and the courtyard beyond.

"Honestly. You're on holiday, on vacation. Stop thinking like a dick and just let it go."

"I tried, but something's not sitting right with me. I just want to ponder things for a bit."

"Well, ponder them at the Chi Chi Club, darling. You can think things over there just as easily as here, and a good martini or glass of scotch may clear your head," Walter said, gazing about the pool area, which was devoid of other guests. "God, this place is like a morgue."

"Walter…"

"What? Oh, sorry, sorry. I just meant there's no one around. Or so I thought! What's that?" he said quietly, stopping in his tracks and gesturing toward something moving low and stealthily against the wall of the building.

Mason squinted his eyes toward where Walter was pointing. "Looks like it's just Marvin's cat, Toujours, on the prowl."

"Oh, yes," Walter said, fiddling with his mustache. "She gave me a fright skulking about like that."

"Looking for dinner, I'm sure."

"She eats early, too, apparently. Ugh, where is everyone? It's so quiet."

"I imagine the Pruitts are in their rooms making arrangements, talking, and whatnot. Miss Atwater is most likely in her room, too. As for Miss Campbell and Miss Schultz, I suspect they're already out on the town. I noticed their car wasn't out front," Mason said as they started moving again.

"And what of Marvin? The office was all locked up just now."

"No idea. Say, did you leave the light on?" Mason said as they reached their room. He pointed to the window, where a lamp was shining through the closed curtains.

"Of course not. It was still very bright out when we left. That's odd."

"It is." Mason unlocked the door, and the two of them stepped inside quietly. A man was there, his back to them. He was holding what looked like a gun. Mason instinctively reached for his own before remembering he left it in Phoenix. The strange man whirled about, a surprised look on his face as Mason prepared for a fight. Then he realized it was Marvin, and what at first appeared to be a gun was actually a crescent wrench.

"Marvin! You scared the hell out of me," Mason said.

"Me too, I must say," Walter said. "Good Lord."

"Sorry. I was just, uh, checking on your room, making sure the heater was working and all."

"The heater? It hasn't been a problem," Mason said.

"Yes, well, Miss Schultz and Miss Campbell stopped in the office on their way out and told me their heater was sparking, and I don't need a fire on my hands on top of everything else. I took a look at theirs, and I think I fixed it, but I wanted to make sure yours and everyone else's was okay, too."

"Oh, so is there anything wrong with it?" Mason said.

"Yours seems to be working fine, fortunately, so maybe it was just theirs."

"What about the heaters in the other rooms?" Walter said.

"I'm sure since yours is okay, it was just the one in the girls' room that was malfunctioning. I thought I would check yours since you were out, but I didn't want to disturb or alarm the other guests."

"Hmm, all right, but since you're here, I'd like to ask you a couple questions, if you don't mind," Mason said.

"Oh? Sure, I guess. What about?"

"Mr. Pruitt's death."

"What about it? I heard it was a heart attack. Not surprising."

"I understand you were in Arlo's room this afternoon, is that right?"

"Yeah, sure I was. He made a real mess of his mattress, spilled a whole bottle of booze, soaked right through, and it may be ruined. I might have to charge him for a new one."

"Did you see anyone or hear anything coming from Angus Pruitt's room while you were there?"

Marvin shook his head. "No, nothing and no one. But I wasn't paying much attention. I was pretty steamed at the whole situation. I had a photography appointment in the afternoon, and I was afraid I was going to be late. The guy ended up canceling on me, but I wasn't aware of that at the time. Say, there is one thing that was odd, though."

"What's that?"

"I went to wring out my rag in the bathroom and noticed a drop of something red on the rim of the sink. I wiped it up, but it looked like blood."

"Curious. Maybe Arlo cut himself shaving," Mason said.

"Yeah, maybe."

"Or perhaps he cut a finger or something," Walter said.

"Could be. Seemed odd, though," Marvin said. "There were little black specks, too. Anyway, just thought I'd mention it. Have you, uh, seen Miss Atwater tonight?"

"No, we just got back from an early dinner. Why?" Mason said.

"Just wondering. I really hope she changes her mind about writing that article about me. Maybe you could talk to her. It could ruin me, you know."

"I imagine it would be pretty bad. I can try and talk to her, but I'm not sure it will do any good," Mason said.

"Probably not, but I'd appreciate it if you'd try. Was there anything else you needed?"

"No, I guess not. Not right now anyway, thanks," Mason said.

"Sure, but why all the questions?"

"I just feel something's not right with Angus Pruitt's death."

"It was a heart attack, plain and simple, that's all. Sorry again about scaring you both. Have a good night," Marvin said, putting the wrench away and picking up the tool box.

"You too," Mason said. He opened the door for Marvin and let him out before turning back to Walter.

"A drop of what looked like blood and little black specks. Interesting," Mason said.

"Hardly. Mr. Pruitt wasn't stabbed. Like we said, Arlo probably just cut himself somehow, and he was most likely intoxicated when he did it," Walter said.

"That makes the most sense, I guess. On another note, it seems odd Marvin was in our room here tonight. I wonder if he was using the heater as an excuse."

"An excuse for what? He was just being conscientious, I'm sure. Or maybe he was fondling and sniffing your dirty underwear."

"Yeah," Mason said.

"I was kidding."

"I know you were, but still..."

"But still, now that we're back from dinner, what are we supposed to do the rest of the night? Oh, I know, *you're* going to ponder. But what am *I* supposed to do? Twiddle my thumbs? Play solitaire?"

"Why don't you go see a movie? There's a theater downtown, I'm sure. I can give you a quarter and you can use my car."

"There *is* a movie theater in town, I noticed it the other day. They're showing *The Postman Always Rings Twice*. But I saw it last week."

"Well, see it again. Or go to the Chi Chi Club."

"By myself? And sit at the bar like a sailor?"

"Why not? Maybe you'll meet a sailor."

"Not likely, especially now that the war's over. Besides, I might run into that click click woman and her pal. If you give me a quarter for the show *and* a dime for popcorn, I guess I could sit through *The Postman Always Rings Twice* again. I am all dressed and everything."

"Fine. Here's fifty cents, but bring me back the change," Mason said, handing him a fifty-cent piece. "The car keys are on the dresser next to our hats. Have fun and behave."

"Well, I can't do both, darling."

Mason laughed. "Well, at least drive carefully. Good night."

"Good night. And honestly, don't dwell on this too much. You'll give yourself a headache. And remember, frowning causes all those nasty lines on your forehead."

"All right. While you're out, maybe I'll go have that chat with Miss Atwater."

"Do that. Maybe you can plead Marvin's case, and perhaps it will put your own mind at ease. Ciao," Walter said as he picked up the keys and his hat from the dresser and sashayed out the door, closing it behind him.

"Ciao," Mason said. He used the bathroom, put some Vaseline on his lips, grabbed his room key, and went out into the courtyard, locking the door behind him. Room four was to his left and just around the corner, the first room in the building that made up the bottom of the U.

Mason knocked upon the door, and Cornelia opened it, dressed in tan slacks and a white blouse, a red kerchief about her neck.

"Oh, hello, Mr. Adler. This is a surprise."

"Good evening. Forgive the intrusion, but I was wondering if I could ask you some questions."

"About what?"

"About Mr. Pruitt and some of the things you said at the club last night."

"Ever the private eye, is that it? Well, I've already said everything I have to say to that police detective."

"Indulge me, please. I won't be but a minute."

She studied him briefly. "All right, I've got nothing else to do at the moment. I was trying to get some writing done, but I couldn't concentrate, to be honest, so come in." She stepped aside and let Mason enter, then closed the door behind him.

"Have you had dinner?" Mason said.

"More or less. A few things from that awful vending machine, but I really wasn't that hungry."

"I suppose not." He looked about, noticing her open suitcase. "Packing?"

"Yes. I plan to leave tomorrow. There's a bus to Las Vegas late in the afternoon. I can catch another from there to Seattle, and then home to Vancouver."

"Sounds like a long trip."

"A couple of days or so. I'm pretty good at sleeping on busses."

"And maybe you can finish reading your book, too."

"Sure. Mr. Gagliardi said I could keep it. I checked the title, by the way, since you were so curious. *The Heart Is a Lonely Hunter*, by Carson McCullers."

"I've not read that."

"I haven't really gotten too far into it, but so far it's good. I like the title, anyway."

"Yes, fitting in many situations and for many people."

"I guess so. I'd offer you something to drink, but I really don't have anything except tap water."

"That's fine, I don't need anything at the moment."

"Okay. Please have a seat. There's just the one chair at the desk, but I can sit on the bed if you don't mind."

"I don't mind at all," Mason said, sitting on the small, wooden desk chair. He glanced at the typewriter, which had a fresh page in it and several typewritten pages next to it. "Still working on your article about Baylis and Ivy?"

"I am. Those pages next to the typewriter are what I have so far."

"I thought perhaps you'd put it to rest given Mr. Pruitt's death."

"Hardly. I still want to get to the truth. Pruitt's death doesn't solve my brother's murder or tell me what my brother discovered. I intend to do some more investigating and finish my articles. I may even need to go back to LA at some point."

"Articles? So besides the one on Mr. Pruitt and his company, you're still going to write the one on Mr. Gagliardi?"

"As I told you last night while we were dancing, there's a story here about the Oasis, and about Marvin Gagliardi and his connection with Angus Pruitt. I think I can tie the two together nicely."

"I see." Mason glanced at the paper in the typewriter, where the title "An Oasis of sin. Perversion in the centre of Palm Springs" had been typed.

"Catchy, don't you think?" Miss Atwater said.

Mason raised an eyebrow. "Indeed." He leaned closer and read on: *What at first glance seemed idyllic, I soon found out was coloured by debauchery in the desert.*

He straightened and looked over at Miss Atwater. "What brought this on?"

"Mr. Gagliardi brought it on. He owns this place, as you know. And he confessed to me last night that he's a homosexual."

"Why would he tell you that?"

"Because perhaps I was flirting with him."

"And you were flirting with him because you suspected he was a homosexual."

"That's right. He said he didn't want me to get the wrong idea, so he confessed."

"Sounds like an honest, brave, and noble man."

"Hardly. I also discovered he takes pornographic pictures of young men in his so-called studio downtown. Debauchery and sin, perversion in Palm Springs."

"The photos he takes are not pornographic, Miss Atwater. The men are covered, and it's perfectly legal."

"You know about all of that?"

"He told me, yes."

"Nonetheless, it's disgusting, and my readers will eat it up."

"That would most likely ruin his business and may even get him arrested."

"Possibly. But it makes a good story, and it's all true, more or less."

"Mr. Gagliardi was pretty upset about you writing this article."

"I know, but one reaps what one sows, as they say."

"He's a good man, Miss Atwater. He even escorted you to the club last night."

"That hardly makes him a good man. He threatened to sue me for libel."

"He probably will if it gets published."

"He most likely won't. And even if he does, he'd lose. His photographs of young men are no secret, and the fact that he's a homosexual would be hard for him to disprove."

"But it would also be hard for you to prove."

"I won't have to. People will believe it. It's nothing personal against him. I actually don't care what he does with his private life, but as I said, it makes a good story, and the tie-in to Angus Pruitt is excellent. Now then, what did you want to talk to me about? Mind if I smoke?"

"No, go right ahead."

She lit an Old Gold, getting up briefly to retrieve the ashtray from the nightstand and setting it on the bed next to her. "So what gives? Are you here to try and talk me out of writing the article? I know you and Mr. Gagliardi are friendly, so to speak."

"I don't know him well, to be honest, but I don't think he deserves to have an exposé written about him and his private life."

"Duly noted. Anything else?"

"Frankly, yes. Something about Angus Pruitt's death has been bothering me."

"Not me. I'm delighted."

"Are you?"

"Yes. He got exactly what was coming to him. The discovery that he was trying to force Mr. Gagliardi to do pornography, the mystery about what was going on at Baylis and Ivy, my brother's murder, and Angus Pruitt's subsequent death will all make excellent columns. My only regret is that I never got Pruitt to confess."

"Not for lack of trying, certainly. I couldn't help but notice you walked over to Mr. and Mrs. Pruitt earlier today out by the pool and said something to him that obviously agitated him."

"That's right. I was sitting at my usual table with my book when Mrs. Pruitt approached me."

"What did she want?"

"To talk. She said her husband had noticed me sitting there, and he didn't like it. She said he wanted to discuss things with me face-to-face and that it was time we met. I figured I had nothing to lose and maybe something to gain by finally confronting him in person, so I went with her back to where he was sitting, and we talked briefly."

"And how did that work out?"

She laughed harshly. "About as well as I expected."

"What was said?"

"Not that it's any of your business, but I basically asked him what it felt like to be a murderer, a liar, a pornographer, and a thief, and he then threatened to sue me."

"Not exactly a friendly start to the conversation."

"I saw no need to be friendly. I know what he did, he knows what he did, and I told him I'd be happy to see him in court if that's what he really wanted, but I knew he'd never go down that path."

"I see you ignored my warnings to proceed with caution."

"I've always favored the direct approach. He did threaten me, of course. He said something about me not knowing what he'd do if I didn't shut up and leave him alone, which I had no intention of doing. But I saw no reason to continue talking to him."

"So, you left and came back to your room here."

"Yes."

"And you didn't come out until the police arrived and knocked on your door?"

"My room is way back in the corner. I can't see the pool from here and had no idea what was going on or what had happened."

"But why choose that moment to go to your room and sit?"

"Because I was furious with him, and he'd given me a headache. I wanted to be alone," she said, taking a long drag on her cigarette.

"So, you came here and just sat?"

"Actually, I wrote quite a bit on my article about Mr. Pruitt. I was inspired."

He just watched her silently for several minutes.

"Why are you staring at me like that?"

"I get the feeling there's something you're not telling me."

"You're really annoying, do you know that?"

"I've been told so on occasion."

"Well, it's true. All right, fine. To be completely honest, I was also waiting for someone."

"Oh, who? A man?"

"Right away you think I was waiting for a man, alone in my room? I'm not that kind of a girl, Mr. Adler. Or maybe I am, but that's not the point."

"I'm sorry, I didn't mean to imply—"

"I think you did, but it's okay. I don't know if it was a man or a woman, but someone claimed to know what *really* happened to my brother. I got a note under my door this morning."

"May I see it?"

"Sure, I suppose." She ground out her Old Gold, got to her feet, and drew a sheet of stationery from the nightstand drawer, handing it to him.

"'I know the truth about your brother,'" he read. "'I will come to your room this afternoon after two to discuss things when the coast is clear.' It's unsigned and written in plain block letters on Oasis stationery. Who sent it?"

"I don't know, no one ever showed. I was still sitting here waiting when that detective knocked on my door. I wasn't even aware what had happened at that point. I think I dozed off."

"Certainly curious."

"It is. Clearly, Angus Pruitt had something to do with Ralph's murder, and someone else besides me knows it. I'm thinking it was Granville Pruitt or maybe Mr. Gagliardi."

"Gagliardi?"

"Yes, it makes sense. Maybe Mr. Pruitt admitted to him he'd had my brother killed for being a troublemaker, and he'd do the same to him if he didn't cooperate."

"I suppose that's possible, but what does that have to do with the note?"

"I think Mr. Gagliardi sent it to me because he wanted to trade something he knew about Mr. Pruitt and my brother's death for not writing the article about him. Only Pruitt croaked before Gagliardi could get here. I'm willing to bet he'll still try to make a deal, only I'm not the deal-making type."

"Clearly you're just guessing."

"I'm a pretty good guesser sometimes. It's one of the things that makes me a good journalist."

"I prefer facts," Mason said. "By the way, I understand your brother left pretty much everything he had to an aunt and a cousin."

"Who did you hear that from?"

"Angus Pruitt. He made inquiries."

"Not surprising, I guess. Well, it's true. Ralph and I discussed it last year, when he was making out his will. I told him I didn't need anything. I'm quite self-sufficient, but our aunt and her daughter did need the money. Aunt Lucy practically raised us after our parents were killed. I made the same provisions with my will. I've really no one else, so it just makes sense from a practical point of view."

"Still, it's charitable of you both. But I can't help wondering, if you're so well off, why did you take one of the least expensive rooms here? With no view, tucked back in the corner?"

"Because I was trying to be discreet, and because there's nothing wrong with being thrifty. I said I was self-sufficient, I never said I was well off."

"Fair enough. Well, I'll leave you to your evening."

"All right. I'm done writing for the night, I think. I'll get a fresh start on it tomorrow."

"About that. Don't you think you'd be better off leaving that story about Mr. Gagliardi and the Oasis alone? Focus on the one about Baylis and Ivy instead."

"The story of what is really going on at that company will sell, but sex, sin, and debauchery will sell even better, they always do. And if Gagliardi does have information about Ralph's death he wants to trade in exchange for killing my article, like I said, I'm not a deal maker."

"Even if that information led you to the truth about what happened to your brother?"

"I think I already know the truth. Angus Pruitt killed him or had him killed. At least that's the way I'm going to write it *and* the Oasis story. Now if you'll excuse me, I'm going to take a bath."

CHAPTER FIFTEEN

Later Thursday evening, May 30, 1946
The Oasis Inn, Palm Springs

Mason left Miss Atwater's room just past eight thirty. He walked around to the opposite side of the pool and down the row of rooms, one by one. The light was on in number twelve, and the drapes open. Mason could see Mrs. Pruitt sitting at the desk, writing something. On impulse he knocked.

"Come in," she called out. He opened the unlocked door and stepped in, leaving it ajar.

"Oh, Mr. Adler, this is a surprise. I was expecting Granville."

"Forgive the intrusion, Mrs. Pruitt. I know it's late."

"It's all right. I was just sitting here trying to compose Angus's obituary, and I honestly can't think of anything to say other than his date of birth, date of death, and who he's survived by."

"Sometimes it's best to keep it simple. Have you eaten dinner?"

She set the fountain pen on the desk and turned toward him. "No, not yet. Granville's going to bring me back something. He went into town a little while ago with Arlo to eat, but I preferred to stay here."

"That's understandable. I'm glad Mr. Gagliardi had a different room available for you for tonight."

"Yes, so am I. Once they took Angus away, I packed my things and had Granville bring them here, just next door. Then I asked him to go back and pack Angus's belongings and put them in the DeSoto. I couldn't bear to do it myself."

"Of course. I'm sorry again about your husband, by the way."

"Thank you. I still can't quite believe it. I keep thinking he'll come swinging through that door any minute."

"It will take time."

"I don't know if I'll ever get used to not having him around, as crude and obnoxious as he was. I'm sure a lot of people are glad he's dead, but he *was* my husband."

"Certainly, for better or worse."

She laughed at that. "With Angus, it was mostly for worse, but I was used to him, even his god-awful snoring. I'm sure that disturbed everyone at the pool when he dozed off."

"It was a bit loud, I admit. You said there are a lot of people who are glad he's dead."

She got up, walked to the dresser, and got a cigarette out of her purse. "Yes," she said, lighting up. "It came with the territory, I'm afraid. There was even someone here at the resort."

"Oh?"

"Miss Atwater. She insisted Angus was involved in her brother's death somehow."

"Was he?"

She took a long drag on her cigarette as she stared at him. "I wish I could say no, but I can't definitively say yes, either. I really just don't know. But *she* certainly believed he was. She started following him and sending him notes after the funeral."

"That must have been unnerving for Mr. Pruitt."

"Angus wasn't the type to get unnerved, Mr. Adler. He usually did the unnerving. Still, it annoyed him. He considered her an irritation, like a bad itch."

"Yes, a pesky fly, as he put it last night."

"And Angus hated flies."

"Do you know what the notes she wrote him said?"

"I have one of them here." She walked back over to the desk and opened a drawer, extracting a sheet of plain white paper. "I'll read it to you: 'I know you're responsible for my brother's death, and I have proof. Pay me five hundred dollars, or I'll go public in my column, and you'll end up the way he did, one way or the other. C. Atwater.'"

"May I?" Mason said, holding out his hand.

"Be my guest," Regina said, handing it over.

He glanced at it briefly. "It's typewritten and unsigned, I see."

"Yes, they were all like that."

"What was his reaction? Five hundred dollars is a lot of money."

"It certainly is. He was furious."

"Did he pay it? Or did he intend to?"

"Of course not. He claims she was bluffing. It made him mad."

"Not frightened?"

"Of her? Hardly."

"May I keep this note?"

"Whatever for?"

"Just curious. I'd like to show it to Detective Branchford."

"I showed it to him earlier."

"Well, then, I'd like to keep it a while for my own sake. I can mail it back to you later, if you like."

She considered that briefly, then shook her head. "No, keep it. The other notes are in Angus's desk at our house in LA. I believe he has them all. I've no use for them now that he's gone."

"Thank you," Mason said, putting it in his pocket.

"You're welcome. She's an awful woman, you know. Of course, my husband's death has been ruled a heart attack, but I must admit, I wonder. She's clever, cunning, and devious. And she certainly hated Angus. He wasn't about to give in to her petty demands, so perhaps she figured out a way to kill him to exact revenge."

"How?"

"I suppose we'll never know for certain. I will say I was surprised she agreed to meet Angus and talk to him face-to-face out at the pool, though she was hardly cordial. Although I didn't think anything of it at the time, she brought her drink with her and set it down next to Angus's and mine. All the cups look alike, so she might have switched drinks with him. When he got up to go inside, he did seem a bit woozy."

"You think she poisoned him?"

"It's a theory," Regina said, taking another puff and blowing the smoke off to the side.

"There was no outward sign of poisoning, though. No vomit and no indication of convulsions."

"It sounds like you're well versed on poison, Mr. Adler."

"Comes with being a detective."

"I imagine it does. It was just a thought. I'm told the coroner feels strongly it was a heart attack, and I'm sure that's what it was. His father died the same way, actually. I can't help but think, though, that her little confrontation with him just beforehand had something to do with it. He was visibly upset by her accusations."

"I noticed. Yet he sent you to get her because he wanted to meet her face-to-face."

"I'm sure he didn't expect her to be quite so hostile out in public and everything." She walked back to the dresser and ground out her cigarette before turning to look at him once more. "We'll all be heading home tomorrow, and we'll have Angus's body shipped to LA as soon as possible."

"All right. I hope you can get some rest."

"Thank you. I plan on taking a sedative or two."

"Good idea. I'll leave you to your evening, Mrs. Pruitt. Good night." Mason left, closing the door behind him, and walked slowly back around the pool to his room as Granville and Arlo came in the front gate, Granville carrying a bag Mason presumed was dinner for Regina.

CHAPTER SIXTEEN

Late Thursday evening, May 30, 1946
The Oasis Inn, Palm Springs

The door opened a little after eleven, and Walter rolled in, dropping his hat on the dresser.

"How was the movie?" Mason said, setting his book down and getting up off the bed.

"Exactly the same as last time, nothing different."

"That's how movies generally work, Walter."

"Ha ha. There was a newsreel, a cartoon, and the film. Not even a double feature, and the popcorn was stale. Worst of all, the ushers were all girls, can you imagine?"

"Sorry to hear it. Do you have my change?"

"The movie was thirty cents and the popcorn fifteen, so here's a nickel," Walter said, handing Mason the five cents as he removed his jacket and tie. "And you'll be happy to know I moved your seat back where it was and readjusted the mirrors."

"Thanks."

"You're welcome." Walter walked over to the closet and hung up his jacket and tie as he took off his shoes. "Ugh, this town is so dusty. These will need a good polishing."

"I'm sure they do that for you at the Triada," Mason said.

"As a matter of fact they do. Oh well, I suppose I'll have to take care of them myself when we get back to Phoenix." He walked over to Mason. "How was your night? Did you get all your pondering done?"

"No, not entirely. As you know, the police detective and the coroner seem certain Pruitt's death was a heart attack, but I wonder."

"What are you wondering?"

"His death was too convenient. Certainly he had a lot of enemies, including nearly everyone here at the Oasis."

"But that doesn't mean one of them killed him," Walter said. "You just said the coroner ruled it a heart attack."

"I think he should retire. He's a little past his prime."

"That may be, but the official cause of death is cardiac arrest, pure and simple."

"I know, but still…"

"But still you wonder."

"Sorry, but I do. I had a little chat with both Miss Atwater and Mrs. Pruitt while you were gone."

"At the same time?"

"No. I talked to Miss Atwater first, in her room, and then Mrs. Pruitt in hers."

"Visiting women in their hotel rooms after dark? My my, what about their reputations? And yours?"

"I don't think any of us are too worried about that, Walter."

"Good. Reputations are overrated anyway. How did all that talking go?"

"Mrs. Pruitt thought Miss Atwater may have poisoned Mr. Pruitt's drink when she came over to him earlier out by the pool."

"It wouldn't surprise me, frankly. She's a nasty woman, and she clearly hated him."

"She definitely did, but I've seen poison cases before. Unless she used one I'm not familiar with, Angus Pruitt's body was not consistent with death by poison."

"What was it consistent with?"

Mason sighed. "A heart attack."

"Well, there you go. And what did Miss Atwater say when you talked to her? Were you able to convince her to kill the story on Marvin, if you'll excuse the expression?"

"No, unfortunately. She's quite determined."

"I was afraid of that," Walter said, fiddling with his mustache.

"Me too, but it was worth a shot. My only hope is that it's only published in Canada, and no one in the United States sees it."

"Unless the newspapers down here pick it up," Walter said.

"That's a possibility, considering it's about Palm Springs, more or less."

"Ugh, I dislike her more and more all the time. What else did she say?"

"She told me someone slipped an anonymous note under her door earlier claiming to have information about the truth regarding her brother's death and that they were coming to her room sometime after two in the afternoon."

"So, that's why she left after talking to Mr. Pruitt."

"Apparently. She said no one ever showed up, though. She told me she thinks Marvin sent it."

"Marvin? Why would he do such a thing? I doubt he knows anything about her brother's death."

"She claims Mr. Pruitt may have told him about killing Ralph Atwater, and Marvin planned to give her that information in exchange for her not writing the article on him and the Oasis."

"Oh dear. I know Marvin's desperate to not have that article published, but still…" Walter said.

"Still, it's possible, like it or not. I wonder, though, if she actually wrote that note to give herself an alibi for being alone in her room in the middle of the afternoon."

"Huh? I'm not following you."

"Well, I was just thinking. What if, when Miss Atwater came back with Mrs. Pruitt to where Mr. Pruitt was sitting, she slipped a sleeping powder into his drink before going back to her room? When he went in to lie down, she could have climbed out her back window and gone around the rear of the buildings into the Pruitts' room. By that time, he would have been fast asleep. She could have smothered him with a pillow or something and slipped back out the way she came."

"Hmm, possibly. She's small enough in stature to fit through that window, I suppose. She's not that tall, though. Wouldn't she have a hard time climbing up there?"

"There was a chair outside the window of Pruitt's room. There's something else, too. When Mr. Pruitt got up to go in the first time, with his wife, he looked a little unsteady. Poison would have been easy to detect, and he could have staggered to the door and called for help when he started feeling ill. A sleeping powder, however, would just make him tired."

"I admit that makes sense, Mason. Perhaps you'd better telephone that handsome detective."

"I don't know. Some of it makes sense, but yet there are parts that don't."

"Such as?" Walter said.

"Well, the location of her room, for one thing. She's in the corner.

Her window basically looks out on the walkway to the side gate and the wall of the other building. She can't see the pool from there. How would she know when Mr. Pruitt went inside?"

"Maybe she just waited in the back and watched through the rear window of his room until he entered."

"Maybe, but it still seems like a risk. How would she know he wouldn't just fall asleep on his lounger out by the pool? Or if he did decide to go in and lie down, how would she know Mrs. Pruitt wouldn't go in with him? And even if Mrs. Pruitt stayed by the pool, she was just outside the door and could have come in at any moment. Plus, Miss Atwater is a petite woman, and smothering a big man like Mr. Pruitt would take some strength and effort. Surely even with a sleeping powder he'd be somewhat conscious and would struggle. Also, how would Miss Atwater have known Mrs. Pruitt was going to come get her, giving her an opportunity to drug him?"

"Ugh, yes, I see. Why must you make everything so complicated?"

"I'm just thinking things through, that's all."

"So, if it wasn't Miss Atwater, who did it? If, in fact, someone did. My money's still on a heart attack."

"The only other people not at the pool the whole time besides Miss Atwater were Arlo, Granville, and Marvin. Arlo and Gran were supposedly alone in their rooms, and neither of them emerged when Mrs. Pruitt screamed. Marvin was in the office, having claimed his appointment downtown was canceled. What if Marvin returned to the desk after cleaning the mattress and waited until Arlo left and Mr. Pruitt went back in alone? I'm sure you can see the door to the Pruitts' room from the front office window. What if he then slipped into room twelve, which was vacant, out that window, and into Mr. Pruitt's?"

"I suppose."

"The chair is an issue, though. I don't think even a small one would fit through that tiny window, so it would have had to have been placed underneath in advance, brought around from one of the ends under cover of darkness. And how would Marvin know ahead of time that Mr. Pruitt was going to go into his room alone and lie down, or that the back window would be open? If he went into room twelve, someone would have noticed. And anyone going back behind the buildings through any of the ends would have been seen by someone out at the pool."

"Exactly. I told you Marvin's innocent," Walter said.

"Perhaps. There's also Arlo and Granville. Maybe when Arlo was in his brother's room, he unlocked the back window. Then he went out the window of his own room and into Mr. Pruitt's, and back again. But the problem I see with that is the size of the window and the size of Arlo, who is as big as his brother was. The window is about twenty-two inches across and up and down. I think it's possible Marvin or even Miss Atwater could have squeezed through, but I don't believe Arlo or Granville could have."

"True. Say, I just thought of something," Walter said, still fiddling with his mustache. "If whoever did it needed the chair to gain access because the window is high off the ground, they would have needed a chair to get back into their own window, too. So, after killing Mr. Pruitt, they would have climbed back out, then moved the chair beneath the window of their own room so they could get back inside."

"But the chair was still beneath Mr. Pruitt's window. Good thinking, Walter."

"Thanks. Perhaps you're rubbing off on me. I was just contemplating what I would have had to do if it had been me. Which it wasn't."

Mason chuckled. "I know that. I suppose they could have climbed down and escaped some other way. Maybe even over the wall."

"For which they would also need the chair. That wall is at least seven feet tall."

"Hmm, true, and the chair was definitely not next to the wall. And there was no one still in Mr. Pruitt's room, I checked."

"Exactly, so it's possible the chair means nothing. Mr. Pruitt went into his room and opened the back window to get some air. He left the front one closed because of the noise from the pool area. He lay down, had a heart attack, and died. That old chair could have been out there for days or weeks."

"Left by a previous guest, a petite Peeping Tom, maybe, as Detective Branchford said."

"It makes sense. Stop trying to make things more difficult."

"Maybe you're right," Mason said.

"I am right. Now let's get some sleep. We've a long day of driving ahead of us tomorrow, and frankly I can't wait to get home."

CHAPTER SEVENTEEN

Early Friday morning, May 31, 1946
The Oasis Inn, Palm Springs

"Rise and shine, Walter," Mason said, opening the drapes and letting the morning sun flood in like a tidal wave.

Walter sat up and peeked one eye out from beneath his sleep mask before snapping it back into place. "Ugh. What time is it?"

"Just past seven thirty. I'm hungry. We had dinner so early last night."

"And whose fault is that? *I* wanted to eat at eight, like civilized people. Close those damned drapes."

Mason pulled them closed again. "Fine. Now get up."

"You're beastly in the morning, do you know that?" Walter said, taking the sleep mask off and blinking slowly.

"So you've said. I didn't sleep very well. Too much on my mind."

"Not surprising," Walter said, sitting up and letting his feet dangle over the edge of the bed.

"I've been up since six thirty. I shaved, washed, and dressed, then I read for a while. I can't believe how soundly you were sleeping. You were snoring almost as loud as the late Mr. Pruitt."

"I *don't* snore, and there's nothing on my mind to keep me awake. *My* head's completely empty."

"As I've always suspected," Mason said with a chuckle. "Come on, let's get going."

"All right, I'm hungry, too. Let me wash and get dressed, and then we can go."

"Casual is fine," said Mason, who was wearing a short-sleeved green paisley knit shirt with gray-blue trousers.

"I assume we're going to the Big Cup again?"

"Yes, unless you have any objections."

"Normally I would, but I'm anxious to get on the road and away from here." Walter stood, smoothed out his red silk pajamas, and padded to the dresser, taking out a blue, white, and red horizontal striped short-sleeved crew-neck pullover, khaki trousers, and a fresh pair of underwear from one of the drawers. "I'll be just a minute."

It was nearly eight thirty when Walter finally emerged and slipped on his white leather sandals. "All right, I suppose I'm ready. Oh, I almost forgot my chapeau." He picked up his straw fedora from the dresser and put it on.

"Fine, let's go," Mason said.

"You're not wearing a hat?" Walter said.

"Not this morning, but I've got my sunglasses. Come on."

They walked out of the room and Mason locked the door behind them, and then out the front gate to Mason's car and the short drive to the Big Cup Café.

"Good morning, gents," the waitress said with a toothy grin. "Table or booth?"

"Booth, please," Mason said.

"Sit yourself down at any of 'em. I'll get you some coffee."

"Thanks," Mason said, as he and Walter slid into the nearest booth beneath a large window overlooking Indian Canyon Drive. "What will you have?"

"Hmm, oh, I think toast, two eggs, and bacon won't kill me."

"Sounds good. I'll have the breakfast platter."

"Scrambled eggs, bacon, hash browns, and biscuits and gravy? My, you are hungry," Walter said.

"I am. And I think better on a full stomach." The toothy waitress brought over two mugs of steaming hot coffee and took their order. It wasn't long before she was back, putting their plates in front of them.

"Anything else I can get you two?"

"No thank you, miss, that will do."

"Sure. I'll be by with more coffee in a bit."

As they drank their coffee and ate, Mason reviewed the events of the last few days again with Walter.

"Honestly, Mason, how many times are you going to go over all of this? It's no wonder you're still single, you bore people nearly to death."

"I happen to like being alone. And what's your excuse? You're just as single as I am."

"I'm particular, that's all."

"That's one word for it."

"It's a very good word. Are you going to finish that biscuit?"

"I was, but I don't need it. Here," Mason said, scooping it onto Walter's plate.

"Thank you. You all finished?"

"Yes, I think so. I've certainly had enough coffee. Good thing it's a short drive back to the inn."

"The waitress was attentive, at least."

"She was. I always appreciate good service," Mason said.

"I appreciate good service by handsome waiters, but when one is at the Big Cup Café, one must accept what one gets."

"Yes, one must. Come on, the waitress left the check with the last refill. We pay at the register."

"I remember. How quaint."

"Isn't it, though?" Mason said, leaving a quarter on the table for a tip.

After Mason paid the bill, Walter put his hat back on, and they both donned their sunglasses as they walked out the door to Mason's car, which was parked in one of the few shady spots on the street.

"What time is it?" Mason said as he climbed in behind the wheel.

"Almost ten, and it's already over eighty degrees."

"Worse back in Phoenix, most likely," Mason said. He started the engine and pulled out, turning the car toward the inn.

"I'm sure," Walter said, putting his hand over his stomach. "Ugh, all that greasy food. This is not at all what I expected when you asked me to come to Palm Springs."

"*You* asked *me* to come to Palm Springs, Walter."

"Well, now I just want to go home."

"We'll leave soon enough," Mason said.

"Good. We should stop by that charming little gas station on our way out of town and have that lovely young man pump up the tires and check the oil."

"I planned to," Mason said. "The radiator, too. I don't want to overheat in the middle of the desert."

"Heavens, no. I'm sure that fellow will take good care of things. What was his name? Lewis?"

"Leroy."

"Oh yes, Leroy. I wonder if he contacted Marvin about getting his picture taken."

"I have no idea. I still think he'd be better off getting a reputable agent. Anyway, here we are. Traffic was light this morning," Mason said as he turned into a spot at the Oasis and switched off the engine.

"Good. Let's go in and finish packing," Walter said.

"It won't take me long, about ten minutes at most."

"That's because you hardly brought anything. And you pack like a sailor, everything the same color and all in one bag."

"You, on the other hand, pack like the Queen of England with all her trunks. All that's missing is the tiara."

"I'd wear one if I could, darling," Walter said, following Mason's lead up to the entrance and through the gate.

As they passed the office, Mason noticed the Pruitt family had assembled inside. "They're all in their traveling clothes. Looks like they're checking out."

"Can't say I blame them," Walter said.

"No, neither can I. Let's go say goodbye."

"Don't you need to use the bathroom?"

"I can wait a bit. Come on, it's the polite thing to do."

"Ugh, if we must."

"We must," Mason said. He opened the door and stepped inside as Walter followed, closing it behind them. "Good morning, everyone," Mason said.

"Good morning," Marvin said.

"Hello, Mr. Adler, Mr. Wingate," Regina said, turning toward them as Granville and Arlo nodded. She looked weary.

"Checking out?" Mason said.

"Yes. We had to wait for Mr. Gagliardi to return, but now we're all set."

"You had to wait?" Mason said.

"I had to use the bathroom in my apartment is all," Marvin said from behind the counter.

"You were gone nearly ten minutes," Regina said tersely.

"My apologies again," Marvin said.

"I hope you all have a safe trip back," Walter said.

"Thank you. They're sending my husband's body the day after tomorrow. This has all been just too much."

"I can't even imagine," Mason said.

"No, I don't suppose you can. Thanks for stopping in to say goodbye. Are you two leaving today as well?"

"Yes, as soon as we finish packing," Walter said. "We've just come from what some people call breakfast."

"It's what everyone calls breakfast, Walter," Mason said.

"Not me. Breakfast is poolside at the Racquet Club."

"We ate at the Big Cup Café. Not Walter's cup of tea, so to speak."

"Ah, I see. We plan on stopping for a bite on our way out of town, though I must admit I'm still not very hungry," Mrs. Pruitt said.

"But you do have to eat," Mason said.

"Yes, I suppose so. Safe travels to you both, as well. I imagine everyone will be checking out today," Regina said.

"Everyone but Miss Campbell and Miss Schultz," Marvin said. "They're here until Sunday."

"I see. And where is Miss Atwater this morning? I'd rather not run into her," Regina said.

"She requested a late checkout. I, uh, haven't seen her yet. She's probably still in her room," Marvin said. "I'm sure she doesn't want to be disturbed."

"No doubt she's waiting until we leave before she shows her face," Arlo said.

"I'm sure she feels terrible about what happened," Granville said.

"She should," Mrs. Pruitt said. "I think it was her accusations that got him so upset and led to his heart attack. Well, we need to get on the road. Arlo, take the bags out to the car, won't you?"

"Sure, Regina."

"I can give you a hand," Granville said.

"No, I want you here with me, Gran," Regina said. "I don't want to be alone right now."

"You're hardly alone, Mother. Mr. Adler, Mr. Wingate, and Mr. Gagliardi are all here."

"But they're not family. You're my only son, and I need you here with me now."

"I can help you with the bags, Mr. Pruitt," Marvin said. "Mrs. Pruitt has paid the bills for all the rooms, so I'm free to assist."

"It's all right, I can handle them on my own. I put a few of them in the car earlier, so there's just these left," Arlo said. He picked up the suitcases easily, and Walter opened the door for him and then closed it again.

"My, he's strong, isn't he?" Walter said. "Some big men like that aren't, you know."

"Er, yes, I suppose he is fairly strong," Regina said. "Well, Mr. Adler, I believe you said you needed to finish packing?"

"Yes, that's right. But it won't take me very long. I suppose I could go and check on Miss Atwater for you," Mason said. "Make sure she doesn't come wandering over to the office while you're still here."

"Thank you. You're very kind, but I'm sure she's sequestered in her room, waiting until we leave, as Arlo said. Actually, I'd like to speak with you and your friend Mr. Wingate here for a moment, if I may."

"Oh? What about?" Mason said.

"Well, you're a detective, correct?"

"That's right, in Phoenix."

"What's your take on all this?" Regina said, stepping closer to him and placing a gloved hand on his forearm.

"On your husband's death? According to the coroner, it was cardiac arrest. A heart attack."

"Exactly," Granville said. "Not surprising in the least."

"Gran, please," Regina said.

"Sorry. But it wasn't, not to me."

Regina sighed and turned back to Mason. "What about the, uh, other things? The accusations Miss Atwater made? What are your thoughts on what she said about my husband's involvement in her brother's death?"

"I'm afraid I really couldn't say. I don't have enough facts."

"Oh, well, what about you, Mr. Wingate?"

"Me? I don't have the slightest idea. Now, if you want my opinion on your outfit or on how to decorate your home, I'd be happy to assist."

"My outfit? What's wrong with it?" she said, glancing down at her clothing.

"Oh nothing, really. I mean, if you like horizontal stripes. And clearly you do."

"It's a striped black and raspberry jacket with a solid raspberry skirt."

"And a black hat, black gloves, and black shoes," Walter said.

"Well, I *am* in mourning. I'm afraid I didn't have any all-black clothes along."

"Of course. As I say, it's completely fine, really. Though I'd wear it belted at the waist."

"Walter," Mason said.

"What? She asked me, didn't she?"

"Only after you brought it up," Mason said, turning to Mrs. Pruitt. "Honestly, Mrs. Pruitt, your outfit is the height of fashion. You dress impeccably."

"Thank you, Mr. Adler."

"Oh yes, of course you do. But I can't help but wonder," Walter said, "if raspberry is really the best choice for your skin tone. I noticed it in your bathing suit, too. I think peach might suit you better."

"I'll keep that in mind."

"Walter, shut up," Mason said.

"What do *you* think about what I'm wearing, Mr. Gagliardi?" she said.

"Me? Oh, gee, it's very nice, Mrs. Pruitt. Though I agree a belt about the waist might be a nice addition. You're so slender."

"Why thank you, Mr. Gagliardi. A belt is an excellent suggestion. I'll give that a try next time I wear this. You've clearly an eye for fashion."

"Wait a minute," Walter said. "It was my idea in the first place."

"Hmm? Was it? Well, Mr. Gagliardi put it so much more succinctly, wouldn't you say, Gran?" Mrs. Pruitt said.

Gran shrugged and looked uncomfortable. "Sure, I guess. But why are we talking about your clothes, anyway, Mother? It seems ridiculous."

"Yes, you're right, dear, of course you're right. It was just a momentary distraction," Regina said.

"It's okay. I suppose you need a distraction."

"I think I do. Don't you need something to take your mind off things?"

"Me? Naw, I'm okay. I just want to get home."

"You were up awfully early this morning, dear. I couldn't sleep, and I saw you strolling about the courtyard just after dawn."

"I couldn't sleep, either. What's taking Uncle Arlo so long?" Gran said. "Maybe I should go see if he needs a hand."

"Arlo can manage, I'm sure. He's quite capable." She turned back to Mason. "So, have you two ever been to Los Angeles?"

"No, not yet, though I've been to San Jose and San Francisco several years ago," Mason said.

"I've been there," Walter said. "I would like to go back again."

"You truly should, and you simply must look us up when you do. I believe you said the other day, Mr. Wingate, that you would like me to introduce you to some of my confirmed bachelor friends."

"It's always nice to meet fellow bachelors, Mrs. Pruitt," Walter said.

"Fine. Let me know when you're in town, we're in the telephone directory. Oh look, here comes Arlo back now."

Arlo pushed through the door, sweaty and a bit disheveled. "God, it's hot out. I'll be glad to get back to LA," he said, wiping his brow with the back of his hand.

"What took you so long?" Gran said.

"I checked the oil and water on the DeSoto while I was at it."

"Good thinking," Regina said. "Everything okay?"

"Yes, all taken care of."

"What's happened to your handkerchief? It was in your breast pocket earlier," Walter said.

"Huh? Oh, it's in my trousers pocket. I had to use it to wipe the dipstick for the oil," Arlo said.

"And you used your handkerchief for that?" Walter said, aghast.

"There was nothing else around." He looked at Regina. "We still need to get some breakfast and get on the road. Everything all set here?"

"Yes, I think so," Regina said. She turned back to Mason. "I bid you a good day and safe travels back to Phoenix, both of you."

"Thank you, good day," Mason said. The Pruitts left the office, and Mason turned back to Marvin. "Everything okay?"

"Sure, I guess. Mrs. Pruitt was kind enough to pay for the full length of their stay for all of the rooms, even though they checked out early, She paid for the ruined mattress, too. And at least I don't have to worry about Angus Pruitt anymore."

"How exactly did this all start with him?" Mason said.

"Oh, we got to talking one time when he was a guest at the Triada. I told him about my wanting to open my own little hotel someday, and he was interested. He said he'd be willing to loan me the money if the opportunity ever arose, and he gave me his card. When I got fired, I heard about the Oasis being for sale. I tried to get a bank loan, but they said I was too high a risk, being unemployed except for my photography studio, so I called Mr. Pruitt. He offered to loan me the money at a fairly decent interest rate in exchange for a certain say in the business, and I foolishly took him up on it."

"Hindsight is always clearer, Marvin," Mason said. "I spoke with

Miss Atwater about you and the article she wants to write on the Oasis, by the way, as promised. I tried to talk her out of it."

"To no avail, I'm sure."

"Sadly, no."

"Figured as much, but thanks for trying. Even with Angus Pruitt dead, I still may end up losing it all as long as she's around."

"I'm sorry, Marvin, truly," Mason said.

"I appreciate that. Anyway, I should get back to work, if you'll excuse me. And after you two check out, I need to get downtown. I have an appointment with someone who wants his picture taken."

"Okay, we'll see you later," Mason said. He and Walter turned and left the office, walking the short distance to their room.

CHAPTER EIGHTEEN

Later Friday morning, May 31, 1946
The Oasis Inn, Palm Springs

Mason unlocked the door and the two of them stepped inside, setting their sunglasses and Walter's hat on the dresser. Mason used the bathroom and then walked back over to the window.

"What time is checkout?" Walter said.

"Eleven, I believe."

"It's past ten thirty now. We should finish packing," Walter said.

"I suppose. I want to talk to Miss Atwater again first, though."

"What for? She's already told you she's going to write the article."

"I know, but maybe the two of us together can convince her to leave Marvin alone. And I have a couple more questions for her. I wouldn't mind taking another look at that note that was slipped under her door, too."

"Oh, good grief, why? It will be a complete waste of time."

"Come on, Walter. I wouldn't mind an extra set of ears and eyes, and I'll give you a hand packing when we get back. Besides, like I said, maybe if we both talk to her about what a good man Marvin is, I mean, you know him better than I do…"

Walter held up his hands. "All right, fine, but let's make it snappy. I imagine if I leave the two of you alone, you're liable to yak with her all morning and we'll be late checking out and heading for home."

"Good. Come on, then."

The two of them walked down to number four, neither of them bothering with hats or sunglasses. The maids were just starting their morning routine on the rooms opposite.

Mason rapped on the door and waited, noting the drapes were closed. There was no answer.

"Perhaps she's gone out to breakfast," Walter said.

"Not sure where she'd go," Mason said, knocking louder this time. "She doesn't have a car, and there's not much in this neighborhood to walk to. And it's already awfully warm out."

"It certainly is," Walter said. He knocked on the door also, but still no response.

"Wait here. I'm going to see if I can look in the back."

"You can't go peeking in windows, Mason."

"I want to see if she's inside, that's all. I'll just be a moment. I think there's access to the walkway through that gate."

"Fine, but if you get arrested, I know nothing."

"That won't be hard to believe," Mason said.

"Rude!"

Mason went out the side gate and up the narrow passage to the back of the building. The first octagonal window he came to was Miss Atwater's, but it was closed and the drapes were drawn, just like in the front. He returned to Walter, who was waiting impatiently, smoking a Camel.

"Well? Is she in there?"

"I couldn't see anything. I think I'll ask Marvin if he can use his passkey so I can take a peek and make sure she's definitely not inside."

"If she were in there, why wouldn't she have answered the door?"

"That's a good question."

"The answer is that she's clearly out, and you just want to snoop, I know you too well. But Marvin's not going to let you peek into another guest's room."

"Then I'll ask him to have a look on his own. We can wait outside here."

"Oh, for heaven's sake, you're impossible. All right, fine, I'll go see if he's still at the desk," Walter said. "But I'm sure he'll think you're utterly mad. She's undoubtedly gone somewhere, probably to avoid the Pruitts."

"Most likely, but I want to be sure. I'll wait here in case she opens up or comes back."

"Good, you can stand in the hot sun and wait for me for once," Walter said, sashaying away toward the office. It wasn't long before Walter came walking back, his left arm looped through Marvin's right as they strolled along the room fronts, giggling over some secret joke.

"What are you two on about?" Mason said as they approached.

"Oh, Walter's just being Walter. We were discussing Granville Pruitt and his form-fitting swimming trunks."

"Why am I not surprised? Well, thanks for coming, Marvin. I'm just a little concerned Miss Atwater hasn't answered her door."

"So Walter said. I didn't see her leave the resort, and I didn't see her around the coffee and doughnut area. Are you sure she's not just taking a nap, sleeping late, or perhaps in the shower?"

"She'd have to be an awfully heavy sleeper to not be woken by the pounding I gave the door, and I've been standing out here knocking for a little over ten minutes now. That would be a long shower."

"Hmm, all right. I'll have a look, but I can't let you two in. I'll just unlock the door and see if she's there or not. Most probably she went out for a walk via the side gate here and I just didn't see her." Marvin stepped to the door and rapped on it with the knuckles of his right hand. "Miss Atwater? It's Mr. Gagliardi, are you in there?" He paused and waited, but she didn't answer. Marvin retrieved the passkey from his pocket, inserted it into the lock, and turned it while at the same time giving the door a gentle nudge. It swung open silently, exposing a darkened room. With his left hand he flipped on the overhead light, and then let out an audible gasp.

"What is it?" Mason said, trying to peer around Marvin. "Is she in there?"

Marvin didn't answer or even stir at first. Finally Mason moved him gently but firmly out of the way and stepped into the room. Miss Atwater was lying face up across the bed, her head hanging over the edge. Vomit had spilled from her mouth onto the tile floor, and her brown eyes were staring blankly at the ceiling. Mason checked for vital signs, but there were none. An empty pill bottle was next to the body.

"What's happening?" Walter said, peering inside. "Oh my God. Is she dead?"

"Yes, I'm afraid so. Marvin, you'd better call the police and that Detective Branchford."

"Hmm? Oh, uh, yes, right. The detective gave me his card. I can't believe this. First Angus Pruitt and now Miss Atwater?"

"Marvin, please go make the call," Mason said. "Walter and I will wait here."

"Okay, sure. This is all too much. I'll be right back." Marvin turned and hurried away toward the office.

"What happened to her?" Walter said, stepping into the room next to Mason. "And what's that awful smell?"

"Death, or the aromas associated with it."

Walter took out his handkerchief and held it to his nose. "It's awful. How did she die?"

"I don't know."

"Look, there's a note on the floor," Walter said, stooping.

"Don't touch that!" Mason said loudly and sternly. "Don't touch anything."

Walter stood back up. "All right, all right. You don't have to yell. It's typewritten. You can actually read it without picking it up."

"Hmm, yes, so I see." Mason hunched down and looked at it closely, putting on his reading glasses and reading it to himself. "It's a suicide note," he said after a moment, "and she confesses to having killed Pruitt."

"What? *She* killed Pruitt? Not that I blame her, and it's not really all that surprising, but I thought he died of a heart attack."

"That was the belief, yes."

"Then why would she confess to killing him, and then kill herself?" Walter said.

"Sounds like a case of a guilty conscience. Look at the note."

Walter leaned closer. The note read: *I can't live with myself for taking Pruitt's life. When I saw the color drained from his body, it was as if the center of the earth opened and swallowed me.*

"I noticed it's not signed, though," Walter said, looking over his shoulder.

"She told us she typed everything, remember?" Mason said, standing erect once more and removing his reading glasses.

"Curious."

"Well, she was a columnist for a newspaper, and by her own admission, she had lousy handwriting, so I suppose it makes sense," Mason said. "Come on, let's wait for the police outside."

"Normally I'd object to standing in the sun again, but the sight of her lying there and that awful smell are turning my stomach, not to mention that awful breakfast."

"The awful breakfast in which you cleaned your plate *and* ate my biscuit."

"Yes, that's the one," Walter said, stepping through the door and moving down the walkway as Mason followed behind.

"That poor woman," Mason said.

"Yes, but I wouldn't feel too sorry for her. After all, she admitted killing Angus Pruitt and then killed herself. And remember, she was planning on writing that tell-all about Marvin, so I'm not exactly brokenhearted."

"I know, but still…"

"Still, she was alone in her room when Pruitt died. And since she's on the end, she could have easily slipped out the side gate and gone up the passageway behind the building, just like you did earlier when you tried to peek in her window. She then could've gone behind the other building, used the chair, which she'd placed there the night before, to climb into Mr. Pruitt's window and kill him. Then she climbed back down and escaped. No one would have noticed because her room is tucked back here in the corner."

"Hmm, yes. I admit that makes sense, more or less," Mason said.

"More or less? It makes total sense. Say, I'm getting pretty good at this detective thing. Maybe I'll join you in the biz. I could be the decorating detective. Catchy, yes?"

"Yes, like a bad cold," Mason said.

"You're just bitter because I figured it out before you did."

"But it still seems risky on her part. As I said before, what if Mrs. Pruitt had walked in while she was trying to suffocate him? And even if Miss Atwater had drugged him previously, wouldn't he be at least conscious enough to struggle and fight back? She's such a tiny woman."

"Sometimes us tiny folk are capable of doing strong things."

"True. Anyway, here comes Detective Branchford along with Marvin and two uniforms," Mason said, nodding toward the four men striding toward them.

"So I see," Walter said.

"Ah, Mr. Adler, we meet again," Detective Branchford said, coming up to him. He was, at five foot eleven, a couple of inches shorter than Mason. Two police officers, different from the ones the other day, stood just behind him. One of the officers was carrying a camera.

"Hello, Detective. You remember my friend, Walter Wingate?"

"Yes, how do you do, Mr. Wingate? The coroner's on his way. What's happened? Mr. Gagliardi said Miss Atwater is dead."

"I'm afraid so. It appears to be a suicide," Mason said. "I don't know for certain, of course, but she left a note, and there's an empty pill bottle on the bed next to her body."

"Interesting." Branchford turned to Marvin. "Who's still here, guest-wise? I believe you said Mrs. Pruitt and her family checked out this morning?"

"Yes, that's right. They're heading back to Los Angeles. It's just the two women from San Diego, and Mr. Adler and Mr. Wingate here now," Marvin said. "I have a few other guests checking in this evening and tomorrow."

"Okay. Once the coroner arrives, we can get started," Branchford said.

"Actually, it looks like he's here now," Mason said, nodding toward the front entrance at the far end of the pool. Silas Drake, wearing the same suit he had on the previous day, was walking slowly down the courtyard, carrying his black medical bag.

"Here we are again, Detective," Mr. Drake said as he finally reached the assembled group.

"Yes, let's have a look, gentlemen," Detective Branchford said. "I'll ask that Mr. Gagliardi, Mr. Wingate, and Officer Smyth wait out here, please. Mr. Drake, Mr. Adler, and Officer Barrows, you're with me."

"Are you married, Officer Smyth?" Mason heard Walter say as the four men walked to the door of the room and the detective opened it, letting it swing inward. Mason didn't hear what Officer Smyth's answer was.

"Was the light on when you entered before?" Branchford said to Mason.

"Uh, no, the room was pretty dark. I saw Mr. Gagliardi turn it on. Mr. Wingate and I waited just outside the door."

Branchford stepped all the way in as the other three men followed behind. "Leave that door open, it's pretty stuffy in here, and that smell…"

"Right," Mason said.

"Officer Barrows, go ahead and take the standard photos."

"Yes, sir," the officer with the camera said as he moved around the others and began taking pictures of Miss Atwater's remains and the room in general.

"As soon as he's finished, you can examine the body, Silas."

"Per usual," the coroner said.

"Correct, Mr. Drake." He turned to Mason, pointing to the sheet of paper on the floor. "Is that the note you mentioned? The suicide note?"

"It is. I didn't touch it, no one did. But it's readable if you get close."

"Hmm." Branchford stepped over to it and bent down awkwardly, slipping on a pair of reading glasses. "So I see. Interesting." He read it briefly before glancing up. "She admits to killing Angus Pruitt."

"Yes, surprising," Mason said.

"Looks like we'll have to reopen the file on him and do a full autopsy after all. Good thing his body hasn't been shipped back to LA yet," Branchford said. He got back to an upright position and put his reading glasses back in his breast pocket as he turned toward the open door and stuck his head out. "Smyth, I'll need an evidence bag in here. There's a piece of paper on the floor I want taken downtown."

"Yes, sir," Smyth said.

Branchford turned back to Barrows. "Be sure and get a close-up of that note, without touching it, of course."

"Will do, Detective."

Finally, Branchford looked at Mr. Drake. "Silas, you said yesterday Pruitt died from a heart attack."

Mr. Drake looked embarrassed. "It certainly appeared that way. I still think he did."

"But in Miss Atwater's note, she admits to killing him and killing herself because she felt guilty."

"Maybe she intentionally induced his heart attack. It's been known to happen. Not common, but possible," Drake said.

"I suppose. Well, as I say, we're going to require a full autopsy—on her as well as him. I'm assuming his body hasn't been embalmed yet?"

"Not that I'm aware of, Detective. He's still on ice down at the morgue, awaiting paperwork," Mr. Drake said. "Lots of red tape, as always."

"Good thing for paperwork and red tape, for once."

"Sure, but I still say it was a heart attack."

"Maybe so, Mr. Drake," Branchford said as Smyth entered with an evidence bag. Using white cotton gloves, he picked up the suicide note carefully and placed it into the bag as Branchford stepped over to the desk. "This must be the typewriter she used to write the suicide note. I'll want that taken in and dusted for prints, too, and examined to be certain it was used to write that note."

"Yes sir."

Branchford glanced at the typed piece of paper lying on the desk. He read aloud, "'An Oasis of sin. Perversion in Palm Springs. What at first glance seemed idyllic, I soon found out was coloured by debauchery in the centre of Palm Springs.' What the hell does that mean?"

"She was a writer," Mason said, unsure how much he wanted to share in that regard.

"Hmm. An Oasis of sin could refer to the Oasis Inn. It makes sense. Oasis is capitalized. I think I'll have a talk with Mr. Gagliardi again. See if he can shed some light on this," Branchford said.

"Anything else, Detective?" Smyth said.

"Not at the moment. Put the typewriter and evidence bag in the squad car and wait outside."

"Yes, sir." Smyth left with the items, leaving the door still open, as Branchford turned to Mason. "So what exactly happened here, Mr. Adler? It all seems odd. Are you the one that found the body?"

"Myself, Mr. Gagliardi, and Walter."

"How did that come to be?" Branchford said, taking out his notebook and pencil.

"I wanted to talk to Miss Atwater about some of the things she'd said earlier. I decided to pay her a visit this morning, and Walter tagged along."

"I didn't tag along. You make me sound like a dog. You invited me," Walter said from the doorway, annoyed.

"Fine," Mason said, looking over at him. "I asked you to come."

"Okay," Branchford said, walking to the door and closing it on Walter before turning back to Mason. "And then what?"

"Well, the two of us came here to her room and knocked. I thought it odd she didn't answer because she wasn't out at the pool, didn't have any friends staying here, and doesn't have a car. The drapes were drawn as they are now. I admit I even went around back to see if I could see in the rear window, but it was closed and curtained, too."

"All done with the photographs, Detective," Officer Barrows said.

Branchford nodded at him. "I think you can get back to the station, then. Don't forget to drop off that typewriter, note, and film in the lab. I'll call and let them know what I'm looking for."

"Yes, sir," Barrows said.

"I want Smyth on the door until I can get the locks changed. And radio the morgue. Tell them the body will be ready for pickup in the next forty minutes or so."

"Will do, sir." Barrows tucked his camera under his arm and left, closing the door behind him.

"Okay, Silas, go ahead with your examination."

The old man went around the double bed and set his case down as he turned on the bedside lamp and put on his thick glasses. "Certainly, certainly."

"And please be thorough and careful this time, Mr. Drake. And accurate."

Silas Drake stared at him through his thick glasses. His eyes looked huge through the lenses. "I *always* am, Detective."

"Sorry, I didn't mean to imply anything." He turned back to Mason. "So then what happened? I believe you said you went around back but couldn't see anything through the rear window."

"That's right, so I came back to the front and knocked again, but still there was no response. Finally I sent Walter, Mr. Wingate I mean, to get Mr. Gagliardi from the front office. They returned shortly and Mr. Gagliardi opened Miss Atwater's door with his passkey. We found her dead, the suicide note on the floor. Obviously, we didn't touch anything, as I said before, except the doorknob and the light switch. Oh, and I did touch the body briefly to check for vital signs."

"That's actually not obvious to most people to not touch anything. You'd be surprised how many people would have picked up that note, opened the curtains, walked around, and made a right mess of things."

"Things we learn in the business, as it were."

"You're right. So Gagliardi used his passkey? I suppose it makes sense he'd have one since he owns the place," Branchford said.

"Yes, only natural."

"Indeed. Hmm. You married, by the way? For the record."

"No, no, I'm not. Never have been. You?"

"I'm a widower."

"Oh. I'm sorry."

"Thanks. She's been gone nearly nine years. We never got around to having kids. I'm married to my work now. In a way, I suppose I always have been."

"I know the feeling."

"Do you visit Palm Springs often?"

"Not really, no. I've been here before, but it's been a while. Mr. Wingate visits more frequently."

"Okay. Well, I guess that's all for now. Would you wait outside, please, with Mr. Wingate and Mr. Gagliardi? You can tell Mr. Gagliardi I'll have some questions for him later, but he can go back to the office now if he wishes."

"Of course," Mason said. He stepped out the door, closing it behind him. Officer Smyth was off to the side, stone-faced. Marvin was near the pool, looking pale and nervous, and Walter was leaning against the wall by the window of Miss Atwater's room and the side gate, smoking a Camel.

Mason walked over to Marvin, and Walter ground out his cigarette and joined them.

"The detective said you can go back to the office, but he does want to talk with you later in private," Mason said.

"He does? Why? What for?"

"I'm not sure exactly, but he knows you have a passkey to all the rooms, and he noticed the start of the article Miss Atwater was writing about the Oasis Inn."

Marvin looked sick. "Oh, he saw that, did he?"

"Yes. It appears all she wrote was just the title and first line," Mason said. "She didn't get very far."

"Well, that's a relief, at least."

"Though had she not been killed, she certainly would have finished it, and it would have been published," Mason said. "Possibly even picked up by the papers down here in the States."

"I know what you're thinking," Marvin said quietly, so as not to be overheard by Smyth.

"Do you?"

"Yes. You're thinking I killed Miss Atwater, aren't you? Because of that article. It would have ruined me, you know, and probably gotten me arrested, deported, or at least investigated. It would have probably shut down the Oasis."

"It's quite possible. I have to admit you could have easily entered her room using the passkey while she was asleep early this morning, suffocated her, typed a suicide note, and put the empty pill bottle next to her. And you were missing from the office for at least ten minutes while the Pruitts waited to check out."

"That's all true. I could have done it, but I didn't. Of course I was upset after she told me her plans. She was flirting with me fairly strongly on the drive home. She asked me all sorts of questions, even wanting to know if anyone else was a homosexual here at the Oasis."

"Oh dear," Walter said. "What did you say?"

"I lied and told her no. It's none of her business. But then she wanted to know about my photography and what exactly Pruitt was trying to force me to do. I foolishly confided in her, as I thought I had an ally in her. I thought perhaps the two of us together could figure out a way to put a stop to him once and for all."

"And all the while she was mentally taking notes about everything you said so she could use it against you," Mason said.

"Apparently. When we reached the Oasis Wednesday evening, she thanked me for being honest and candid with her. Then she said that it would make an interesting, possibly prizeworthy piece for her column. I was shocked and angry. Angry with her and angry with myself for being so stupid. I walked her to her room, all the while pleading with her not to write it. Perhaps to appease me, she said she'd consider not using my name or the name of the inn, but she couldn't make any promises. Then she went into her room, bade me good night, and closed the door."

"And that's the last time you spoke with her?" Mason said.

"Yes. I saw her around the resort yesterday, but we didn't talk."

"If you were in her room this morning and *had* killed her, there's no way you would not have seen the title page of her article. It was in her typewriter last night. I know because I stopped in to chat with her briefly. You would have had to remove it to type the suicide note."

"But I didn't kill her."

"But if you had, why wouldn't you destroy it or at least take it with you? The title alone is rather incriminating. Surely you'd have no way of knowing that I or anyone else would have seen it previously, so why not get rid of it? Leaving it in the room would be foolish."

"Exactly. That's proof right there that I didn't do it."

"Yes, perhaps," Mason said. "Why don't you go back to the office or your apartment and relax for a bit, have some water, and maybe lie down until the detective needs you?"

"Yes, I think I'll do that. I'm not feeling all that well," Marvin said. He turned and walked away.

"I'm confused," Walter said when Marvin had gone. "Didn't Miss Atwater kill herself?"

"That's how it appears, but I suspect Detective Branchford is looking at every possibility."

"Ugh, that man. I can't believe he slammed the door in my face."

"He didn't slam it in your face, he just closed it. You shouldn't have been eavesdropping."

"I wasn't eavesdropping, I just happened to overhear, that's all. It couldn't be helped. Then when he slammed the door in my face, I had to resort to listening at the window, but I didn't catch everything, so tell me what I missed."

Mason shook his head. "You really are something else. There's not much else to tell. The coroner is examining the body now. Has anyone else made an appearance out here?"

"No, all quiet. But the only ones still here are those two annoying women from San Diego. God knows where they are. By the way, Marvin said it wasn't a problem that we've missed checkout time because our room isn't rented for tonight. It sounds like most of the rooms aren't, and all this death business probably isn't going to help. You don't really think Marvin killed that woman, do you?"

"To be honest, he could have."

"But why wouldn't he have destroyed that page to her column? Why would he leave it in her room to be found, possibly incriminating him?"

"Because maybe instead of using his passkey while she was asleep, he just knocked on her door while the Pruitts were waiting for him. She let him in, he pleaded his case one more time, and she mentioned that I had also visited and had discussed her article. He would have known I was aware of the page in the typewriter, so destroying it would actually be even more incriminating than just leaving it. He could have even killed Mr. Pruitt the other day, and perhaps confessed to Miss Atwater thinking it would get him in good with her and stop her from writing about the inn, but instead she threatened to go to the police."

"Ugh, this all makes my head hurt," Walter said. "What about the note Miss Atwater got under her door?"

"Maybe Marvin did send it, like she thought."

"I don't believe it. And I don't believe he killed her or Pruitt."

"I wish I could be as certain. Though I do wonder about Granville. He certainly wasn't upset about his father's death, and his mother said he was up at dawn this morning, pacing the courtyard. And I'm still curious as to why he didn't come out of his room when his mother screamed."

"Maybe he didn't emerge because he was napping on his good ear. Remember, he's deaf in his right."

"Yes, that's the theory I presented to Branchford earlier, but maybe Granville wasn't in his room at all. Perhaps *he* killed his father and wanted to frame Miss Atwater by killing her and typing that note."

"Do you really think that beautiful man could be so horrible?"

"Beauty has nothing to do with it, Walter. Anyway, let's wait in the shade over there."

"For what?"

"For the detective and the coroner to finish. I want to hear what they have to say."

After about ten more minutes, Branchford stepped out and over to the two men, nodding at Smyth, who was now looking bored.

"The coroner puts the time of death about an hour ago, more or less. He believes she overdosed on the pills."

"So it *was* suicide?" Mason said.

"Do you have any reason to believe otherwise?"

"No, not really, I guess. I bet Mr. Drake was surprised she admitted to killing Pruitt."

"Mr. Drake, is, shall we say, pretty much ready for retirement."

"Frankly I'm surprised he's still on the job."

"He's not as old as he looks. That job ages a person."

"I can imagine it does."

"And so does mine sometimes. You told me yesterday Miss Atwater felt Mr. Pruitt had something to do with her brother's death, and she confirmed it when I spoke with her."

"Yes. Certainly it gave her a motive in his death," Mason said.

"And she had apparently been trying to blackmail Mr. Pruitt. Mrs. Pruitt showed me the note Miss Atwater sent him, and supposedly there had been other notes, too."

"She showed me that note, too," Mason said.

"I told Mrs. Pruitt yesterday to let me know if she wanted to press charges against Miss Atwater."

"Press charges?" Walter said. "What for? Yesterday everyone thought he died from a heart attack."

"For attempted blackmail, Mr. Wingate. It's against the law, you know," Detective Branchford said.

"What did Mrs. Pruitt say?" Mason said.

"She said she didn't see the point now that her husband was dead, but people often say things in the heat of a crisis that they later reconsider, so I told her to call me if she changed her mind."

"And that's pointless, too," Mason said. "Now that Miss Atwater is also dead."

"Yes. She apparently killed Pruitt, but even though she probably would have gotten away with it, her conscience got the better of her. It happens sometimes. Guilt can be powerful."

"So, even though Pruitt was utterly contemptable, she felt guilty taking his life, and so took her own," Walter said.

"Apparently. It's all rather convenient, though," Branchford said. "And that article she had started writing. I'd like to know what that was all about. There were some other typed pages in there, too. An article she had started on a company called Baylis and Ivy. I read through it while waiting for Drake. She's pretty ruthless with Angus Pruitt and her accusations regarding her brother's death."

"She was adamant he was responsible," Mason said.

"Indeed she was. I wonder if we'll ever fully know the truth about any of this, but I'm not prepared to close the case on either death just yet."

"If I may make a suggestion," Mason said. "Your lab should verify those blackmail notes Miss Atwater sent to Mr. Pruitt were written on her typewriter."

"That's a good idea," Branchford said. "The one she showed me was typewritten and had Miss Atwater's first initial and last name at the bottom, but it was unsigned. Hopefully, Mrs. Pruitt still has it in her possession. I can contact the Los Angeles detective division and have them get it for us once she's home."

"I can save you some time and effort with that," Mason said. "I actually got Mrs. Pruitt to give me that note. I have it here in my pocket." He pulled it out and handed it to Branchford, who was quite surprised.

"Thanks, Mr. Adler," he said, glancing at it before putting it into his own pocket. "I'll be sure the lab does an analysis on it."

Mr. Drake stepped out of Miss Atwater's room just then and put his hat back on as he walked over. "I'm all through in there. I was as thorough as I could be considering the circumstances. I'll know more once we get the body downtown and I can do a complete autopsy in the laboratory, but it definitely appears to be suicide by overdose."

"It appears that way," Branchford said, "but I want to be absolutely certain this time."

Drake chewed the inside of his cheek. "Of course you do. We'll do that autopsy on Mr. Pruitt, too, as soon as possible."

"Right, we'll get to work on the necessary steps and let you know."

"Sure. See you back at the station, then," Drake said, ambling away before Branchford could respond.

"Now what, Detective?" Mason said.

"The men from the morgue will arrive and take away Miss

Atwater's remains shortly. Since she was a Canadian citizen, there'll be more paperwork and red tape, and the feds will have to be notified, as well as her next of kin."

"She mentioned her parents were dead. She said her and her late brother were raised by their aunt Lucy, her mother's sister, in Ottawa. I'm sorry but I don't have a last name. As far as I know there's no one else."

"Okay. By law we have to notify Mrs. Pruitt and Miss Atwater's family of our intent to do the autopsies. Without their permission, we'll probably need a court order, which will delay things a couple of days or so, less if we can get Mrs. Pruitt to agree and we can find this Aunt Lucy and she has no objections. We can get her surname and address from the newspaper Miss Atwater worked for, and I have Mrs. Pruitt's contact information in the file. How long are you in town for, Mr. Adler?" Detective Branchford said.

"We're checking out today."

"Oh, I see. Well, perhaps you'd better give me your Phoenix number in case I need to reach you for further questioning."

"Further questioning?" Walter said. "But it was a heart attack and a suicide. What further questioning could there be?"

"It was apparently a *murder* and a suicide, Mr. Wingate. But things are not always as they seem."

"Oh. Well, won't you need my number, then, too?"

"Just Mr. Adler's will suffice. I'm sure I can reach you through him if necessary. Is that all right, Mr. Adler?"

"Yes, of course," Mason said, "I'll write my telephone number down for you. I'd give you one of my cards, but they're in our room."

"Thanks." Branchford handed him his pencil and a piece of paper from his notebook. "Call me crazy, but I just have a funny feeling things aren't quite right, so I may be telephoning you. Do you two, uh, live together in Phoenix?"

"Walter and I? Oh no, we're friends but not roommates. I live alone," Mason said. He jotted down his name and telephone number and handed the paper and pencil back.

"Oh, good. I mean, so do I. Live alone, I mean."

"Do you ever get to Phoenix, Detective?"

"I was there once a few years ago. It's only about a five-hour drive from here, isn't it?"

"That's right."

"I might have to make a trip again one of these days."

"If you do, please give me a ring. It doesn't have to be business related. I'd be pleased to show you around."

"That's nice of you, thank you, Mr. Adler."

"Mason, if you like."

"Mason, then. And please call me Brian. Ah, it looks like the fellows from the morgue are here now."

Two attractive young men dressed in white and carrying a stretcher walked over to them. One had a black leather bag slung over his left shoulder.

"Morning, Detective," the one with the bag said.

"Good morning. Room four, boys. She's all yours."

"Yes, sir." The two went down the walkway and entered, leaving the door ajar behind them.

"My goodness, such strapping young men," Walter said. "When I die, I want those two fellas to carry me away."

"Walter," Mason said.

"What?"

"It's all right," Branchford said. "They *are* strapping young men. Is Mr. Gagliardi in the office, Mason?"

"I believe so. Either there or in his apartment across from it."

"Okay. I need to call the lab and give them instructions, and I want to ask Gagliardi more about that strange article she was writing. I'll need to get a locksmith over here to change the lock on her door, too, so Smyth doesn't have to stand there all night. I don't want anyone nosing around in there until the investigation's complete."

"Certainly," Mason said.

"If you'll excuse me, then, gentlemen."

Branchford gave Mason a shy, gentle smile, shook his hand, and then strode off, nodding at Walter.

CHAPTER NINETEEN

Early Friday afternoon, May 31, 1946
The Oasis Inn, Palm Springs

The men from the morgue carried Miss Atwater's body away, and Walter sashayed back to their room to analyze his wardrobe, Mason having convinced him they should stay one more night. Mason sat alone, pondering on a lounger beside the pool, just out of sight of Officer Smyth around the corner.

"Hello, there," Miss Campbell called out from over his right shoulder. Mason got to his feet as she approached, dressed once more in her swimming suit.

"Ah, Miss Campbell. I was wondering where you two had disappeared to today."

"We were out to breakfast, then Myrtle wanted to take a drive by the Kaufmann House. Have you seen it yet?"

"No, I haven't."

"It's not quite finished but really different. Anyway, after that we stopped at a café downtown and had lunch, then we came back here, and I thought I'd lay out by the pool for a bit. You two are going home today, aren't you?"

"We were planning on it, but now we're staying another night."

"You are? Even after everything that's happened? I mean, first Mr. Pruitt, then that Miss Atwater. She didn't strike me as the type to off herself, but who can tell? Anyway, Myrtle and me were thinking of checking out and leaving early. We didn't want to be the only ones left here, too spooky. But now that you're staying, well, I guess it's okay."

"Er, yes. So, you heard about Miss Atwater."

"We sure did. We ran into Mr. Gagliardi when we came back.

He was just getting ready to go to his studio downtown after finishing talking to that detective fellow. He looked pretty shaken."

"That's understandable."

"Yeah, I guess so. Me and Myrtle just couldn't believe it. I hear that Canada dame confessed to killing Mr. Pruitt, and here we all thought it was a heart attack. Well, it just gives me chills. I knew there was something off about her."

"Everyone has their secrets."

"Sure, I guess, but to kill someone like that. And then she goes and commits suicide. I just can't believe it. Of course, those Canadians are kinda funny."

"Funny?" Mason said.

"Yeah. They look like us and act like us sometimes, but they're different. Did you know they even speak French in some parts of Canada?"

"I'm aware of that, yes. It's called French Canadian."

"That makes sense, I guess. But even their English is a little off. They spell some words wrong and pronounce some of them wrong, too."

"Not wrong, Miss Campbell, just differently."

"Seems wrong to me. Don't tell Mr. Gagliardi I said that, though. I heard he's from Canada, too. Poor man, all this isn't going to help his business."

"At least he has his photography work to keep him busy and his mind occupied. I believe he said he had a client this afternoon, actually," Mason said. "A much-needed distraction, I'm sure."

"Gee, he's a real professional. I only do it for fun. Just a hobby, you know, but I enjoy it. I'd rather be behind the camera than in front of it."

"Oh? Why is that? You're an attractive woman."

"Aw, you think so? Really? I was beginning to wonder, because, you know, you never seemed to want to go out with me or nothin'."

"Well, I do have my lady friend back in Phoenix. I believe I mentioned her."

"Oh yeah, her. Still, I thought we could have some laughs or something while we was both here, you know?"

"I am sorry about that."

"Sure. Well, anyway, thanks for the compliment. Fellas tell me I'm pretty and all, but I hate looking at photographs of myself. I don't think I look like me at all."

"I find that a lot of people don't like the way they look in pictures. My friend Mr. Wingate actually has a theory about that."

"Yeah? What's his theory?"

"That few people's faces are truly symmetrical. We're used to seeing ourselves in the mirror, the opposite of how others see us, so when we see a photograph of ourselves, we're seeing us as others do, and it's off-putting."

"Huh. That's kind of confusing, but I guess it makes sense."

"Yes, I certainly think so. What is Miss Schultz doing this afternoon?"

"Oh, she said she was bored with the pool, so she hitched a ride back downtown with Mr. Gagliardi."

"Really? Why?"

"She said she wanted to go back to the café we ate lunch at. Her and the waitress hit it off, instant friends, and Myrtle wanted to go back and see if she wanted to get a drink or something after her shift at the diner. They was chatting about all kinds of stuff, totally ignoring me during breakfast. If Myrtle had any sense about her, she'd go look for a man instead of more friends. Honestly, for as smart as she is, she can really be a dope sometimes."

"Can't we all? As I said before, everyone has their secrets."

"Sure, but what's that got to do with Myrtle?"

"Nothing. I'm just thinking out loud."

"I do that sometimes, too."

"Another thing I'm thinking about is your photographs. You took pictures out here on Wednesday afternoon shortly after we arrived, didn't you?"

"Yeah, some candid shots. I think they're much more interesting than posed photographs."

"I agree. You also took some candids on Thursday afternoon, yes?"

"Sure I did. I got pictures of you two fellas, Mr. and Mrs. Pruitt, their son, pretty much everybody. Sad to think that's probably the last picture ever taken of Mr. Pruitt."

"Yes, quite sad. I guess we never know when that last picture will be taken."

"I don't think I've ever taken a picture of someone right before they died before. Not that I know of, anyway."

"Would you mind terribly if we had your film developed, Miss Campbell? I'd like to see your photos."

"Well, the roll's not quite finished. But when it's done, I can send you some prints. Just give me your address in Phoenix. There's a few of me in my swimsuit that Myrtle took, too, that I can send you."

"Thanks, but I really want to see those pictures now, as well as the ones on the rolls you took since you've been here. I'll pay for the developing and for a new roll of film."

"Gee, I suppose in that case it would be all right, but why the hurry?"

"I've had a thought, but I'm not trusting my memory entirely, that's all. I think we can get Mr. Gagliardi to develop them at his photography studio, and he should be there by now."

"Okay. My camera and the film is in our room, but it will take me a while to change and get ready to go downtown."

"Actually, if you don't mind terribly, I'll just take the film and go with Walter. Walter's a personal friend of Mr. Gagliardi's, and it might be better if it were just me and him."

"Oh, I see. Well, okay. I'll be back in a minute or two, then."

Mason watched her walk away and into her room, and then he walked into his, where Walter was standing in front of the closet, shaking his head. "Have your wardrobe all figured out?"

Walter turned and looked at him. "No, it's hopeless. I've worn everything I've brought except for some evening wear, and nothing can realistically be combined. I'm also out of clean underwear."

"Well, I've an idea. Why don't we take a drive downtown to Rudy's, and you can buy something new to wear tomorrow, along with more underwear."

"That sounds expensive."

"Considering you've barely spent a dime on this trip, I think you can manage. Besides, maybe Rudy will be in, and he'll give you a discount."

"Well, I suppose it wouldn't hurt to look, and it would be nice to see him. But since it's your fault we're not leaving today, I should think you would be willing to buy me a new outfit."

"I'll spring for underwear for both of us, but that's it."

"Oh, all right. And if you really think that Branchford fellow may suspect Marvin of killing Pruitt and Miss Atwater, I guess it is better we stick around for a bit. I trust you to get to the truth of the matter. You have a talent for that, I must admit."

"Why thank you, Walter, I appreciate that. You should know, though, that the truth may just be that Marvin did do it."

"I refuse to believe that. Did you want to go downtown right now?"

"No time like the present. We can grab a bite to eat if you like, too. We haven't had anything since breakfast, and it's already after one."

"Not the Big Cup again, please."

"I'm sure we can find someplace else. And while we're downtown, we can stop in to Marvin's photography studio, too."

"What for?"

"I want to get Miss Campbell's film developed."

"That sounds incredibly dull. Why doesn't she get it developed herself?"

"Because *I* want to see the pictures. It has to do with what's been going on around here. At least I think it might."

"What is that supposed to mean?"

"I think it's possible Mr. Pruitt's death wasn't a heart attack after all."

"We know that now. Miss Atwater confessed to killing him, and then she killed herself."

"Actually, I don't think she did."

"You don't think she confessed, or you don't think she killed herself?"

"Perhaps both," Mason said.

"Ugh, stop being so vague and mysterious. I hate it when you do that."

"Sorry, but other people had motives for wanting both Mr. Pruitt and Miss Atwater dead—Marvin, Granville, Arlo, Mrs. Pruitt, and even perhaps someone else. So come on, she's probably waiting."

"Who? Mrs. Pruitt? She's on her way to Los Angeles."

"No, Miss Campbell." Mason didn't wait for a reply. He grabbed his car keys, sunglasses, and hat and went out while Walter trailed behind. "Don't forget to lock the door," Mason called out over his shoulder.

Ermengarde was indeed waiting, still in her swimming suit. In her hands were four rolls of film, which she gave to Mason as he approached.

"My, you seem to have taken a great many photographs since you arrived."

"Uh, I guess I have, but you never know which ones will turn out. Three full rolls plus the partial one. So, you'll pay to get them developed, then give me the prints for free plus a new roll of film?"

"That's right."

"Seems funny, but I guess it's your money."

"I'll take good care of the film and prints and get them back to you as soon as possible. Enjoy your afternoon, Miss Campbell." He tipped his hat and turned, Walter waiting for him by the gate.

"Here," Mason said. "Hold on to these, will you?"

"Four rolls of film? She's only been here a few days."

"I was surprised, too."

Walter put the film rolls into his pockets. "Why exactly are you doing this? What is it you hope to see?"

"I'd rather not say just yet. I may be completely mistaken."

"Let's get this over with then. I look all bulgy with these in my pockets."

The two of them walked out the gate to Mason's car. It was a quick drive downtown, and Mason managed to find a parking space about a block away from the studio.

CHAPTER TWENTY

Later Friday afternoon, May 31, 1946
Downtown Palm Springs

"There's a little café that looks passable," Walter said, pointing across the street as they exited the car and stepped onto the sidewalk.

Mason took in the little restaurant with a green-striped awning. "Sure, looks okay, but let's go see Marvin first. While he's developing the film, we can grab some lunch over there and then shop at Rudy's."

"Assuming Marvin's willing and able to drop whatever he's doing and develop four rolls for you."

"Only one way to find out," Mason said.

"Let's go, then," Walter said. They pushed through the single wooden door to the left of the hardware store, which led to a steep, narrow staircase. At the top of the stairs was a small landing with another door directly ahead, marked in gold letters with the words *M. Gagliardi Photography, hours by appointment* stenciled on the frosted glass. It wasn't quite closed. Mason knocked on the glass, but there was no response. "That's odd. The door's ajar, and he's not answering."

"Maybe he's gone out for a late lunch," Walter said.

"Perhaps, though he said he had an appointment this afternoon." Mason pushed the door fully open and stepped into a small reception room, Walter following behind.

"Hello? Marvin? It's Mason and Walter," Mason called out, but there was still no answer. The walls were lined with photographs, presumably taken by Marvin. There was an uncomfortable-looking chair and a small sofa with a round coffee table in front of it, upon which was a ringed scrapbook of still more photographs. Two small windows overlooked the back alley. A wooden desk piled with papers and books was against the wall, and a battered old file cabinet stood beside it. A door to the right of the desk was closed and labeled *Restroom*. The wall opposite the windows held the door to the stairs and two more, a wood framed-glass one labeled simply *To Studio* and the other *Darkroom*. A red light, turned off, was above the darkroom door, and a sign beneath it read *Do not enter when red light is on.*

"We should have called first," Walter said, picking up the book of photographs that was on the coffee table and flipping through it. "Waste of time if he's not here."

"It's awfully quiet."

"It's a photography studio, Mason, not a dance hall," Walter said. "What did you expect?"

"I'm not sure, exactly. But if he went out, you would think he would have closed and locked the main door and maybe posted a sign." Mason tried the studio door. "Hmm, it's locked."

"Hmm, what? Hardly mysterious. I'm sure he has a lot of expensive equipment in there."

"True, so why leave the front door open?"

"He probably just forgot. You're thinking too much."

Mason peered through the glass door. "This leads to a short hall, and there's another door at the end, which must go into the studio. Maybe he's in there and can't hear us."

"Or maybe he's out. Oh my, some of these photographs are quite good. Lots of weddings, portraits, babies, and school photos, but some nice scenery shots, too. I wonder where he keeps the more risqué ones, though," Walter said, still flipping through the book from the coffee table.

"Probably locked in his desk or the file cabinet." Mason knocked on the glass studio door. "Something's not right."

"There you go again, being all detectivy. Maybe he's in the bathroom."

Mason considered that for a moment. "Maybe." He rapped on the restroom door, and when no answer was forthcoming, he tried the knob, which turned easily. It was empty, just a toilet, sink, and small shower. The darkroom door was also unlocked. He stepped in and switched on the light.

"What are you doing?" Walter said. He put the binder down and came up behind him. "We shouldn't be nosing about like this. Better to just sit and wait until he gets back. Or better yet, let's get some lunch and then go next door to Rudy's and pick up a few things. By the time we're finished, I'm sure Marvin will have returned."

"Unless he's already here," Mason said.

"Don't be a goose. If he were here, he'd have answered when you knocked and called out his name."

"Not if he couldn't," Mason said.

"Now you're making me nervous," Walter said, his mustache twitching.

"Sorry." Mason stepped farther into the small, windowless darkroom, noting lots of professional-looking equipment and shelves of mysterious bottles and jars. Walter followed closely behind.

"He's not in here, either. We should go," Walter said quietly.

"Not yet. There's another door there." Mason walked over to it and found it too was unlocked.

"I have a bad feeling about this all of a sudden," Walter said, standing beside him.

"Shh, quiet." Mason pulled the door open, revealing the brightly lit studio at the front of the building. A man was lying on his back in the center of the room, his feet splayed out. His face was hidden from view by a screen.

"Oh my God," Walter said, peering around Mason, his eyes huge. "That's Marvin's body! Is he dead? Those are his shoes, I'm sure of it!"

At the sound of their voices, Marvin sat up. He was holding his camera in his hands. "Oh, hello, Mason, Walter. What are you two doing here?"

They stepped into the studio, closing the darkroom door behind them. A young man Mason recognized as Leroy from the gas station was standing on a platform with his legs spread, wearing only a small posing strap.

"Forgive the intrusion, Marvin, I knocked but there was no answer," Mason said. He couldn't help but stare at Leroy.

"So you just decided to press on through? I'm in the middle of a session, as you can clearly see. I was trying to get some photos looking up at Leroy from the floor."

"Yes, I'm sorry. I didn't know," Mason said, embarrassed.

"That's why the studio door was locked. I didn't think I had to lock the door to the darkroom, too," Marvin said, getting to his feet and dusting himself off.

"I sincerely apologize."

"It's all right, I suppose," Marvin said, though he was clearly annoyed.

"It's just that the front door at the top of the stairs was ajar. I must admit I was a bit concerned for your welfare, considering all that's happened."

"Oh, gee, that's my fault," Leroy said, stepping down from the platform. "I must not have closed it all the way when I came in. Hey, you're the fellows from Phoenix. Mr. Wingate and the other man, the guys from the filling station. You're the ones who told me about Mr. Gagliardi here."

"Yes, that's right," Walter said, stepping up to him and looking him over from head to toe. "My, you're all sweaty and glistening."

"It's just baby oil. Mr. Gagliardi says it picks up the light better."

"It does," Marvin said, setting his camera on a nearby table. "I think I'm all through here, Leroy. I've gotten some good shots."

"Gee, you sure? I don't mind if you want to take a couple more."

"I'll see how these turn out. If I need you to come back, I'll let you know. Go ahead and get dressed. Leave the posing strap on the hook. You can take a shower, too, if you want, but I need to get back to the Oasis soon. I have guests checking in late this afternoon." Marvin turned off the spotlights and picked up an envelope. "Here's your payment, cash."

"Great, thank you, sir," Leroy said as he took the envelope, his muscles rippling. He looked over at Walter, who was staring at him, mouth agape. "Hand me a towel, would ya, Mr. Wingate?"

"Hmm? What? Oh, yes, a towel," Walter said. He picked one up and handed it to Leroy, who used it to wipe his forehead, chest, and arms.

"Guess I was kinda sweaty. Those lights are awfully hot."

"I can imagine. Do you need a hand cleaning up or wiping yourself down?" Walter said hopefully.

"Thanks, but I can manage okay," Leroy said. "My clothes and stuff are behind the screen here in the corner, so I'll just get dressed. No need to shower until I get home."

"Oh, all right," Walter said, clearly disappointed as Leroy disappeared behind the folding screen.

"It is awfully warm in here," Mason said. "I can see why Leroy was sweating."

Marvin nodded. "Yes. Normally I like to shoot in the mornings or evenings when it's cooler, but this is the only time Leroy could get away that also worked for me."

"I'm sorry again that we interrupted," Mason said.

"It's okay. I really was just about finished. I wanted to get a couple of shots from the floor, looking up at him, and I did. Those were the last ones of the session. So, what brings you two here? Any news from the detective?"

"No, not yet. But I have a few rolls of film I was hoping we could get developed as soon as possible," Mason said. "I know you're busy, but it's important. I think the photos may contain a clue as to what really happened to Angus Pruitt and Miss Atwater."

"You don't believe it was murder and suicide?"

"Let's just say I'm skeptical."

"Then what did happen? What do you know?"

"Let's wait and see what the photographs show. Do you think you'd be able to develop the film? There are four rolls, three full and one partial, from Miss Campbell's camera. Walter has them in his pockets."

Marvin nodded. "I was wondering what you were carrying around in your trousers."

"Yes. I don't mind a bulge in my pants, but not in all the wrong places," Walter said, pulling out the rolls and handing them over.

"You said they're from Miss Campbell? Does she know you have these?"

"Yes, she gave them to me."

"I see. Well, I suppose I could do it if you think it will help. I can't stop thinking about all of this and how some people seem to think I may have been involved."

"Let's hope this will answer everyone's questions, then. I'll pay you for your time, of course," Mason said.

"Buy me a drink sometime. If it helps uncover the truth, it will be more than worth it. Besides, I guess I owe you both for recommending Leroy to me. He's a fine-looking young man, and I think his photographs will do quite well."

"I've no doubt," Mason said.

"Me neither," Walter said, trying to discreetly peek around the screen without success. Leroy stepped out from behind it just then, dressed in a white short-sleeved shirt, blue jeans, and brown leather work boots. He was still looking oily and sweaty and almost ran into Walter.

"Let me know how the photos turn out, would ya? I'd like to see them," Leroy said.

"As soon as they're ready, I'll let you know."

"Thanks, Mr. G."

"I'd like to see them, too," Walter said.

"Buy the magazine when it's published," Mason said.

"Uh, nice seeing you again, Mr. Wingate and Mr...." Leroy said.

"Adler, Mason T. Adler."

"A pleasure, Mr. Adler. I'm Leroy Brewster. You may see my name up in lights someday. You gents heading back home to Phoenix soon?"

"Hopefully tomorrow," Mason said.

Walter nodded. "Yes, though I'm sure we'll be back, Leroy. And if you're ever in Phoenix, please look me up. Walter Waverly Wingate, interior decorator. I'm in the telephone directory."

"Much appreciated, Mr. Wingate. Bye now," Leroy said as he unlocked the door to the small, short hall that led to the reception room and went on through.

"Nice young man," Marvin said.

"Young being the operative word. What is he, twenty?" Mason said.

"Twenty-two," Marvin said. "He suffers a bit from shell shock, goes crazy when he hears a loud noise. He was in the Army in Italy during the war, poor kid. Now he has his heart set on being a movie star."

"So he told us. And I told him he should go out to LA and get himself a legitimate agent," Mason said.

"I suppose you don't approve of what I do here, but you'd be surprised at who looks at my photographs in the magazines. I've had a hand in at least one young man getting a start in the movies. All it takes is one producer or director to take a liking to Leroy's looks."

"And there's certainly a lot to admire," Walter said.

"Well, I hope it works out for him," Mason said. "And it's not that I don't approve of what you do, Marvin. I mean, he is over twenty-one. You are paying him, and it's not illegal, but I just think there has to be another way. But what do I know about the movie or photography business?"

"About as much as I know about the private detective business, I guess," Marvin said.

"Indeed. And now with Mr. Pruitt and Miss Atwater dead, you can focus on your regular work. You also may be able to get out of that loan contract, and you don't have to worry about the article anymore."

"It sounds like you still think I'm guilty. If I was afraid of being arrested on pornography charges, I certainly wouldn't risk a murder rap, much less two, would I?"

"Probably not, but..."

"But desperate people sometimes do desperate things, is that it?" Marvin said.

"Sometimes," Mason said.

"Yeah, I guess so. I'm curious to see what you think these photographs will show," Marvin said.

"Me, too. We've got a few things to do. How long will it take to develop them?"

"Three full rolls and one partial? About an hour and a half to get the contact sheets, if I hurry. The prints will take longer, but I really need to be back at the Oasis no later than four thirty for the weekend check-ins."

"Okay, the contact sheets should be fine for now. It's coming two o'clock. What time does Rudy's close, Walter?"

"Five, I believe."

"Perfect. We'll get some lunch, do a little shopping at Rudy's, and stop back about three thirty. It shouldn't take me long to see what I'm hoping to see, or not see, in the photographs."

"Okay, I'll do the best I can to have them ready, though I still need to eat something."

"Can we bring you lunch?" Walter said.

"No, I have a thermos and a sandwich in my desk, but thanks."

"Okay, see you in an hour and a half or so, then," Mason said.

CHAPTER TWENTY-ONE

Late Friday afternoon, May 31, 1946
Downtown Palm Springs

"Let me put my packages in the car," Walter said as they exited Rudy's clothing store and walked toward Mason's vehicle up the block.

"You certainly bought enough clothes. I thought you were only going to get an outfit to wear for tomorrow."

"I was, but Rudy was having that marvelous sale, and he gave me such a nice discount on top of it. It was nice seeing him again," Walter said as he deposited his purchases in the trunk along with the underwear Mason had bought.

"Good. I enjoyed meeting him, but right now let's go see if Marvin's finished. It's nearly three thirty." Mason closed the trunk lid and put his keys in his pocket, and they walked back to Marvin's studio. Marvin was sitting at his desk, but he whirled about in his chair at the sound of them arriving.

"Good timing, gentlemen. I still have the contact sheets on the line in the darkroom, but they should be dry and ready by now. Let me get them for you."

"I'm actually only interested in one roll, but I'll have to look at them all to find the ones I want."

"I hope you find what you're looking for," Marvin said as he walked into the darkroom.

"You still haven't told me exactly *what* you're looking for in Miss Campbell's pictures," Walter said.

"If the pictures are there, you'll learn soon enough. If we have to sort through forty plus photos, we might as well get comfortable. Let's have a seat on the sofa," Mason said, setting his hat down on a side table.

"An excellent idea, my feet are killing me," Walter said, sitting beside Mason on the small settee.

"Well, here they are in glorious black and white," Marvin said, coming back into the reception room. He pulled up his desk chair and handed the contact sheets to Mason, who set them on the coffee table next to the ringed binder. "Just handle them by the edges, please."

"Certainly. Let's take a look and see what we've got," Mason said as he put on his glasses and viewed the contact sheets one at a time. "Hmm, a couple shots of Miss Campbell's thumb, these ones are blurry and out of focus, this one she had the lens cap on, here's seven almost identical photos of the mountains, some of what I believe is the Kaufmann House, a few of cactus plants, lots of pictures of palm trees, and here's several of Miss Campbell, including the cheesecake pictures she alluded to."

Walter and Marvin both glanced at the pictures. "Yes, I noticed those as I was developing them. Actually not bad from a photography perspective. If she were a little younger, she could probably model for certain magazines."

"And I suspect she'd be willing," Mason said. "Even though she said she doesn't like the way she looks in pictures. There's a few here of Miss Schultz, too, though not as revealing as those of Miss Campbell. Oh, and here are a couple of the two of them together. They must have gotten someone else to take those."

"Seems like they were taken at a restaurant, judging from the background. Perhaps by the waitress. Look, here's a photo of Miss Schultz and a waitress together, too," Walter said, pointing to a shot of Myrtle and an attractive woman in a uniform and apron, both beaming happily.

"Ah yes, so I see. I'm glad Miss Schultz made a friend," Mason said.

"The rest of the photos are mostly candid shots from around the pool area at the Oasis," Marvin said.

"Those are the ones I'm most interested in," Mason said. "The ones from around the pool, I mean. Please tell me they're not blurry and out of focus."

"No, those are pretty clear but lots of repetition, including four pictures of her bare feet."

Mason sighed. "A professional photographer she's clearly not."

He picked up the last contact sheet and examined it carefully. "Here's one of Miss Atwater sitting at the table, pretending to read her book. You can see she was looking over the top of it as she was watching Angus Pruitt."

"Probably the last photo ever taken of her," Marvin said.

"Yes. I asked her to be careful, to forget about it all and go home, but she was stubborn," Mason said, pointing to another photo. "Good grief, I look awful."

"You look exactly like that picture," Walter said, looking from the photo to Mason.

"Gee, thanks a lot," Mason said.

"It's true, but I must say, that next one's not a very flattering photo of me," Walter said. "She didn't capture my best side."

"Probably because she couldn't photograph you from behind."

"You're hilarious."

"You started it." Mason looked from the top row of images to the bottom row. "Ah, here are the ones I was looking for."

Marvin glanced at them. "Angus Pruitt?"

"Correct. Look here. In this photograph, taken Wednesday afternoon I believe, you can clearly see the crude heart tattoo on Mr. Pruitt's chest. The arrow is pointing to the right, away from the diving board. But in this photograph, taken the day he died, the arrow is pointing to the left, toward the diving board."

"That's odd. Maybe I reversed the negative in the processing," Marvin said.

"No, because everything else in the photographs is the right way around, including the room number on the door behind him. It's only the tattoo that's backward."

"But that doesn't make any sense," Marvin said.

"There are other differences, too," Mason said. "Look here. In the picture on the top, Mr. Pruitt is just a bit thinner. His hat is covering his face, but his body is not exactly the same."

"I'm confused," Walter said. "I mean, I can see what you're saying. He *does* look different, and the tattoo is definitely the opposite in the one picture, but how can that be?"

"Because one of these men is an imposter. Someone was pretending to be Angus Pruitt. I had my suspicions based on what I thought I remembered seeing when it came to the tattoo. It was your remark actually, Walter, that made me think of it."

"Oh? What did I say?"

"You said people dislike photos of themselves because the camera shows them how they really are, versus the mirror image they're used to seeing."

"Glad I could help, but I'm afraid I still don't understand."

"I don't either," Marvin said.

"I don't think Miss Atwater killed Mr. Pruitt. And I don't think she killed herself."

"Then what did happen?" Walter said. "And who killed them? Surely not Marvin here?"

"I didn't, I swear," Marvin said, his eyes wide.

"I believe you, Marvin," Mason said. "I think it was all premeditated and planned out. Miss Atwater suspected Mr. Pruitt of having something to do with her brother's death because her brother discovered something shady going on at Baylis and Ivy, just as the other woman who worked there had."

"The woman who died in a car accident," Walter said.

"Yes, but I'm willing to bet that was no accident," Mason said. "And Miss Atwater and her brother suspected as much, too."

"So she was right?"

"About some of it, yes. Only I think Angus Pruitt was innocent."

"Innocent how?"

"Oh, he was no angel. He wasn't above dirty tricks, lying, cheating, and carousing, but I don't think he was involved in whatever Ralph Atwater discovered, and I don't think he had anything to do with either Ralph's death or the other woman's."

"Then who did?" Walter said.

"Unless I'm completely wrong, it was Arlo in cahoots with Regina Pruitt."

"Mr. Pruitt's brother?" Walter said.

Mason nodded. "And his wife. Mr. Pruitt suspected them of being sweet on each other, and I now think they were. Arlo also boasted at the club that he was making money unbeknownst to Mr. Pruitt. I think his lips got a little too loose for Regina's liking that night."

"So, they were having an affair and embezzling?" Walter said.

"I think so. But after Ralph Atwater and the woman found out what was going on at Baylis and Ivy, Arlo and Mrs. Pruitt had to get rid of them. Remember, Arlo carries a gun, and Ralph was shot to death."

"Lots of people carry guns, Mason," Marvin said.

"True, but not lots of people had a motive to eliminate Ralph Atwater. However, neither Arlo nor Mrs. Pruitt counted on Cornelia

Atwater nosing around and asking questions after Ralph's death. Miss Atwater, of course, incorrectly fingered Mr. Pruitt as the guilty party, since it was his company."

"And she tried to blackmail him," Walter said.

"Maybe. I think Mrs. Pruitt may have made that part up, trying to make it look like Miss Atwater truly hated Mr. Pruitt. I suspect they'll find that blackmail note was written on a different typewriter than the suicide note."

"You mean you think Mrs. Pruitt faked them?" Walter said.

"Yes. Miss Atwater admitted sending Mr. Pruitt notes, but I don't think she was blackmailing him. I think Mrs. Pruitt was writing and delivering the blackmail notes and putting Miss Atwater's name on them to anger Mr. Pruitt. Maybe she hoped he'd have her done away with."

"Oh my," Marvin said. "So he was receiving the threatening notes *and* the fake blackmail notes from her?"

"I believe so. After the funeral, Miss Atwater started following Mr. Pruitt, asking questions about him at the company, trying to figure out the truth. I suspect she was motivated not only by wanting to find out what really happened to Ralph, but also by the chance to write an excellent exposé on what was going on."

"Quite the journalist," Marvin said. "She was certainly very driven in that respect."

"Yes, only she kept hitting dead ends, so she followed Mr. Pruitt and the rest of the Pruitts here to Palm Springs. Mrs. Pruitt found out who she was when she asked you about her, Marvin."

"That's right. It was just after she checked in. Mrs. Pruitt saw her leaving the office and inquired who she was."

"Up until that point, I don't think either Mrs. Pruitt or Arlo had ever laid eyes on her, though they were both aware of her because of the threatening notes. I'm sure Mrs. Pruitt was surprised to find out the woman at the Oasis was Cornelia Atwater. Later that afternoon, she and Arlo discussed it at the pool, probably plotting. I remember Mr. Pruitt complaining about Mrs. Pruitt and Arlo talking to each other when he went in to use the bathroom. They had already planned to kill him, but when Miss Atwater showed up, they decided to eliminate both of them. Kill Mr. Pruitt, make it look like Miss Atwater did it, then kill Miss Atwater and make it look like a suicide because of guilt. And at the same time, blame any crooked dealings that may be uncovered at Baylis and Ivy on Mr. Pruitt."

"But how did they manage it?" Marvin said.

"I suspect Mrs. Pruitt slipped her husband a sleeping powder right before she got Miss Atwater to come over."

"Why would she do that?" Marvin said. "Get Miss Atwater, I mean."

"So that if an autopsy was done and the sleeping powder was found in his system, Mrs. Pruitt could say Miss Atwater dropped it into his drink and then later killed him. I think Mrs. Pruitt is the one who sent that mysterious note to her. She wanted to make sure Miss Atwater was in her room alone while the murder was being committed. If she'd been out at the pool the whole time, she would have had an alibi."

"Devious," Walter said.

"Definitely. After the altercation with Miss Atwater, Mr. Pruitt got sleepy because of the sleeping powder, and he and Mrs. Pruitt went inside. Arlo was watching through the window of his room. Shortly after they went in, Arlo went to the office to tell Marvin about the spilled bottle of scotch. That was a ruse to give him an excuse to be in his brother's room for a while. He came back, knocked on his brother's door, and Mrs. Pruitt let him in. Mr. Pruitt was probably already asleep by then. Arlo smothered him with a pillow or something, then took off his own shirt and put on his brother's red trunks, along with his wide-brimmed hat and sunglasses. He probably had already applied the fake tattoo. Then he and Mrs. Pruitt left the room and went out to the pool, and everyone thought Arlo was still inside and Mr. Pruitt was still alive."

"I certainly thought he was," Walter said.

"That was the plan. And Mrs. Pruitt came over to us to talk, but also to make sure we noticed what was supposedly going on. When Marvin finally came out of Arlo's room, she went over to the fake Mr. Pruitt and he got up and went into the room where the real Mr. Pruitt was dead on the bed. He stepped in and off to the side of the open door so he was out of sight and took off the hat, sunglasses, and red trunks. He put his own shirt and swimsuit back on and left the room as himself, pretending to say something to Mr. Pruitt. He then went back to his own room. All was calm until Mrs. Pruitt went to check on her husband a little later and 'found' him. She screamed, and all hell broke loose. If foul play was suspected, Arlo and Mrs. Pruitt would both be in the clear, as witnesses saw the person they thought was Angus Pruitt go into his room alone, and Arlo was only in there with him less than a minute."

"But what about the backward tattoo in the photo?" Marvin said.

"The tattoo was key in making everyone at the pool believe Arlo was Angus Pruitt. Only Arlo made a crucial mistake. While he was waiting for Mr. and Mrs. Pruitt to go in, he drew the heart on his own chest using the bathroom mirror, either from memory or a photograph."

"Ah, I see. Because he drew it using the mirror, he got it backward," Marvin said.

"Exactly. The fact that Mrs. Pruitt had purchased art supplies downtown made me wonder, especially since Mr. Pruitt was surprised when I mentioned it and didn't seem to know anything about her having an interest in art. Mrs. Pruitt claimed she wanted to paint the mountains, but there were no art supplies in their room, and she hadn't purchased any canvas. The real reason was to create the fake tattoo."

"Clever, I must say," Walter said.

"And do you remember when you mentioned finding that drop of red and the specks of black on the bathroom sink in Arlo's room, Marvin?"

"Yeah, sure, I wiped them up."

"Do you still have the rag you used?" Mason said.

"It's in the laundry room at the Oasis, but I haven't washed it yet, why?"

"Because I don't think that drop of red was blood. It was paint from Arlo coloring the fake tattoo, and the black was used for the arrow. There's something else, too. When the fake Mr. Pruitt was supposedly napping on the lounger by the pool, he wasn't snoring, all was quiet. Walter even remarked that one could hear the proverbial pin drop. But we know from several accounts, including our own, that the real Mr. Pruitt snored like a freight train, especially on his back. The other piece of the puzzle is Arlo's fairly recent weight gain. Mr. Pruitt mentioned it that night at the club. He blamed it on Arlo's drinking, but I think it was to make his body match his brother's more."

"But everyone thought Mr. Pruitt's death was a heart attack," Marvin said. "Why go to all the trouble to turn around and make it look like Miss Atwater killed him and then killed herself?"

"To get her out of the way. They had to have a good reason for her to kill herself, and guilt over killing Mr. Pruitt seemed plausible. It was apparent to everyone that she hated him, especially after the confrontation Mrs. Pruitt arranged for us all to witness."

"Why not just make Miss Atwater's death look accidental?" Walter said.

"That may have been suspicious, especially after everything that had happened. Plus, if they did end up doing an autopsy on Mr. Pruitt, they'd see he'd been given a sleeping powder, as I said before, and that he did not, in fact, have a heart attack. They needed a scapegoat. A dead scapegoat."

"I'm surprised Mrs. Pruitt didn't want to press charges against Miss Atwater and put her away for attempted blackmail. That would have shut her up just as effectively, I would think," Marvin said.

"I can't agree. If she'd been arrested for that, they'd want to know why she was trying to blackmail Mr. Pruitt. It would have stirred everything up in the press and made things even worse, especially if Miss Atwater wasn't really blackmailing him, and I don't think she was. No, I think Mrs. Pruitt and Arlo wanted to get her out of the way for good. They didn't want her writing her exposé, and they wanted to lay the blame for Mr. Pruitt's death on her."

"So how did they arrange Miss Atwater's murder? And what made you suspect it wasn't a suicide?" Marvin said.

"Something Miss Campbell mentioned, actually."

"Ugh, that awful woman," Walter said, fiddling with his mustache.

"In some ways, she is rather uncouth, but she was talking about people from Canada, and how they say and spell certain words differently than we do."

"I can't say I've met enough Canadians to say one way or the other," Walter said.

"Well, it's true. They tend to add the letter *u* to some words we don't, like the word *color*. In Canada, it's spelled c-o-l-o-u-r."

"Seems silly, but what does that have to do with anything?"

"Do you remember the title of that article she planned to write on Marvin and the Oasis?"

"Ugh, *I* definitely do. I'll never forget it," Marvin said. "That detective asked me about it over and over. *An Oasis of sin. Perversion in the centre of Palm Springs.*"

"Yes. There was a subtitle, too, or first line. *What at first glance seemed idyllic, I soon found out was coloured by debauchery in the desert,*" Mason said.

"Certainly attention grabbing. But what about it?" Walter said.

"The word *color* was spelled the Canadian way, with the *u*."

"That would make sense, since she was from Canada," Marvin said.

"Yes, but in her suicide note, *color* was spelled without the *u*, and the word *center* was spelled as we do in the United States rather than the Canadian way," Mason said.

"Good grief, don't tell me they add a *u* to *center*, too," Walter said.

"No, but in Canada we spell it c-e-n-t-r-e," Marvin said.

"That doesn't make any sense," Walter said.

"There are an awful lot of words we use in the United States that don't make a lot of sense, either, Walter, but the point is, someone else typed that note, not Miss Atwater," Mason said. "Most likely Arlo Pruitt." He looked at Marvin. "You're from Quebec, born and raised. If you'd faked the suicide note, you would have spelled the words the way Miss Atwater would have, correct?"

"That's true. I wouldn't have even thought about it."

"The suicide note was flowery, too," Mason said. "Like something someone with an English degree would have written, which is what Arlo Pruitt has."

"Interesting. But how did Mrs. Pruitt and Arlo kill her and make it look like a suicide?" Marvin said.

"Remember this morning when we were saying goodbye to the Pruitts in the office of the Oasis? Mrs. Pruitt told Arlo to take the luggage out to the car."

"Yes, of course," Walter said.

"And Granville offered to help, but Mrs. Pruitt insisted he stay with her," Mason said.

"I offered to help, too, but they refused. I thought it was a bit odd," Marvin said.

"And she did her best to keep me and Walter there, too. In thinking back, she was all set for us to leave and finish packing until I said I could go and check on Miss Atwater for her and make sure she didn't come wandering to the office while they were still there. After I said that, she was suddenly interested in mine and Walter's opinion on what Miss Atwater said about her husband's involvement in her brother's death, as well as our opinion on her clothing, and inviting us to visit her in LA sometime."

"That was strange, I must admit," Walter said. "It didn't seem typical of her. Even Gran was exasperated by it, but I just chalked it up to stress and duress."

"The reason she wanted us all to stay in the office with her was to give Arlo a clear shot at murdering Miss Atwater. Arlo took the suitcases out to the car and then went in the side gate of the resort, knocking on Miss Atwater's door. He most likely said he wanted to talk to her on

Mrs. Pruitt's behalf or something like that and let her know there were no hard feelings. When she let him in, he attacked her, probably forcing the sleeping pills down her throat, and then I imagine he smothered her. Most likely while she was gasping for air, she vomited some of the pills, though a few probably remained in her stomach."

"Why go to the trouble of forcing sleeping pills down her throat if he was going to smother her?" Walter said.

"Because Mrs. Pruitt probably figured there would be an autopsy. I doubt the pills would have had time to dissolve in her stomach, but I'm guessing they didn't think about that."

"It gives me the willies," Walter said.

"Me too. Arlo must have put her body on the bed, then put the empty bottle of pills next to her. He typed the suicide note on her typewriter, then used his handkerchief to wipe the keys clean and to remove the sheet of paper and place it on the floor. Then, again using the handkerchief, he opened the door and went out after closing the drapes. I imagine he stuck the handkerchief in his pants pocket, perhaps after wiping up any vomit he may have gotten on his clothes. When you asked him about it being missing from his breast pocket later, he used the excuse of checking the oil on their car. It seemed odd to me he wouldn't just go to a service station and have them do that for him."

"What about the chair under the open window, though?" Walter said.

"That was put there by Arlo sometime the night before under cover of darkness to further the illusion that Miss Atwater killed Angus Pruitt."

"Poor Granville," Walter said. "Imagine having your mother and uncle conspire to kill your father, and then murder him and an innocent woman. I should make a trip to Los Angeles. Granville's going to need consoling."

"If he needs consoling, I'm sure his fiancée can manage it just fine," Mason said. "Besides, we don't know for certain Granville wasn't complicit in the plot."

"Surely you can't believe that bronzed god had anything to do with all this?" Walter said.

Mason shrugged. "I think he's probably innocent of the murder of Miss Atwater, anyway, given that he wanted to help Arlo with the luggage and all, but he certainly had good reason to hate his father. He definitely had a motive in wanting him dead."

"What now?" Marvin said.

"Please print all of these photos when you have time and give them to Miss Campbell. I also promised her a new roll of film, which you can also put on my room bill. I'll take this contact sheet with the images of Angus Pruitt and his imposter and show them to Detective Branchford. And speaking of, I need to contact him and let him know what I found out. Hopefully he'll agree with me, and he can get in touch with the Los Angeles police to have Arlo and Mrs. Pruitt arrested on suspicion of murder. Mind if I use your telephone?" Mason said, taking off his reading glasses and putting them back in his front pocket.

"Not at all. It's on my desk. The number for the police is on the inside of the telephone book, top left drawer. I'll put the contact sheet you want in an envelope."

"Thanks," Mason said, getting to his feet and stepping over to the desk against the wall. He retrieved the number, picked up the receiver, and dialed. It was just a few seconds before a voice answered.

"Palm Springs Police, Sergeant Greco speaking."

"Would you connect me with Detective Branchford, please?"

"He's not here, can I take a message?"

"Oh, this is Detective Mason Adler, from Phoenix, Arizona. I have information regarding the deaths at the Oasis I think he'll want to hear. It has to do with the Pruitts."

"Adler, right. He mentioned you. Actually he's heading out Highway 60 now to speak with the Pruitts."

"Really? But they left this morning for Los Angeles."

"It seems their car broke down fifty miles or so out. Apparently, they'd been sitting along the roadside for about an hour before someone finally stopped. Not much traffic this time of day. The motorist contacted us when he got to town and told us the man gave his name as Arlo Pruitt, and that there was a woman and a younger man with him. I recognized the name and contacted Branchford, figuring he might be interested. Turns out he was. He decided to take a drive out and talk to them, saying something about renewed suspicions. We contacted the highway patrol and a garage and asked them to send a truck, too."

"I see. Well, thank you for the information, Sergeant. I appreciate it. Please tell Detective Branchford I called. Goodbye." Mason returned the handset to the cradle as he looked at Marvin and Walter, who were staring at him intently.

"So, he wasn't there?" Walter said.

"Where is he?" Marvin added.

"On his way to talk to the Pruitts. Apparently their car broke down about an hour or so out of town."

"But they left the Oasis around ten thirty this morning," Marvin said. "It's three thirty now."

"Yes, but they told me they were going to stop for breakfast, which probably took them until noon, then they most likely drove an hour or so before breaking down around one, then apparently they sat along the road for about an hour before someone finally stopped about two. And it would have taken that person an hour to get into Palm Springs and notify the police about half an hour ago."

"I suppose that makes sense," Walter said.

Mason nodded. "The police contacted the California Highway Patrol, but the sergeant said Branchford decided to go out there himself and use the time to talk to them some more. Most likely their car will have to be towed back to town, and they'll need a ride back, so he can give them a lift. Plenty of time to get them to talk."

"But he doesn't have any jurisdiction outside the city limits, does he?" Marvin said.

"I don't think so, but I'm sure he just wants to grill them off the record. Like me, I bet this has all been gnawing at him."

"It sounds rather risky, going out there by himself. As we discussed before, Arlo carries a gun," Walter said.

Mason frowned. "You're right."

"Certainly the highway patrol will be there by the time the detective gets to their car," Marvin said.

"Maybe. I'm sure they have lots of other more pressing things to do, though," Mason said. He nodded toward Walter. "Stay here with Marvin or have him take you back with him to the Oasis. I've decided I'm going to go and see what's going on out there. I don't trust any of them."

"Not on your life," Walter said. "If you're going, I'm going with you."

"No, it may be dangerous. Arlo carries a gun, as you just reminded me, and as you may recall, you insisted I leave mine back in Phoenix."

"That's right," Walter said. "I must say I regret that now, but it's all the more reason for me to go with you. There's safety in numbers."

"Fine, if you insist. Let's go, then, we're wasting time," Mason said, picking up his hat and the envelope with the pictures in it and heading out the door and down the stairs as Walter followed.

CHAPTER TWENTY-TWO

Later Friday afternoon, May 31, 1946
On the highway to Los Angeles

Mason anxiously scanned Highway 60 ahead of him as they searched for signs of either Branchford's car, though he wasn't exactly sure what it looked like, or the Pruitts' black sedan, but there was no sign of either. In fact, there was nothing much to see at all except cactus, thistle, sand, asphalt, and the occasional buzzards circling overhead.

Walter fiddled with the tuning knob on the dash. "I can't get anything on the radio out here."

"You should be able to pick up an Ontario, California, station soon."

"Ugh, when are we going to get there? We've been driving just over an hour already."

"I'm not sure, but it can't be too much farther," Mason said, gripping the steering wheel as Walter continued turning the radio knob, getting mostly static. "Detective Branchford had about a half hour's head start on us, so I'm sure he's already talking to them, which I must admit has me a little worried."

A few miles on, an old Ford rumbled past, the first car they'd seen for some time, but otherwise the road remained empty. Then, finally, as they rounded a bend in the highway, Mason spotted the Pruitts' black DeSoto sedan, just barely off the roadway, its hood raised and the windows all rolled down. A gray 1938 Buick Century was parked in front of their car. Arlo, his jacket open and his tie and collar loose, was talking to Branchford as Regina Pruitt stood nearby. Mason could just make out Gran sitting alone in the back seat, probably glad to be out of the sun. All four of them turned as Mason slowed and stopped fifty yards or so behind the DeSoto.

"Why are you stopping way back here?" Walter said.

"For safety's sake. I can't be worrying about you."

"You worry about me? How sweet."

"Look, I brought you along because you insisted, but now *I* must insist you wait here, okay? Stay in the car."

"All right, fine. It's too hot outside anyway, and I did finally get a decent station tuned. But if you need me, just give me a yoo-hoo or a wave, and I'll come running."

"I'll do that," Mason said. "And I'll leave the keys so you can listen to your radio program."

"Thank you, darling," Walter said. "Do you want the envelope with the pictures?"

"Not yet. Let's keep those in the glove box. I want to show them to Branchford in private."

"I'm sure that's not all you want to show him in private," Walter said, lighting a cigarette and reclining in his seat.

Mason shook his head, got out, put his hat on, and walked toward the DeSoto.

"Mr. Adler, this is a surprise," Detective Branchford said. "I thought you'd be on your way back to Phoenix by now."

"I decided to stay one more night."

"Oh, well, good," Branchford said. "So, what brings you out this way?"

"I, uh, heard what happened," Mason said. "Thought I might be of assistance."

"Only if you have a tow truck in your back pocket," Branchford said, nodding toward the front of the Pruitts' car. "Not only is their radiator bone dry, but the engine's seized up. Looks to me like a piston welded itself into the cylinder."

"I'm impressed," Mason said. "You know your way around a vehicle."

"I used to work at a garage before I joined the force."

"Speaking of garages, where the hell is that stupid truck? We've been stuck here nearly four hours now," Arlo growled as Granville got out from the back seat, stretching and yawning.

"Hello, Mr. Adler," Gran said. He had taken off his coat and tie and had rolled up his sleeves.

"Hello, Gran," Mason said.

"As Mr. Pruitt mentioned," Branchford said, looking at Mason, "a truck from one of the garages is supposed to be coming. They were called around three, so they should have been here over an hour ago. I'm guessing you didn't pass any?"

Mason shook his head. "No, sorry, I didn't. They're probably busy."

"Most likely. The highway patrol's supposed to be sending someone, too, but no sign of them yet, either. I was told they're dealing with a pretty bad accident involving a couple of cars and an overturned truck just off the highway near Beaumont. That's most likely where the tow truck is, too. Anyway, I looked over their car, determined it was pretty much a lost cause, and now I was just having a chat with Mr. Pruitt and Mrs. Pruitt, reviewing things one more time. I informed them of what happened to Miss Atwater."

"Simply horrible. I can't believe it," Regina said. "Detective Branchford was going over all the details with us when you pulled up."

"And over and over and over in the hot sun for the last half hour," Arlo said as he turned to the police detective and snarled. "This is pointless and stupid, and so are you, Branchford."

"Arlo, being rude won't help anything. We just have to be patient," Regina said.

"I'm through being patient. I'm hot, tired, and thirsty. It's got to be close to a hundred degrees with no shade, and we have at least three more hours of daylight. I don't suppose you have anything to drink in your car, Adler?" Arlo said. "We finished off the water we had two hours ago."

"Sorry, no. I'm actually surprised your vehicle overheated and broke down like that, considering you told me you checked the oil and water before you left the Oasis."

"I guess there must have been a leak in the radiator," he said, taking off his hat momentarily and wiping his brow as he glared at Mason.

"We'll have the garage check for any leaks," Mason said, "just to be sure."

"It is still rather warm," Gran said. "I'm going to sit back in the car if you all don't mind."

"That's fine, dear," Regina said as Gran climbed into the back seat once more and lay down on his good ear.

Mason turned toward Branchford. "Detective, I wonder if I could have a word with you in private?"

Branchford looked at Mason with a puzzled expression. "Of course. Since you took the time to drive all the way out here, I'm assuming you have a good reason."

"Yes. It's regarding what happened at the Oasis. Would you mind walking back to my car with me?"

"All right. Excuse us, folks," Branchford said as Arlo and Regina exchanged worried looks.

"I want to know what you have to say," Arlo said loudly.

Mason and Branchford both stopped and stared at him.

"Excuse me?" Mason said.

"What about what happened at the Oasis?" Arlo said, squinting at the two of them under the brim of his hat. "We all *know* what happened because Branchford just told us. Miss Atwater killed my brother, and then she killed herself. What else is there? Huh? We have a right to know." His tone was angry.

Mason turned toward him. "It's *assumed* that's what happened, but I have some new evidence Detective Branchford will want to know about."

"Oh yeah? Then just say what you have to say. To all of us, big shot. I'm willing to bet you're full of crap."

"Arlo, please," Regina said, putting a hand on his left arm.

"Shut up, Reg."

"That's no way to talk to a lady, Arlo," Mason said.

"Reg ain't no lady. Not much of one, anyway. So spill your guts, Adler. What evidence do you think you got?"

"All right, if you insist."

"What's this all about, Mason?" Branchford said warily, looking from Arlo to Mason. "Perhaps we should wait for the highway patrol to get here."

Mason glanced at the detective. "That's probably a good idea. Always wise to have reinforcements."

"Why do you want reinforcements? What are you afraid of? And what do you know?" Arlo said nervously.

"I know more than you think," Mason said.

"Like what?" Arlo said. "Sounds like something you don't want Regina and me to know. And it sounded like you didn't believe me earlier about the radiator springing a leak."

"I'll discuss it in private with Detective Branchford once the highway patrol arrives."

Arlo reached into his coat and yanked out his gun, aiming it at Mason and Branchford before Branchford could get to his. "Hands up, boys." When Mason and Brian had raised their hands, he pointed the gun at Mason. "You'll discuss it now, big shot. With all of us. *Before* the highway patrol arrives."

"Why do you want to know right now?" Mason said. "So you can shoot us if I'm correct?"

"Arlo, stop it," Regina said. "You're making things worse."

"*He's* making things worse. Tell me what you think you know. Now."

"Might as well tell him, Mason," Branchford said.

Mason considered this. Telling him slowly might stall him enough to allow the highway patrol to get there. "All right. I'll tell you. But this is between you and me, Arlo. Allow Detective Branchford to drive away."

Arlo laughed loudly. "You're a funny guy, Adler. Now tell me. I'm still willing to bet you're full of crap."

"Maybe I am, but I have evidence you switched places with your brother poolside the day he died, faking the heart tattoo. Only you got it backward."

"Got what backward?"

"The tattoo. Photos that were taken of Mr. Pruitt earlier and of you pretending to be your brother that day show it to be true. His faced one way, yours faced the opposite. There's inconsistencies on the fake suicide note, and other things, too." He glared at Arlo. "I'm right, aren't I?"

"I'm not admitting anything because I think you're just guessing. Show me these photos you claim to have."

"I don't have them with me," Mason said, hopefully lying convincingly, "but they exist, believe me. No wonder you broke down out here. You never really checked the oil and water on the DeSoto this morning, did you? Instead you killed Cornelia Atwater shortly after leaving the Oasis office, and you killed your brother with Mrs. Pruitt's help, and possibly Granville's. The three of you are facing jail time and possibly the gas chamber."

"Gran's innocent," Regina said, suddenly alarmed. "This was all me and Arlo. My husband was a stupid, nasty man who deserved to die."

"Did Miss Atwater deserve to die, too?"

"That was unfortunate. We hadn't counted on her showing up. I thought Angus would scare her off after he got the blackmail notes I sent. I didn't want her hurt, but Arlo—"

"I told you before to shut up, Reg!" Arlo said, staring at Branchford. "I figure you got a gun, Detective, so take it out nice and slow with your left hand and drop it in the sand. Now."

Branchford hesitated.

"Weighing your chances?" Arlo snarled. "We're in the middle of the desert. No one around. If you go for your gun, I'll shoot you both stone cold dead."

"And if I do drop my gun? What then? Most likely you'll still kill us," Branchford said.

"I've no reason to. I don't need two more murder raps hanging over my head. Drop it and give me your car keys. Yours, too, Adler. Reg and I will take whichever of your cars has the most gas and head for Mexico. We'll leave the two of you with Gran."

"With no vehicle and no water?" Mason said.

"That stupid truck will show up eventually along with the highway patrol. Or you can always flag down a passing motorist when there is one."

"All right, I guess we have no choice," Branchford said. Slowly he reached awkwardly into the left side of his jacket with his left hand and took out his revolver, which he dropped into the sand.

"Good boy. Now your keys."

Branchford dropped them next to the gun.

Arlo looked at Mason. "You packing, too?"

"No," Mason said, still dressed in his short-sleeved shirt and trousers. "Where would I put it?" He turned slowly around so Arlo could see he had nothing in his back pockets.

"All right, fine, so what are you waiting for, Adler? An engraved invitation? Drop your keys in the sand."

"I left mine in the ignition of my car. I'll go get them."

"I don't think so," Arlo said. "I'm not stupid, I have a college education. Reg, go take a look in Adler's car and see if the keys are there. If they are, bring them to me."

"Sure," she said, "but is this really a good idea? Leaving them here, I mean? When that truck finally shows up, it may have a radio, and the highway patrol most definitely will. These two could identify the vehicle we took, even the plate. They'd have us arrested before we even reached the border."

Arlo considered this. "Good point. So, what do you suggest?"

"Take them with us. We could tie them up, gag them, and put them in the trunk. Let them go once we cross into Mexico or at least get close to it."

"Tie them up with what? We don't have any rope."

"We could look. There must be something."

Arlo shook his head. "Nah, we're wasting time. That truck or the highway patrol could be here any minute. Let's shoot them both dead right now and put their bodies in the trunk of one of their cars. We'll dump them in a ravine somewhere in Mexico. When the truck and the highway patrol arrive, all they'll find is our sedan and one of their cars. They won't know what happened, which way we went, or what the car we're in looks like."

Regina looked worried. "I don't like the idea of killing two more people, Arlo."

"I don't either, but we don't have a choice."

"And what about Gran?"

"We'll take him with us. Once we're in Mexico, he can do as he chooses."

Regina considered this briefly. "Okay, as long as he's safe, but I still don't like this. Why can't we just tie them up?"

"Because that truck and the patrol could be here any minute, like I just said. Now then, which one should I shoot first?" Arlo said, pointing the gun at Mason and then at Branchford.

From behind him came the sound of an engine roaring to life and tires spinning against asphalt and sand. Arlo turned, a surprised look on his face as Mason's 1939 Studebaker Champion came charging at him. Walter was peering over the top of the steering wheel, the accelerator to the floor. Chaos erupted as Mason, Branchford, Arlo and Regina dove for cover. Arlo wasn't fast enough, and the front fender clipped him, sending him flying over the hood and off to the side, the gun bouncing off the fender. Walter slammed on the brakes and brought the car about, honking the horn and grinning from ear to ear. He jumped out and ran to Mason while Branchford retrieved his gun and pointed it at Regina and Arlo, who was lying unconscious along the side of the road, a trickle of blood coming from his mouth. Granville had scrambled out of the back seat of the sedan, looking bedraggled, confused, and stunned.

"What the hell is going on?" Gran said, starting for his mother.

"Stay where you are," Branchford growled. "Your mother and uncle are under arrest for murder."

Granville froze in his tracks, a shocked look on his face.

"You okay?" Walter said.

Mason clamped a hand on Walter's shoulder. "Thanks to you, my friend." He looked over at Branchford. "Brian, you all right?"

"I'm fine. Get Arlo's gun and help me keep them covered."

"Sure," Mason said as he glanced back up the highway. "No sign of the truck or the highway patrol yet, but I suspect they'll be here soon."

"No doubt they will, darling," Walter said. "And I'm sorry, Mason, but I just had to move your car seat up so my feet would reach the pedals."

Chapter Twenty-Three

Thursday morning, June 7, 1946
Mason's apartment, Phoenix

"Another doughnut?" Mason asked, offering the plate to Lydia across his dining room table. "There's two left."

"No, thanks, but you go ahead if you like," Lydia said, sitting back in her chair.

"I've had enough, too, I think," Mason said.

"I'll take one to go when I leave, though, if you don't mind."

"Be my guest." Mason glanced about. "Gee, it's good to be home."

"You've been back almost a week already."

"I know, but it was quite a trip. Not exactly relaxing."

"I should say not, though the postcard you sent made it sound like you were having a marvelous time."

Mason chuckled. "That was the first day."

"Ah, I see. By the way, besides all the murder and intrigue, how did it go with Walter? Just the two of you in the same room for three nights?"

"Four nights, since we stayed an extra day. To my surprise, it went rather well. We both got to know each other better and understand each other more. And I can say in all honesty, he saved my life. If it hadn't been for him running down Arlo Pruitt with my car, Arlo would have shot both Branchford and me, and probably Walter, too, when he was discovered."

"Goodness, it seems murder and danger follow you everywhere," Lydia said, taking a sip of her coffee.

"It does seem that way. I think I need a vacation from my vacation."

"Good idea. Maybe you and I can go to Sedona or Flagstaff sometime this summer and escape the heat for a bit."

"I'd like that. I have a new case I just signed on, but let's plan something as soon as it's wrapped up. There's also a certain someone I met in Palm Springs I wouldn't mind visiting again."

"Oh? Do tell. All you've told me so far is about the murders. Who is this someone you'd like to visit?"

"The police detective on the case, Brian Branchford."

Lydia raised an eyebrow. "Interesting. Two dicks together."

"Not together yet. I don't know anything for certain, but I have my suspicions, and I wouldn't mind confirming them."

"Your suspicions are usually right on target. Is he handsome?"

"I think he is. In his fifties, a widower."

"Hmm. I should like to meet him."

"Maybe. Someday, depending. He's five hours away, you know."

"That's not so far. He spends a weekend here, you spend a weekend there…"

"And my long distance phone bill goes through the roof."

"You could always write letters."

"You're jumping the gun, Lydia. I barely know him."

"Fair enough, but I have a feeling. So, what's the latest on the two murders?"

"Mrs. Pruitt and Arlo were both arrested for murder and attempted murder. Arlo had a broken arm but is otherwise okay. Surprisingly, they've both pleaded not guilty even though Walter, Branchford, and I gave statements they tried to kill us, so it will most likely go to trial. They'll use our testimony and the two photographs Miss Campbell took of Mr. Pruitt and of Arlo pretending to be his brother, along with the fake suicide note. They also found traces of red and black paint on Arlo's chest that matched the paint on the rag Marvin used to wipe up Arlo's sink and the paint Mrs. Pruitt bought at the art supply store."

"I would think all that should be enough to convict them."

"Yes, and I think Detective Branchford will uncover more. He telephoned the other day and told me an investigation is under way at Baylis and Ivy. If it can be determined that Arlo *was* embezzling funds, that would give them a strong motive. With Mr. Pruitt out of the way, Arlo would take over the company. If any crooked business was discovered, they figured they could blame it on Mr. Pruitt."

"Pure evil," Lydia said.

"Yes. An autopsy was done on Mr. Pruitt's body, even though Mrs. Pruitt objected. The detective obtained a court order."

"Did it show anything?"

"Yes. Mr. Pruitt was indeed given a sedative, most likely administered by Mrs. Pruitt, and it was still in his system. And he died by suffocation, not heart attack. I suspect his supposed symptoms were all made up by Mrs. Pruitt."

"What about Miss Atwater?"

"Her death also came from suffocation, according to the autopsy."

"So, not suicide."

"Definitely not. The unfinished exposé she was writing on Baylis and Ivy and the suspicions about her brother's death and the other employee's death will also be used as evidence, I'm sure."

"Even though she was accusing Angus Pruitt?"

"Yes. Neither Arlo nor Mrs. Pruitt could afford an investigation into the company or the two deaths, so they needed her done away with. And the bullet extracted from Ralph Atwater's body will be compared to Arlo's gun, now that he's under arrest. I suspect there will be a match. Along with that, testing showed the supposed blackmail notes were typed on Mrs. Pruitt's home typewriter, not Miss Atwater's. Plus, the keys of Miss Atwater's typewriter showed no fingerprints whatsoever."

"Aha, but they *should* have shown Miss Atwater's since she supposedly typed her suicide note on it, but Arlo wiped them clean," Lydia said.

"Exactly. In wiping off his own prints, he wiped hers away, too."

"So, they'll both definitely be proven guilty," Lydia said, finishing her coffee.

"No doubt about it in my mind, though Mrs. Pruitt will probably be named an accessory, since I think it was Arlo who did the actual killing in each case."

"And what of the son? What was his name again?"

"Granville. It's hard to say. I believe he really didn't have any knowledge of what Arlo and his mother were up to, and they both say he's innocent."

"What a horrible thing for him to discover. So, now what?"

"I imagine he'll inherit Baylis and Ivy and whatever else Mr. Pruitt had his hands in. I'm not a lawyer and don't know about what will happen with the loan contract Marvin Gagliardi and Pruitt signed regarding the Oasis. It may be null and void if it can be proven illegal, but if not, Granville sounds like he's more honest than his father. Perhaps he'll rewrite the loan with standard terms and interest rates. I also suspect he'll marry that girl he's in love with, and hopefully they'll be happy. Gran's got a lot of demons to sort out, though, including everything that just happened."

"And what of Mr. Gagliardi? Will he be all right?"

"With Mr. Pruitt out of the picture and Miss Atwater dead, I think he'll be just fine. He told me Walter and I could have a complimentary room at the Oasis anytime we're in town."

"That's kind of him. Will you keep in touch with those two women from San Diego?"

Mason chuckled. "You mean Miss Campbell and Miss Schultz? Ermengarde Campbell gave me her telephone number and address as we were leaving the inn."

"I bet she did. What about Miss Schultz?"

"I didn't get to say goodbye to her. Miss Campbell told me Miss Schultz and a waitress she'd met had gone for a drive up into the mountains, just the two of them."

"She met a waitress?" Lydia said.

"Yes. As I mentioned to you when Walter and I got back, she seemed to be fond of women, though Miss Campbell is clueless about it."

"That's often the case. They don't see what they don't want to. I hope it works out for them."

"Me too. I have a feeling Miss Schultz will be making a few return visits to Palm Springs."

"So, that's the lot of them and another case closed, then. Good job, Detective Adler."

"Thanks, but I actually couldn't have figured it out without the comments from Walter and Miss Campbell. And of course, Brian, I mean Detective Branchford, is handling the final details of the case quite well."

"He certainly sounds competent, attractive, and eligible. So, what will it be, Mason? A trip to Sedona or Flagstaff? Or will you be making a few return visits to Palm Springs, too, like Miss Schultz?"

Mason grinned. "How about you and I take a trip to Catalina Island? There's an older woman there who wants me to investigate a missing family jewel."

"Oh, that sounds nice! I've never been to Catalina Island. I guess I wouldn't mind relaxing on a veranda overlooking the ocean while you look over the family jewels."

"Indeed. And afterward we can make a stop in Palm Springs. I might just take Marvin up on his offer of a complimentary room."

"So you can get to know that Brian Branchford," Lydia said, finishing off her doughnut.

"A guy's gotta have a hobby," Mason said with a toothy grin.

MYSTERY HISTORY

- The Oasis Inn is fictional but is based on resorts and motels that started to appear in the late 40s and early 50s.
- The Chi Chi Club was located at 217 North Palm Canyon Drive and first opened as Freeman's Desert Grill in 1936. It became the Chi Chi Club in 1938 and was known for its images of a topless, bronzed woman on everything from matchbooks to glasses and dinnerware. The Starlite Room opened there in 1948, with Desi Arnaz and his orchestra as the first musical guests.
- The Triada in Palm Springs was built in 1939 and soon attracted a large number of Hollywood's elite, including Elizabeth Taylor, Tyrone Power, and Howard Hughes. It still exists as of this writing. The events and people mentioned in this book regarding the Triada are fictional.
- The Racquet Club in Palm Springs opened in 1934 and catered to Hollywood stars as well. It was demolished after a devastating fire in 2014.
- The Palm Springs Hotel was built in 1934, the same year the Racquet Club opened. The two-story building was designed in the Mission Revival style and demolished in 1967 to make way for an enclosed mall. In 2010, that mall was also demolished.
- The Cactus Cantina in Phoenix is fictional but based on typical small, family-owned restaurants of the time.
- Roy's Buffet at 307 E. Roosevelt Street originally opened in 1939 as Larry's Buffet. It changed to Roy's in 1940 and was renamed again in 1947 as Hubbard's 307 Club. It was considered to be gay-friendly by the 1950s. In the 1980s, drag performances were held there, including one drag show that started at six in the morning.

It finally closed in 2000, and the property was redeveloped into apartments.

- Muscle and physique magazines began to appear in the United States in the 1930s. Though the early magazines especially were supposedly designed to promote physical fitness, many of the readers were gay men who appreciated the photographs of scantily clad young men.

- Sinclair gas stations were quite popular in the 30s and 40s and still exist today. The well-known Sinclair green dinosaur was introduced in 1930. The author owns a small plastic Sinclair dinosaur he received with a fill-up back in the 1980s.

- Ethyl gasoline is basically mid-grade leaded gas, introduced in 1923.

- Gas station trading stamps were given out to customers with the purchase of gas and oil. They could be pasted into a book, which could then be redeemed when full for a variety of products such as glassware and dinnerware. In the United States, they were first distributed by Schuster's department store (which has been mentioned in many of the author's mysteries) in 1890.

- Dorothy Dandridge was a popular singer, actress, and dancer who was born in 1922 and died tragically in 1965. Her recordings can still be found online.

- Hildegarde was a well-known singer known as the Incomparable Hildegarde. She was born in Adell, Wisconsin, in 1906 and toured nightclubs all over the United States. Her recordings and songs can also be found online.

- The Orpheum Theatre opened in Phoenix in 1929 and was originally used for vaudeville acts and silent films. In the 1940s, it was purchased by Paramount Pictures and renamed the Paramount, then it became the Palace West in 1968, and finally went back to the Orpheum again.

- Danny Kaye was a red-haired, green-eyed actor, popular in the 1940s and 50s, and known for his comedy and dancing. He paired with Bing Crosby in the musical *White Christmas*.

- The Kaufmann House was built in 1946 in Palm Springs and was considered an architectural marvel, very modern and ahead of its time.

- Cigarette smoking was actually thought, in some circles, to help with weight loss and to be good for you. The same with sun exposure. Of course, we now know cigarette smoking and too much sun exposure can have serious health repercussions.

- *The Postman Always Rings Twice*, starring Lana Turner and John Garfield, and based on the book by James M. Cain, was released on May 9, 1946.
- *The Heart Is a Lonely Hunter*, by Carson McCullers, was written in 1940 and made into a film in 1968.
- The California Highway Patrol, also known as CHP or sometimes CHiPs, was created by an act of legislature in August of 1929 and is still active today.
- The author's first cat was named Je t'aime Toujours, which means *I love you always*. She was called Toujours for short.
- The author could not determine for certain if Palm Canyon and Indian Canyon were two-way streets in 1946, but for this story, it is assumed they were.

About the Author

David S. Pederson was born in Leadville, Colorado, where his father was a miner. Soon after, the family relocated to Wisconsin, where David grew up, attending high school and university, majoring in business and creative writing. Landing a job in retail, he found himself relocating to New York, Massachusetts, and eventually back to Wisconsin. He and his husband now reside in the sunny Southwest.

His third book, *Death Checks In*, was a finalist for the 2019 Lambda Literary Awards. His fourth book, *Death Takes A Bow*, was a finalist for the 2020 Lambda Literary Awards.

He has written many short stories and poems and is passionate about mysteries, old movies, and crime novels. When not reading or writing, David also enjoys working out and studying classic ocean liners, floor plans, and historic homes.

David can be contacted at davidspederson@gmail.com or via his website, www.davidspederson.com.

Books Available From Bold Strokes Books

Murder at the Oasis by David S. Pederson. Palm trees, sunshine, and murder await Mason Adler and his friend Walter as they travel from Phoenix to Palm Springs for what was supposed to be a relaxing vacation but ends up being a trip of mystery and intrigue. (978-1-63679-416-7)

The Speed of Slow Changes by Sander Santiago. As Al and Lucas navigate the ups and downs of their polyamorous relationship, only one thing is certain: romance has never been so crowded. (978-1-63679-329-0)

Felix Navidad by Nathan Burgoine. After the wedding of a good friend, instead of Felix's Hawaii Christmas treat to himself, ice rain strands him in Ontario with fellow wedding guest—and handsome ex of said friend—Kevin in a small cabin for the holiday Felix definitely didn't plan on. (978-1-63679-411-2)

Manny Porter and The Yuletide Murder by D.C. Robeline. Manny only has the holiday season to discover who killed prominent research scientist Phillip Nikolaidis before the judicial system condemns an innocent man to lethal injection. (978-1-63679-313-9)

Corpus Calvin by David Swatling. Cloverkist Inn may be haunted, but a ghost materializes from Jason Dekker's past and Calvin's canine instinct kicks in to protect a young boy from mortal danger. (978-1-62639-428-5)

Murder at Union Station by David S. Pederson. Private Detective Mason Adler struggles to determine who killed a woman found in a trunk without getting himself killed in the process. (978-1-63679-269-9)

A Champion for Tinker Creek by D.C. Robeline. Lyle James has rescued his dad's auto repair business, but when city hall condemns his neighborhood, Lyle learns only trusting will save his life and help him find love. (978-1-63679-213-2)

Heckin' Lewd: Trans and Nonbinary Erotica, edited by Mx. Nillin Lore. If you want smutty, fearless, gender diverse erotica written by affirming own-voices folks who get it, then this is the book you've been looking for! (978-1-63679-240-8)

Inherit the Lightning by Bud Gundy. Darcy O'Brien and his sisters learn they are about to inherit an immense fortune, but a family mystery about to unravel after seventy years threatens to destroy everything. (978-1-63679-199-9)

Pursued: Lillian's Story by Felice Picano. Fleeing a disastrous marriage to the Lord Exchequer of England, Lillian of Ravenglass reveals an incident-filled, often bizarre, tale of great wealth and power, perfidy, and betrayal. (978-1-63679-197-5)

Murder on Monte Vista by David S. Pederson. Private Detective Mason Adler's angst at turning fifty is forgotten when his "birthday present," the handsome, young Henry Bowtrickle, turns up dead, and it's up to Mason to figure out who did it, and why. (978-1-63679-124-1)

Three Left Turns to Nowhere by Jeffrey Ricker, J. Marshall Freeman & 'Nathan Burgoine. Three strangers heading to a convention in Toronto are stranded in rural Ontario, where a small town with a subtle kind of magic leads each to discover what he's been searching for. (978-1-63679-050-3)

One Verse Multi by Sander Santiago. Life was good: promotion, friends, falling in love, discovering that the multi-verse is on a fast track to collision—wait, what? Good thing Martin King works for a company that can fix the problem, right...um...right? (978-1-63679-069-5)

Fresh Grave in Grand Canyon by Lee Patton. The age-old Grand Canyon becomes more and more ominous as a group of volunteers fight to survive alone in nature and uncover a murderer among them. (978-1-63679-047-3)

Loyalty, Love & Vermouth by Eric Peterson. A comic valentine to a gay man's family of choice, including the ones with cold noses and four paws. (978-1-63555-997-2)

Bury Me in Shadows by Greg Herren. College student Jake Chapman is forced to spend the summer at his dying grandmother's home and soon finds danger from long-buried family secrets. (978-1-63555-993-4)

Best of the Wrong Reasons by Sander Santiago. For Fin Ness and Orion Starr, it takes a funeral to remind them that love is worth living for. (978-1-63555-867-8)

A Different Man by Andrew L. Huerta. This diverse collection of stories chronicling the challenges of gay life at various ages shines a light on the progress made and the progress still to come. (978-1-63555-977-4)

Death's Prelude by David S. Pederson. In this prequel to the Detective Heath Barrington Mystery series, Heath discovers that first love changes you forever and drives you to become the person you're destined to be. (978-1-63555-786-2)

Death Overdue by David S. Pederson. Did Heath turn to murder in an alcohol-induced haze to solve the problem of his blackmailer, or was it someone else who brought about a death overdue? (978-1-63555-711-4)

Death Takes a Bow by David S. Pederson. Alan Keys takes part in a local stage production, but when the leading man is murdered, his partner Detective Heath Barrington is thrust into the limelight to find the killer. (978-1-63555-472-4)

Death Checks In by David S. Pederson. Despite Heath's promises to Alan to not get involved, Heath can't resist investigating a shopkeeper's murder in Chicago, which dashes their plans for a romantic weekend getaway. (978-1-163555-329-1)

Death Goes Overboard by David S. Pederson. Heath Barrington and Alan Keyes are two sides of a steamy love triangle as they encounter gangsters, con men, murder, and more aboard an old lake steamer. (978-1-62639-907-5)

Death Comes Darkly by David S. Pederson. Can dashing detective Heath Barrington solve the murder of an eccentric millionaire and find love with policeman Alan Keyes, who, despite his lust, harbors feelings of guilt and shame? (978-1-62639-625-8)